WARPED

WARPED

A MENAPACE COLLECTION OF SHORT HORROR,
THRILLER, AND SUSPENSE FICTION

JEFF MENAPACE

MIND MESS
PRESS

2018

CONTENTS

INTRODUCTION

Short stories are hit or miss with some people.

I love 'em.

I look at them like a sort of middle ground between fast food and fine dining: go in with realistic expectations, and you'll be more than satisfied—maybe even wowed if the rotisserie chicken is cooked just right that day. You might not get the strong backstory, deep character development, and elaborate ending that fine dining offers, but you came here on your lunch hour, didn't you? You *want* that middle ground between a greasy flat burger and a ten-course meal with all the trimmings. And the author (at least this one) is always going to do his or her best to give it to you so you can leave your lunch hour satisfied, maybe even wowed if they cooked that chicken just right.

For me, ideas for short stories usually happen via two ways. Dreams (to which I have many, never lacking in *WTF!?*-ness), or observing something in everyday life I found peculiar, something my mind—off its leash now—begins to create an explanation to, the more bizarre the better.

"The Straw Man and a Murder" was based on a dream I had about a scarecrow dancing in a cornfield as it rained blood (*WTF!?*-ness), while something like "Princess" was based on my observing one of the most depressed-looking middle-aged men I'd ever seen in my life, sitting in a mall food court, looking like he was dreading something. As I window-shopped after lunch, I came upon a creepy-looking mannequin in a shop window. Still thinking about the depressed guy, my mind started its typical churn. Maybe the guy is really lonely, goes home to a mannequin of his own and pretends it's his wife. In my car now, and I'm barely concentrating on the road (at least I wasn't texting), and all I can think about is the depressed guy and the mannequin. *SO* much fucked-up potential there…

I may have lied a little: sometimes stories come from good old-fashioned ideas. Ideas that had novel-sized aspirations but fell short in length (insert phallic joke here) once the story was told. "Torment" is one such story. *Wooowee!* did that story go through some changes. There are at least four different versions of that story (my preferred version is in here, of course), and many people simply did not like the majority of them. And I kinda can't blame them—of couple of those versions ended up falling a little flat. I had always been fascinated with cannibalism and the legend of the Windigo (read the story to learn more) and wanted to write a story about it, *however*, I wanted to do it in a very unique way, one of my few attempts at social commentary within a story. That coupled with a lot of ambiguity and an abrupt ending that left the audience scratching their heads, and what I had was a lot of annoyed readers. So I pulled the story and said screw it, I'm gonna play with this. The result was the version in this anthology. Still somewhat ambiguous, still a bit of a noodle-scratcher when it comes to figuring out what's real and what's not, but a much more satisfying ending—one to hopefully make you whisper "*Oh shit!*" to yourself once you read what the child ends up "taking" from Kane (you'll know what I'm talking about when you read it).

Ah shit, I lied again. There are three stories in here that were not spawned through dream or observation. These stories ("Business is Business, James," "Five Card—DRAW!" and "Fish and Biscuits in a Barrel") are really short. Less than 1,500 words each. Why? I was going to submit them into a contest years back. The rule was that they had to be less than 1,500 words. *This is not an easy thing to do*. But what it *does* do is give the writer a fantastic tool in which to sharpen his trade, utilizing one of William Strunk's and E.B. White's timeless rules: omitting needless words. I would encourage every fledgling writer to give this little exercise a shot. You'd be amazed at how many words you can do without in order to tell your tale.

And, of course, there are stories like "Job Interview" and "Get off My Ass." These are prequel stories involving characters from my *Bad Games* series. They were originally exclusive to my *Bad Games Box* Set, but I decided to throw them in here too. Short and pure popcorn, these stories are for those who have read the *Bad Games* books and wanted another fix, no matter how little. And no, you don't need to read the *Bad Games* series first to follow them, and they won't spoil any of the books if (*and when!*) you decide to read them.

So here it is, guys and gals: a collection of my short fiction over the years. I hope you can select a story, sit down during your lunch hour, and I hope I can fill your belly with something satisfying, maybe even wow you if my rotisserie was working particularly well that day.

All the best, my friends.
Jeff

THE STRAW MAN AND A MURDER

The crows were not afraid of the scarecrow. Maybe the first day or two after it had been erected they steered clear of it, but as soon as Thomas Bowen started smuggling bread outside to feed them, and as soon as Thomas began his habitual chats with his best and only friend—the once imposing straw man—the crows were never wary again.

The feeding of the crows was therapeutic for Thomas. It gave him the delight of watching the black birds soar and dive like toy planes as they plucked the pieces of bread he tossed from the air, and it allowed him time to think—of what he and his straw friend would talk about that day. It mattered little whether it was new territory or old that they covered; it had all been discussed before. He had told the scarecrow about the kids at school who bullied him; the teachers who told him his drawings were a waste of time; the unfair judge who wouldn't let him live with his mother because of what she had done with Todd. And of course, the alcoholic father he was forced to live with who was relentless with his verbal and physical abuse.

Before each chat, Thomas would present his straw friend with a drawing. Today's was a brilliant black and white sketch of the boy and scarecrow: a close-up of their smiling faces, their heads tilted and leaning on one another, the sketch easily on par with any competent teen as opposed to the ten-year-old boy who drew it.

Initially, Thomas had stapled the drawings to the outside of the scarecrow's clothing—a patchwork of sorts in the medium of paper and ink. When Hunter Bowen became aware of what his son had been doing it all stopped; the drawings were snatched off and ripped to pieces. This was followed by the predictable hiding and punishment, of course, yet Thomas remained undeterred; he soon began *stuffing* the drawings safely inside his friend where they would remain out of sight—their clever little secret.

The crows never flinched when Thomas jostled the straw man. Never flinched when he would hug him tight, or break out in laughter from a joke they shared. The birds simply looked down from the wide straw shoulders, black eyes blinking, observing, monitoring, approving—parents watching their child play.

And so today, after his drawing had been stuffed deep inside the straw man's shirt—the crows sitting regally on their perch, bellies full from bread, their calls light and content—Thomas Bowen sat near the foot of the pole and looked up at his friend to begin their chat.

But the crows interrupted him. They screeched angrily, flapping off the scarecrow's shoulders in a feathery black gust. Thomas Bowen needn't turn around to see why the birds had fled. He knew, and he felt it before he saw it.

Hunter Bowen slapped the side of his son's head hard enough to rock him on his side. The boy put up no fight; he just lay there, hoping his submissive posture would signal acquiescence. It did not. Hunter reached down and grabbed hold of his son's hair, ripping him to his feet. Thomas stifled a cry of pain.

"Goddammit, boy! What good is a damn scarecrow if it don't scare crows?!" He tightened his grip on Thomas's scalp, leaned in, and jammed the boy's face into his own, their eyes all but touching—the boy's blue, wide, and scared; the man's black, narrow, and blazing. "Those filthy bastards are hell on my crops, and you're out here feeding the sons of bitches with food off *my* table!" He pulled the boy's face away from his and slapped him. "Ungrateful little shit … maybe a night with no supper will teach you to respect the food I put in your stomach."

Hunter Bowen, still gripping his son's hair, dragged him backwards through the rows of corn towards their home. Eyes blurred with pain, Thomas watched the straw man grow smaller and smaller as the heels of his shoes scuffed the earth and his scalp ached like a hat of tacks. Still, despite the pain, he managed to wave goodbye to his friend. The crows were gone.

·   ·   ·

Thomas sat at the kitchen table, his arms folded on top of one another, his head down. The boy's father loomed over him.

"I don't see why you can't be no normal boy. Spendin' all that worthless time talking to a stupid scarecrow. Drawing all those sissy little pictures. Can't be a normal boy and play some football or baseball, can you?"

Thomas spoke without lifting his head. "Momma liked my drawings."

Hunter Bowen latched onto the boy's scalp and jerked his head backward. Thomas gasped from the breath that was squeezed from his throat.

"*What did you say, boy?*"

Thomas said nothing; he couldn't even if he wanted to.

"Come on, boy; say what you just said about your momma."

Hunter let go of his grip and Thomas's head sprung forward. The boy took several breaths, and then, for some reason even he himself didn't understand, he repeated his previous statement.

"Momma liked my drawings."

Hunter's eyes crackled, his mouth fell open. The boy's defiance had apparently rattled him, and violence was his only means to debate an insolence he couldn't comprehend. He hoisted the boy out of his chair and threw him into the corner of the kitchen. Thomas landed hard on the dirty linoleum floor.

Hunter removed his filthy cap, wiped his balding head with the forearm of his sleeve, put the cap back on. "Your whore of a momma gets no mention in this house, you hear me?" Hunter turned to leave the kitchen, stopped, and returned to his son. He was grinning. "You know what a *whore* is, boy?"

Thomas didn't reply, but it hardly mattered; his father's question was now rhetoric.

"A whore is a woman that *screws* men for money. Did ya know that, son? Did ya? But here's the thing … " He snorted, phlegm bubbling in his throat. "Your momma was *worse* than a whore. You know why? Because she didn't *take* no money—she screwed everyone for *free*." He kicked Thomas lightly with his boot until the boy looked up at him. "You hearing me, boy? You hearing what I'm saying?" Hunter looked hard at his son, a sneer curling his lip, the disgust in his eyes hinting he may spit bile instead of the phlegm that gargled his voice. "You *look* like her, boy. All that ridiculous blond hair of yours. Those girly blue eyes..." He bent over and gripped the boy's arm, his thumb and index finger touching. "Weak spaghetti arms...skin as soft and as white as a baby's. *God Almighty,* you actually *look* like her."

The more Hunter spoke the more his revulsion seemed to fester like an infected wound. "Sorta makes me wonder about you, boy. Her spendin' all that time with you— encouragin' you to keep drawing all those stupid little pictures. I wonder what happens to a girly-looking boy who spends all his time with a whore. I wonder if it makes that boy go a little bit *funny.*"

Thomas looked away, and Hunter kicked him again.

"How 'bout it, boy? That whore make you go all funny on your old man? Hell, I bet she did. I bet it's why you spend all your time talking to a scarecrow and playing with little birdies. I imagine you'll be wearing dresses soon too. You gonna start wearing dresses, boy?"

"No sir."

Hunter squatted down into a catcher's stance. His voice was low and intense. "You damn well better not, boy. I swear to the Almighty Himself, you better not. Because ten years old or not, I catch you in a dress and I'll kick you right the hell out this house, just like I did that whore of a mother of yours. You understand me?"

"Yes sir."

Hunter stood to his feet, lifted his cap and wiped his brow again. "Good. Now I want you to get started on supper early today. *You* won't be having any, but I got Earl coming over and we plan to do some celebrating tonight. Earl's little boy just made captain of his football team. Lucky bastard, that Earl. Now there's something to be proud of." He snorted again, spit a wad of yellow into the sink, then called over his shoulder as he walked out of the kitchen. "Get supper started." He did not notice the three crows perched and watching from the kitchen windowsill.

·　　　·　　　·

It was after six. Dinner was cooked and eaten. Thomas stood on a small stool to scrub the dishes and pans in the kitchen sink. Hunter and Earl sat slack and slovenly at the dinner table, their bellies full, bloated, and peeking through the bottoms of their shirts. A third-of-a-bottle of Jim Beam, two half-empty whiskey glasses, and beer bottles gripped tight in the meaty palms of both men were all that remained on the table.

Earl had spoken of nothing but his son's accomplishments on the football field during the meal, and it continued—intensified and embellished now—during drinking time.

Hunter listened with both awe and envy. He called to his son by the sink. "You hearin' this, boy?"

Thomas kept his back to the pair and his hands in the suds—seemingly hopeful his obedient labor would excuse him a reply.

Hunter drained the whiskey in his glass then sipped his beer. He belched, felt the familiar disgust threaten to raise the booze back up his throat, then waved his hand at the sink as though shooing away a fly. "Look at what *I* been dealt, Earl. Christ, from the back you'd think I had a daughter. Reckon he ain't even fit to be a *place kicker.*"

Earl snickered. He was a big man in clothes, and that's the way he always kept it. Come summertime you had a better chance of finding a leprechaun than you would Earl at the local swimming hole or the lake. Called on it, he would always reply that swimming was a sissy's sport; a girl's sport. Truth was—and Hunter and a few of the guys ribbed him a time or two about it—Earl didn't want to give the town an eyeful of his bountiful man boobs when he could just as easily throw a hefty shirt over them and look as though he could bench press a refrigerator instead.

"What do *you* do, Thomas?" Earl asked.

"Tell him, boy," Hunter said. "Answer our guest."

Thomas replied without turning around. His voice was soft. "I like to draw."

Hunter belched again. "He likes to *draw*, Earl. And that's all he does—doesn't even bring home good grades. Hell, maybe I could stomach it if he was fittin' to be a doctor someday, but this one just *draws*. Tell 'em what else you do, boy."

Thomas finished scrubbing a pot and started drying it.

"I'll tell you what he does, Earl—he plays in my cornfields with a scarecrow. Can't make any friends in school so he plays with a lump of straw all day. Feeds the crows too. Feeds 'em with food from *my* cupboard. You believe that? I got a scarecrow that don't scare shit, all because of my son."

Earl finished his beer and asked, "That true, Thomas?"

Hunter answered. "Sure as shit it's true. He's out there every chance he gets. Even caught him sneaking out of bed a few times to go out there and do whatever the hell he does with those winged rats and that stupid straw friend of his."

Hunter stood and fetched two fresh beers from the refrigerator. He sat back down and handed one to Earl. "Used to draw pictures for him, didn't ya, boy?"

Earl gave Hunter a funny look.

"That's right," Hunter said. "He'd draw pictures for him—used to hang 'em up all over the damn thing. I put a stop to that though."

Earl twisted off the top of his beer and took a deep pull. He let out a satisfied gasp, wiped his mouth and said, "Well let's see one of 'em then."

"I told you I took care of them—tore them all up."

"Let's see a *new* one then."

"Don't encourage the boy, Earl. This drawing's going to *stop*."

Earl leaned in his chair and gave his friend a playful shove. "Come on, Hunt. Let's see what the boy can do."

Hunter's anger grew. "I told you—"

"I'll do one," Thomas said. He was turned on the stool and looking at the two men. His face held an odd purpose.

"The hell you—"

Earl shoved Hunter again. "Come on, Hunt, I want to see what the fuss is about."

Hunter filled his glass to the top with whiskey, nearly emptying the bottle. He did not sip from his glass—he gulped from it, his brow a mess of tight wrinkles in the middle. "Well, go on then, boy. Go get your stuff. Show my friend what you can do."

Thomas wiped his hands, hopped off the stool, and left the kitchen.

Hunter glared at Earl. "You're encouraging my boy to be a sissy."

Earl laughed; his belly and meaty breasts shook. "Oh come on, Hunt, it ain't *that* bad."

Hunter took an angry swig from his beer. "Says the man with an athlete for a son."

Thomas returned with a thick piece of white paper and a pencil. "Can I work in the living room?"

Hunter waved him away with less courtesy than he'd give a mongrel dog. "Go on then."

.   .   .

Thomas returned to the kitchen an hour later. The bottle of Jim Beam was now dry; empty beer bottles littered the cracked oak table.

"Took your time, didn't you?" Hunter said. His words were slurred, his eyes bloodshot.

"Let's see what we got," Earl said. His words were more pronounced, but his torso rocked gently. He was equally drunk.

Thomas handed the drawing to Earl. The man looked at it close, held it away at arm's length, and then pulled it close again.

"Boy's got some talent," he said.

Hunter snatched the drawing from Earl's hand. He glared at it. His vision was blurred from drink, but he squinted and focused intently. He thrust it back into Thomas's hollow chest knocking him back a step. "What is this, boy? Explain it."

Thomas's posture straightened—he appeared confident in front of his drunken father and friend. He held the drawing out with his left hand and traced his right finger over the picture as he explained it.

"It's a boy, holding hands with his mom and dad," he said.

Hunter blinked. Blinked several times. A feeling of empathy surfaced for a fleeting moment before it was buried quickly by years of conditioned rage. "Boy, I told you about your mother. Drawing a picture about me an' her back together ain't gonna make it so. You need to start accepting—"

"*It's not you,*" Thomas said. He pointed to the far corner of the picture. The details were small but there. A man was being enveloped by crows. A scarecrow looked on. "*This* is you."

Hunter blinked some more. Drunk or sober he wasn't getting it. "Well, then who's that there holding hands with—"

"That's *Todd*—Mommy's friend. That's me, Mommy, and Todd. I see them every day after school. Todd buys me ice cream. He's nice to me. He likes me. He likes my drawings." Thomas lowered the picture to his side and drilled his father with the eyes of a grown man. "*My mother's not a whore.*"

Hunter leapt to his feet, banging the table, the bottles clanking and rolling to the ground, shattering. He was on Thomas in two steps, snatching the boy by the shirt. Thomas went spark-out from the first blow, his body going limp, nearly slipping out of the shirt gripped tight in his father's fist. Hunter adjusted his grip and flung Thomas against the wall where he bounced off and crumbled to the ground like a large puppet.

Earl hopped up from his chair and grabbed Hunter from behind in a bear hug. Hunter became a wild animal—growling, fighting, roaring. Earl held tighter, but Hunter was wearing boots; Earl was wearing sneakers. Hunter brought his foot high in the air then down with his heel onto Earl's instep. The big man cried out, releasing his grip. Quick as a gunslinger, Hunter grabbed one of the remaining bottles from the kitchen table and whipped it down onto his friend's skull.

Earl dropped to both knees, clutching his bloody scalp. "*You crazy son of a bitch!*"

Hunter picked up a second bottle, cocked it back. "*Get out! Get the fuck out of my house!*"

Earl turned on all fours, his heavy frame doing its best to scurry along the floor and out of the kitchen until the distance was safe enough for him to rise to his feet and run. The back door slammed, an engine roared, tires screeched. The sounds of the fleeing car dwindled to nothing in seconds.

The quiet kitchen hummed with recent tragedy, Hunter Bowen's heavy breathing the only constant. His rage and adrenaline had sobered him some, but he would remedy that soon enough. As for right now, he had one final thing to take care of. He walked towards his unconscious son, bent over, snatched his drawing in one hand, the boy's ankle with the other, and dragged him out of the kitchen, through the hall, out the back door, and towards the cornfield.

.   .   .

Hunter Bowen faced the scarecrow high up on its wooden pole. A crow was perched on either shoulder, standing their ground. His son's ankle was still in one hand, his drawing in the other.

If he thought the straw man and the crows could understand him he would have berated them. He spoke anyway—the alcohol made the notion of venting to birds and a scarecrow credible. Besides, it was not the scarecrow and the crows he was addressing.

"You want him? You want to look at his sissy pictures? You want to encourage him to draw this crap?" He held up the drawing, spit on it, then crumpled it into a ball and flung it at the base of the wooden pole. "*You can damn well have him.* Come judgment time, you'll all burn. You'll all fuckin' *burn.*"

Hunter dropped his son's ankle. The boy was still unconscious—a starfish position on his back. The two crows kept their place. They did not squawk; they did not twitch. They just watched—beady black eyes zeroing in on Hunter, not even blinking. To the onlooker they could have been a fine work of taxidermy.

Hunter turned and stormed through the stalks of corn, swatting and punching them out of his way en route back to his house. His whiskey was gone, but he had plenty of beer left. And he was going to drink it. Drink it until his rage succumbed to inebriation.

.   .   .

Thomas was still out, the crumpled picture still at the base of the pole. Gloved hands reached down and took hold of the drawing, fanning it out, taking it in. More crows appeared on the scene. There were squawks now, but not frightened, fleeing squawks—they were chattering calls. The gloved hands dropped the drawing back to the ground and tightened into fists.

When Thomas woke minutes later, his vision was hazy. He rubbed his eyes and stared at the wooden pole—unoccupied.

.   .   .

Hunter Bowen had already drained his fifth beer since returning to the house—his sixteenth that night in addition to the half-bottle of Jim Beam he'd consumed. He sat slumped in his living room, a drunken sleep seconds from taking him. He mumbled gibberish into the air: His wife's name. Todd. His son. The scarecrow. His wife's name again. Profanities.

The half-empty beer bottle dropped from his hand and hit the rug. He cursed that too and didn't bother reaching for it. His eyes were heavy. He did not want to submit to sleep just yet. There was still more beer—more medicine that needed drinking.

He stumbled from the sofa, his body bouncing off each wall as he entered the kitchen. He bent forward to open the fridge and fell back on his bottom. He did not curse his equilibrium; he embraced it now, giggling like a fool. The gibberish continued but its hateful tone had now taken on a carefree, indifferent one—the alcohol doing the job he had hoped it would.

"Stupid cheating bitch," he slurred, getting back to his feet. "*Todd*, huh? Bought you ice cream, did he? I'll take that ice cream and shove it straight up his—"

He stopped. There was an image in his periphery. He turned too fast and swayed, latching out to the refrigerator's handle to stay upright. Someone was standing in the distance—past the kitchen's entrance through the hall, and into the adjoining mudroom by the back door. His drunken vision was poor, and for a second he thought it was the boy, but the figure was far too tall. He took a step forward.

What he saw was impossible.

The lighting in the mudroom was dim, and the figure was more a silhouette than anything. But even his drunken eyes knew a scarecrow when he saw one.

"No fucking way."

Hunter staggered to his left, back into the living room. He stood alone in the room, his heart thumping in his ears. A trick of the eyes. Yes—he was drunk; a drunken trick of the eyes is all it was. He took cautious steps back into the kitchen, peered out through the hall into the mudroom.

The scarecrow was gone.

He sighed, smiled, then laughed. Hunter took his intended beer from the fridge and went back into the living room. The scarecrow was there. No mistake now. It stood tall, far taller than him, its inanimate face and button eyes somehow looking deep into Hunter—he felt it.

"*No fucking way!*"

Hunter dropped the beer, turned and bolted from the room. He was a pinball through the house, bouncing and colliding with everything in his path until he reached the back door, ripped it open, and sprinted out into the dark. He managed ten feet down the path. The scarecrow was blocking his exit. Hunter screamed like a woman, his terror superseding any pride for the pitch that squeaked from his mouth. He banked right off the path and headed towards the cornfield.

·   ·   ·

Thomas had started to wander throughout the cornfield. He did not head back to the house. His head was still foggy from his beating, but his only thoughts were concern for his friend; he feared his father had ripped him down and destroyed him in his drunken rage.

The boy wandered aimlessly in the dark throughout the stalks of corn, desperately worried he may find the straw man dismembered and discarded somewhere along the ground. His compass came in the guise of screeching and screaming—the crows were screeching; his father was screaming.

·   ·   ·

Thomas followed the shouts until he returned to the wooden pole where his best friend used to be. His father had now taken his place on the pole, stuck fast and hammered against the wooden beams like a giant T. His body was littered with crows, perched on every conceivable ledge of his body.

Standing in front of his father was his straw friend. The scarecrow turned and looked at Thomas as he came into view. The straw man's button eyes and sewn mouth were as inanimate as they'd been in Hunter's living room, yet Thomas saw love in those plastic eyes.

The scarecrow waved Thomas close. The boy went to him. When he arrived by the straw man's side, the boy latched onto his waist and hugged. The straw man bent forward and hugged him back.

Behind the pair, the crows were very busy. They plucked flesh from the body of Hunter Bowen like rabid piranha, swallowing it as greedily as they had done with the bread Thomas always offered them. Hunter cried out and called to his son who was deaf to everything but the warm embrace of his friend. Besides, the cries were short-lived—Hunter Bowen's tongue and throat were devoured soon after.

The assault's final act saw one of the crows pluck the discarded drawing from the ground then drill it into the gutted ribcage of the now dead man on the pole.

.   .   .

Thomas ultimately turned and looked at his father. The crows were gone, but he could still hear them nearby. His father had been reduced to nearly a skeleton—only random bits of flesh remained on his body. Thomas was not shocked. Nor was he upset. He had wished this. *Drawn* it. And it had come true. He only began to express concern when he realized what was happening next.

The crows had returned and started undressing the straw man. The flock of black birds started with the straw man's hat, lifting it off his head and flying it towards the skull of Hunter Bowen. But they did not drop the hat onto the skull just yet; they needed something to cover the face first. More crows flew back to the straw man and tugged at the burlap sack with the button eyes and sewn mouth that was his face. Thomas cried out to interject, but the straw man extended his gloved hand, caressed the boy's cheek, and nodded his reassurance to Thomas who was certain he saw the sewn mouth curve upward into a smile before the burlap sack was finally tugged off, spilling the straw inside to the ground where the limp body of the scarecrow fell seconds after.

The crows worked faster now, meticulous and precise in their movements. Their black wings and beaks flapped and clicked, working in unison as they pulled the hood down over Hunter Bowen's skull, setting the straw hat over it, tugging it snug to his crown.

The straw man's shirt was next—the crows working furiously at freeing the buttons, half a dozen lifting the shirt into the air, wrapping it and fitting it around the torso of what used to be Hunter Bowen.

The pants were last, and before long another scarecrow had been erected upon the pole—a dead ringer for its previous occupant.

Thomas looked down at the pile of straw that had once been his friend. He was crying, but not sobbing—he understood. The crows squawked, and Thomas looked up at them. There were dozens perched mightily atop their new home.

Thomas opened his mouth to thank them, but his mother's voice cut him off. She was rushing through the stalks of corn with Todd close behind. She dropped to her knees before her son, spotted the welts on his face, and pulled him into her. Todd looked on with angry tears in his eyes.

Mrs. Bowen, crying, explained that Earl had phoned and told them what had happened. When Todd asked where Hunter was, Thomas did not hesitate.

"He said he was leaving…and he was never coming back."

Mrs. Bowen hugged her son again, and then Todd took his turn. Moments later the three of them walked through an open path of cornstalks—Thomas in the middle, his mother holding his hand on the right, Todd holding on the left.

.   .   .

Mrs. Bowen insisted on sitting in the back seat with her son. Backing out of Hunter Bowen's driveway, Todd wheeled the car around, but stopped before going any further. A crow had landed on the hood of the car, a folded piece of paper in its beak. A second crow landed soon after—then a third and a fourth.

Todd went to hit the horn, but Thomas quickly shouted his objection. Instead, the boy unbuckled his seatbelt and went to open the door. His mother grabbed his arm, but her son's expression assured her it was all right. He told her they were his friends. She let him go.

Thomas exited the car and approached the crows. They greeted him with quiet clicks and calls, and Thomas gently took the folded piece of paper from the first crow. He opened it and looked at the drawing he had done earlier that day. The one of him and the scarecrow together, their smiling faces side by side—the same drawing he had hid deep inside the straw man's chest. A solitary piece of straw was stuck to the picture. Thomas smiled and tucked the piece of straw into his pocket before pressing the drawing to his heart. The crows flew off the hood of the car and were soon invisible in the black sky.

Thomas re-entered the car. His mother could only stare incredulously at her son. Thomas simply repeated what he had said earlier. "They're my friends."

Todd spoke up from the front seat, his tone was warm, a shot at levity. "Thomas, did you know that a group of crows is often called a *murder?*"

Thomas smiled and said, "Yeah, I did." He hugged the drawing again.

BUSINESS IS BUSINESS, JAMES

"Murphy?"

The voice—deep and rough—spun Jen Murphy on the spot. She stared eye to chest with an enormous man, the width of his shoulders nearly matching her diminutive height.

"Yes?" she whispered, shocked she even got it out at all.

"You alone?"

She managed another yes.

The giant man waved her inside the entrance of the warehouse. Outside, the urban environment showed Jen a pathetic building that looked as though a determined termite could fell it. Inside, it was solid and meticulous; a place of business that demanded secrecy.

Jen followed the giant man's steps along the smooth concrete floor, her tiny taps to his booming thuds. She took her surroundings in without turning her head. It felt wrong to take in any more. It made her feel… what? Like an accomplice? She *was* an accomplice though, right? Yes. Maybe. You could rationalize it anyway you wanted, but she *was* here to have her husband killed. And you better believe it was her idea.

What Jen did take in revealed nothing of significance anyway. She saw rows of new cars, and she saw rows of office doors—each door shut, the shades drawn tight over their windows. The warehouse could have been a secret car dealership.

"You confirmed the appointment?" the big man asked once they were stopped before one of the office doors.

Jen looked up and met the big man's eyes for the first time. They were deep set and empty. She was fairly certain the color was black, but with the shadow cast by the canopy that doubled for his bald head she couldn't be sure. "Yes," she said. "This morning."

The big man reached out with his meaty index finger and touched her gently on the cheek. His movement shocked her and she flinched. The big man's stone affect never changed, but his tone did. It was soft, despite its inescapable bass.

"That happen this morning too?" he asked.

Now it was Jen's turn to touch the purple bruise on her cheek. She glided her fingertips over it and winced; it was still tender. "Last night," she said.

The big man nodded once, turned, and rapped his thick knuckles on the door. A voice inside told them to enter.

The big man opened the door and allowed Jen to walk past him. He then turned and left without another word.

Inside the office Jen faced a handsome man behind a desk who looked like your everyday successful executive—neat; professional; dignified. But what had she expected? A patch over his eye? Gold teeth? Cigar chewed and dangling from one corner of his mouth? The big man seemed to fit the stereotype she had conjured days before to a T. But this man? He could have been a wealthy neighbor in her affluent little suburb miles away from here.

The man stood and leaned over his desk to shake Jen's hand. He smiled a pair of straight white teeth and offered her a seat in front of his desk.

"It's nice to finally put a face to the name," the man said.

Jen smiled and crossed her legs, her skirt rising above knee level. She instantly pulled it down.

"I see a lot of that," he said, pointing at her thigh.

Jen thought the man's remark was sexual. Her face went flushed, and she felt a brief moment of panic.

"That, and *that*." His finger left her thigh and pointed towards her swollen cheek. "It's why you're here."

Jen exhaled with a quick smile and started nodding, the panic washing away. She inched her skirt up, and looked down at the large blue welt just above her knee. She'd forgotten all about that one. She was so used to them by now they could have been birthmarks.

"Yeah—that's why I'm here." She lowered her skirt again. "Mr. Smith, right? That's your name?"

"It's what I want you to call me."

"I'm not a psycho," she said. "And I'm not stupid. I wouldn't have gotten involved with him if I knew—"

Mr. Smith held up a hand. "Irrelevant. I don't need to know anything."

The man was firm, succinct. But she needed to elaborate—for her own reasons; her own justification.

"I genuinely fear for my life." She pointed to her cheek and thigh. "This and this? Child's play. The things he's done. My *God* the things he's done." She started filling up. "He even killed my *dog*…"

Mr. Smith raised another hand, but Jen finished.

"…did it right in front of me. Broke the poor thing's—"

Mr. Smith raised both hands. "*Stop.*"

She did, crying quietly now, her chin on her chest.

"I have only one question," Mr. Smith said. "Are you certain?"

Jen lifted her chin and wiped her eyes.

"Are you certain you want it done?"

"*Yes.*"

"Then there's nothing more to say, Mrs. Murphy. You have the information I asked for?"

Jen slid a folded piece of paper across Smith's desk. He took the paper and unfolded it, giving it a quick but concentrated glance.

He lifted his eyes off the paper. "Will you be paying in advance?"

Jen slid him an envelope; it was thick with money.

Mr. Smith took the envelope and placed it in his top desk drawer. He stood and extended his hand. "Goodbye, Mrs. Murphy."

"It will be Mitchell soon—*Miss* Mitchell," she said, taking his hand and allowing herself a small smile.

"As you say."

Jen turned, and the big man was at the door again. She hadn't even heard it open. She wasn't sure why, but she felt the need to speak to him. Perhaps she wanted the comfort of small talk during this frightening, albeit exhilarating moment—whistling in the graveyard, if you will.

Or perhaps it was the earlier gesture with the finger. The gesture of warmth from a man who seemed incapable of providing warmth.

Likely, it was both. So she spoke to him, allowing herself a big smile now. After all, life was beginning again.

"You startled me," she said. "I didn't even hear you come in."

The big man said nothing in return. But he did make another gesture with his finger; this one was past her shoulder, aimed behind her. Jen turned to follow his finger and instantly felt the big man's powerful embrace. A second later she was dead.

·   ·   ·

The big man held Jen Murphy tight around the waist with one hand and gripped her under the chin with the other. With a quick tug he jerked her neck to one side until it popped. Jen's eyes rolled back into her head and he let go, her lifeless body slapping the concrete floor.

The big man bent over Jen's body and lowered her skirt as far as he could so her thighs weren't exposed—her dignity in death important to him. He slowly stood upright and faced Mr. Smith. "Okay? I can go now?"

Mr. Smith shook his head. "No—you've got one more. It's a home visit. Here's the address." Smith handed the big man the folded paper Jen Murphy had given him.

The big man read it and frowned. He was confused.

"She paid in *advance*. Business is business, James."

James glanced down at Jen, then back up at Smith.

"Abusive son of a bitch just beat her to it," Smith said. "Met with him yesterday. He paid in advance too." Smith glanced down at Jen's body as though inspecting a spot on his tie. "Business is business."

James frowned harder, his giant brow almost jutting off his skull.

"I know this one was unpleasant for you, James. I know you liked her. When you visit her husband you can take your time with him. Just don't leave a mess."

The frown vanished at the thought, and James actually smiled. He *would* take his time with the man who hurt the beautiful woman. He hurried out of the office, keen on meeting up with Mr. Murphy.

TORMENT

"Only the foolish visit the land of the cannibals."

MAORI PROVERB

NORTHERN MINNESOTA

WINTER 1890

Father, mother, and son sat freezing, huddled around the fireplace that was roasting a rat. The rat was a treasured find—the other rodents they'd been dining on for the past few weeks lacked sustenance. Rats were larger. Plump.

The fire flickered a dim, inconsistent light off their gaunt faces, filling the sunken corners of their cheekbones and eyes with black—a collective reflection of skulls to one another; a cruel reminder of their inevitable fate.

The cabin shook hard from the wind and snow that incessantly hammered it. Its painful chill crept through cracks of wood and down the chimney, teasing the fire and shrinking its flame, bringing a weak collective gasp until the gust would stop, and the fire would stand tall again, licking the undercoating of the charred rat.

The boy was the first to speak that night, his voice soft and weak.

"Is it ready?" he asked.

The father glared at the boy, affording him only a brief shake of the head. Words seemed as valuable as food. Conversation was something long forgotten among the family, each one seemingly believing it would drain what precious energy they still had.

There was nothing to discuss anyway. No false hopes of escape. No remembrance of better times. Their fate was inevitable, as painful and as brutal as the elements that had long since blackened, and then taken the mother's nose.

Several tips of the fingers on the father's right hand were gone too. It was only the boy who remained intact, covered at all costs at the expense of his parents.

The father resented this. Equally sure was the resentment for his wife's insistence that the boy receive the most nourishment as well. *He* was the man, was he not? What possible use could the boy provide with a stomach fuller than theirs? The boy was barely ten. Frail and weak. The *man* should be the one to receive the most rations. *He* should be the one to build his strength in case the storm cleared. Only *he* would stand a chance at saving them if he were to make his way out into the harsh wilderness in search of help.

The mother spoke next, her voice accompanied by a faint whistle from the hole that used to be her nose. "Best not to burn it," she said. "I think it may be done."

The father fit a leather glove over his disfigured hand and gripped the iron poker by the handle, lifting it from the small rack that was their makeshift rotisserie. The rat sizzled on the poker as the man brought it towards his face. The smell of cooked meat was maddening. His stomach gurgled and pleaded. He opened his mouth and tore a hunk of meat from the poker, nearly taking the rat whole.

The mother scowled, opened her mouth to scold her husband, and he rammed the searing poker into it.

The boy screamed.

The father tried tugging the poker free, but his dead wife's body flew towards him, her head stuck to the iron rod. He placed a hand on her forehead and shoved it away, ripping the poker from her mouth and skull, the half-eaten rat now pushed up to the handle. The mother's body hit the floor inches from her son, dead eyes looking up at him.

The boy leapt to his feet and ran to the cabin door. The father rose with him, the rat meat bulging his cheek, strings of drool on either side of a mouth that now formed a madman's smile. The boy flung the cabin door open and tumbled out into the snow. He crawled on all fours, sobbing and screaming. His father was on him in three giant strides. There was no hesitation. The father plunged the poker deep into his son's back, pinning him to the frozen earth.

The father swallowed the rat meat with pleasure, and then waited there under the snowfall until his son stopped moving.

.   .   .

For the weeks that followed, a strong smell of cooked meat wafted its way out of the cabin's chimney. The storm had not let up, and when every last morsel was gone, the father faced hunger once again. Except now his hunger was different. It consumed him. Disturbed his sleep and filled his dreams. He could have a dozen rats over the fire and it would not matter. There was only one thing he craved. One thing that had seized his mind and soul complete. The strength he felt, the power that surged through him. He was something different now, no longer the petty man he'd been. His fingers had grown back, longer now than they'd ever been. The mirror reflected a yellow tint to his eyes, gray to his skin. He was taller too—several inches at least.

The storm was no longer an obstacle. It could not stop him from claiming what he needed. His desire and newfound strength would enable him to ignore the harsh climate and seek out the precious flesh that beckoned him like a drug. Of this he was certain.

I
NORTHERN MINNESOTA

PRESENT DAY

Andy said, "We're lost."

"We're *not* lost." Tim snatched the map from Andy's hands and read it with one eye on the road. "Here—see?" He slapped the map on the dashboard and pressed a finger to a location.

"What are you showing me?"

"I'm showing you where we are."

"You're showing me where you *think* we are."

Tim tossed the map into his friend's face then clicked off the overhead light.

Andy smirked and stole a quick glance at the girls in the back seat. They smiled back, knowing Andy was riling up his friend for the umpteenth time in as many years.

Michelle leaned forward and massaged the back of Tim's neck. "My man's just taking the scenic route. Right, honey?"

Andy snorted. "Scenery's like people running in a Hanna-Barbera cartoon—same shit over and over."

It started to rain. Tim hit the wipers. "Great," he said, "as if trying to find the Unabomber's cabin in the dark wasn't bad enough."

Rachel said, "This is the part when you say, *what else could go wrong? And then it starts to snow too."*

"Not even a little funny," Tim said. "In fact, nobody's allowed to say the S-word during the rest of the trip. We've had horseshoes up our butts so far; it'd be nice to keep it that way."

Michelle made a face. "You've got such a way with words, baby."

Andy looked out his window. "He's right though. We have been lucky. There's barely any sno—uh … white shit on the ground."

Rachel looked at Michelle. "Both our men are poets."

Tim squinted through the windshield. Each pass of the wiper gave him little. "Tough to see," he mumbled, flicking the wipers up a notch.

"You have the high beams on?" Michelle asked.

"Duh."

She flicked the back of his head.

The increased speed of the wipers helped, but the rain wasn't the primary culprit for Tim's lack of view and whereabouts: they were on some back road in Northern Minnesota. Thick forest lined both sides of the narrow road, and, had their journey started earlier—had they not all been hungover and slept late—it was likely that sunlight wouldn't have been much of an ally anyway: they were city kids through and through. All four born and raised in Minneapolis. All four alumnus of

The University of St. Thomas in Saint Paul. Northern Minnesota, as far as they knew, was another country.

It had been Michelle's idea to venture this far north. She had found the cabin online, reserved and paid for it online. Tim now only wished that the package deal included a GPS for his old Toyota. Though he wondered if his sentimental relic with its (broken) tape deck and odometer that passed six digits a lifetime ago, would spit the new technology out the window as quickly as an old man his spoon of gourmet soup—because they just don't make 'em like they used to. Tim smiled at the thought.

Michelle noticed her boyfriend's smile. "What?"

He shook his head, still smiling. "Nothing… thinking of a *Simpsons* episode."

"Well maybe we should stop," she said.

"Stop where?"

"At the next town. We can ask for directions."

"We'll hit Canada before we find another town," Andy said.

Rachel leaned forward and tweaked Andy's ear. "Don't be negative. Here, let me see the map."

"What for?"

"Just let me see it."

Andy handed the map back to her. Rachel clicked on the overhead light again and studied it.

Tim leaned forward and squinted. "Hurry up. I can't see with the light on."

"Oh shush." Rachel studied the map a bit longer. Her eyes suddenly jumped with discovery. "There's a town coming up," she said. "At least it looks like a town. It's really small. Here." She thrust the map into the front seat, index finger on her find.

Eyes still on the road, Tim waved the map aside as if shooing away an incessant pet. "I saw that," he said. "But I don't think it's anywhere near our cabin."

"I know that, Tim," Rachel began with harmless condescension, "but we could stop and ask for directions. Please don't be that guy. Don't be that guy who refuses to stop and ask for directions."

Michelle barked out a laugh before slapping a hand over her mouth.

"What?" Tim asked, eyes now on the rearview mirror, trying to catch Michelle's gaze. "I have no problem stopping for directions."

Michelle took her hand off her mouth. "Honey, if we ended up on the *moon*, you wouldn't stop for directions."

"That's bullshit. I've stopped for directions plenty of—" He stopped, threw his hands up. "You know what? I don't care. We'll stop at your little town. But can we all remember this though? Can I get some points for this, please?"

Rachel handed the map to Andy and said, "Up to Michelle. Are we talking *Pussy Points* or *Get-Out-of-the-Doghouse Points*?"

Michelle laughed. "He needs the latter more often than the former."

Tim said, "I will *always* need, nay, *want* the former. However, if I need the latter, then the former becomes irrelevant, no matter how many I've accrued."

Michelle laughed again. "Very true."

Tim glanced towards his friend. "It's a flawed system."

Andy nodded and raised a hand. "Choir."

Tim smiled and asked, "How far to that town?"

Andy glanced at the map. "About an inch," he said. "Like your knob."

Both Rachel and Michelle laughed.

Tim laughed too. He clicked off the overhead light. "So how far is an inch?"

Andy shrugged. "I don't know … ten minutes?"

Tim said, "Okay, well I'm cool with stopping for directions, *despite* what my loving girlfriend might—"

"*STOP!!!*" Michelle screamed.

Tim slammed the brakes and the car fishtailed on the wet road before coming to a crooked stop.

The Toyota sat idling, the three inside upright and rigid, wide eyes locked on the fourth that was Michelle, demanding answers. She did not meet their collective stare; her eyes were fixed out the window.

"Well what is it?" Tim finally asked. Leave it to his girlfriend's hawk eyes to spot something significant in a dim maze like this.

Michelle rolled down the window and craned her head out as far as it would go.

"It's a little girl," she said to the night, and then, pulling her head back inside, to everyone: "It's a little girl tied to a tree."

II
BEMIDJI, MINNESOTA

EARLIER

Professor Jon's lectures on cryptozoology and folklore were popular at Bemidji State. He held only a handful a semester, but they were worth a pleasant four to the usual three credits. Commonly referred to as an *easy* (a term the professor loathed), the truth was that every freshman or sophomore was entitled to build their credit pile with a few easies before hunkering down with the prerequisite *toughies* their majors demanded. And so when searching for easies, mythical monsters (with an additional credit to boot) were a heck of a lot more appealing than any turn of the century philosophy class.

Professor Jon began his lecture with a slide show. Dimming the lights by remote, his silhouette visible in front of the big white screen, the professor spoke over the excited chatter in the auditorium. "Shout them out," he said. "If you know them, shout them out."

The professor's silhouette strolled towards one side of the screen. He hit a second remote. An image flashed in the room, igniting eager faces.

"*Vampire!*" the majority called.

Another image flashed.

"*Werewolf!*"

Flash.

"*Loch Ness Monster!*"

Flash.

"*Bigfoot!*"

Flash.

An eruption of laughter.

It was a black-and-white still of Gene Wilder as Dr. Frankenstein, and Peter Boyle as The Monster, both dressed in tuxedos and dancing to "Puttin' on the Ritz"—the infamous scene from Mel Brooks' comedy classic, *Young Frankenstein.*

Professor Jon's silhouette said: "Sorry—couldn't resist."

Once the laughter softened, another flash.

There was a brief pause, then what sounded like an uncertain but unanimous: "*Werewolf...*"

The lights rose back to full strength. The image the class believed to be a second werewolf remained on-screen.

"Another werewolf?" the professor asked. He turned and looked at the giant image shining above him. The monster had many of the characteristics of the traditional werewolf, but there were differences: it stood exceptionally tall on its hind legs. Its body appeared painfully thin, almost emaciated—each rib was visible, each joint by the elbow, shoulder, and knee protruding, its coat a furless display of grey, sinewy muscle. The eyes glowed yellow, its menacing fangs not stained red as the werewolf's had been, but dripping, almost pouring with saliva. Its hands were not the paw-like hands of the werewolf; they were the hands of man, each finger twice the normal length, fingernails like yellow talons on a predatory bird.

"Did I make a mistake?" Professor Jon continued, a smile forming on the corner of his mouth as his planned ruse built momentum.

The class hummed with uncertain whispers to one another.

"It's a Windigo," a voice from the front row called.

Professor Jon's smile dropped, but the old eyes behind his glasses jumped. He zeroed in on the voice. It belonged to the man the professor had noticed the very moment he'd entered his class. And why not—the man was a *man*; not a student. He was also the first to arrive ... by thirty minutes.

"Correct, you are," Professor Jon said, his smile returning. "It is indeed a Windigo."

Professor Jon gave the mysterious student a second going-over. The first had been lacking; the professor was too busy setting up his presentation. It was only the man's extreme punctuality, and perhaps his age of what the professor guessed fifteen or twenty years the senior of his average student that managed a brief register in his preoccupied mind before being discarded less than a minute later.

But not now. The mystery man had recognized a Windigo. Just as exciting, the professor was fairly certain the man was Native American; had the mystery man sported long black hair as opposed to a shaved head, he would have been dead certain (a bit guilty of stereotyping, but dead certain all the same).

"Curious," Professor Jon said to the man. "A whole class in Northern Minnesota, an area ripe with mythology of the Windigo, and yet you are the only one to recognize it."

The mystery man said nothing in return.

The professor took a chance, followed his gut and asked: "Cree or Ojibwa? Or—"

"Cree," the man said.

The professor closed his eyes and nodded, paying his respects to the man's tribe while trying to contain his excitement. If his class only knew what this meant, the correlation to what he was about to discuss…

A hand in back shot up. "So what is it? What's a Windigo?"

Professor Jon could not stop his smile from returning. It felt too perfect. The mystery student might as well have been a gift—a clever plant to pique then raise the interest of his class that much higher on a subject he'd planned for his primary lecture today; a subject he loved more than any other: the legend of the Windigo.

Except the mystery student was no plant, and when he stood, turned and faced the class and spoke first, it was grimly apparent he did not share the professor's exuberance on the subject:

"My people do not believe in your devil. But we believe in evil. We believe in the Windigo."

III

The car had been maneuvered accordingly off the narrow road to prevent traffic (*as if there'd ever* be *any*, Tim had regrettably thought), and more importantly, to position the headlights onto the scene everyone doubted Michelle saw the moment she voiced it.

But Michelle had been right. The scene was there: a little girl tied to a tree.

All four of them huddled around her now, their anxious breaths like constant exhales of smoke in the damp cold. The child appeared four, maybe five. Her clothes were rags. Long dark hair was wet and matted to her face, the recent rainfall somehow enhancing the tangled mess as opposed to helping. And the soiled face beneath the twisted vines of hair—to suggest mere soap and water was laughable.

Assuming the little girl had been neglected, Tim thought, fell directly into the *No Shit* column. And if the child's appearance somehow failed to clue anyone in, the fact that she was tied to a tree out in the middle of nowhere should certainly hammer that assumption home.

Except for one thing. One thing Tim didn't get.

The little girl was overweight.

Those innocent cheeks, so caked with what might be months if not *years* of filth, were plump. And not *little-kid* plump, but *little-kid-who-eats-too-much* plump. In fact, if Tim had seen the child at the mall, or the movies, or wherever, he would have admittedly thought her chubby—borderline fat. If the child had been neglected and left for dead, why did she appear overfed? It didn't make sense.

Rachel immediately went to work untying the girl. It was not a difficult task; the finger-thin ropes were wrapped around both the torso and the tree in a layer of three passes. The child's wrists and ankles were left free.

Andy squatted next to his girlfriend and helped with the knot at the back of the tree. "Didn't tie much of a knot," he said, loosening it without trouble then displaying his palms as though he'd just performed a magic trick.

"Probably because they didn't have to," Tim said. "Look at her."

They all did—again. Tim's statement did not rely so much on the girl's age when it came to the inability to free herself, but more on her apparent state of mind: once the ropes fell slack and she was free, the child didn't move. She sat stoically in the cold wet earth, mouth ajar, eyes transfixed on the Toyota's headlights some twenty feet away.

Michelle dropped into a catcher's stance and inched close. "Sweetie? Can you hear me?"

The child showed no signs of human acknowledgment; the headlights' trance still held her full attention.

Rachel and Andy moved back to their previous spots. Andy bent forward and snapped his fingers in front of the girl's face. Rachel instantly slapped his hand away.

"What?" he said.

"Don't do *that!*"

But the girl responded. She blinked, then looked at all four of them, slowly and one at a time.

Michelle, still squatting, said, "Sweetie?"

The little girl looked at her, eyes as transfixed on Michelle as they'd been on the headlights.

"Who did this to you?" Michelle asked.

The child continued to stare with what Tim was beginning to think were not mesmerized eyes, but vacant eyes. And her mouth—always ajar despite her body's innate response to chatter from the cold. "*Catching flies*" his father used to call it before smacking little Tim in the head for "… *looking like a damn retard.*" What would delicate Dad say here? Or was the obvious so obvious that even a charmer like his father would find futility in ridicule? Futility because, as Tim wanted to think, any remarks from his father about this little girl would not be an insult—they would be fact.

"I don't think she understands, honey," Tim said to Michelle's back.

Michelle repeated herself, slower, louder: "Who did this to you?"

"No—Michelle, I don't think she *understands.*"

Andy said, "You think she's deaf?"

"I don't know."

Michelle stood. "Foreign maybe?"

Tim shook his head. "I think she might be … you know … " He began spiraling one hand as though trying to waft the right word towards his mouth. "I think she might be a little slow."

All three of them looked at the child as if to refute Tim's statement. The girl continued to stare at them blankly, still not moving despite the recent absence of her binds.

Andy said, "Slow, like retarded?"

Rachel slapped him again, on the chest this time. "Don't use that word."

"Oh come on, you know what I meant."

Rachel was firm. "I don't like that word. It's wrong."

Andy splayed his hands. "Fine. So what should I call—"

"*Eat?*" the little girl said.

Everything stopped. Everyone stared.

"*You eat?*" the little girl said.

All four exchanged looks.

Michelle dropped back down into her catcher's stance. "What was that, sweetie? What did you say?"

The little girl looked at Michelle. "Eat now. Eat. You eat?"

Michelle said, "I think she's hungry."

The child showed no response to Michelle's words. No eager nods in the affirmative. No verbal confirmation. Her face appeared as lost as ever. Tim found this curious.

Rachel said, "Of course she is. My God, the poor thing. This goes beyond any and all neglect. This is like … *attempted murder.*"

Tim studied the child. Her wide eyes were now shifting curiously back and forth between each of them. "Ask her something else," he said to Michelle.

Michelle brushed some matted hair out of the child's face. "Like what?"

"Anything. Ask her anything."

Michelle thought for a moment, then touched the little girl's shoulder to get her attention. "Do you know where you live?"

"Eat now," the child said. And then, loud enough to make Michelle flinch and nearly tumble backwards: "*Eat!*"

"She's hungry, man," Andy said to Tim.

Tim stepped forward and crouched in front of the girl. "Are you hungry?" he asked. "*Hungry?*"

The child cocked her head to one side like a puzzled dog. Tim nodded to himself. He still wasn't sure exactly what it was, but something was coming together. He stood. "She doesn't know the word 'hungry,'" he said.

"So?" Michelle said.

"But she knows 'eat?'"

Michelle frowned. "You're the one who said she might be slow ... "

"I'm not so sure anymore—at least not like I was thinking before."

"You lost me," Michelle said.

Rachel added, "Me too."

Tim pointed to the child and kept his finger on her as he spoke to the group. "We can all agree that this child is a victim of serious neglect, yes?"

They nodded.

"So then why ... ?" He paused, once again looking for the right words.

Andy blew into his cupped hands and rubbed them together vigorously. "Why *what*?"

Tim just said it. "Why is she so heavy?"

Rachel said, "*Tim!*"

Tim shrugged innocently. "Look, I'm not trying to be a dick, but look at her. She's filthy. Her clothes—if that's what you wanna call them—are something a bum would turn away. Wouldn't logic tell you she'd be pretty damn skinny too?"

They all looked at the girl again. The girl looked back, still in a state of both confusion and wonder.

Andy eventually said, "He does have a point."

Michelle got to her feet and looked at Tim. "I'm still lost. What are you saying exactly?"

"I'm not sure. All I'm saying is something here doesn't make sense."

"Does it matter?" Rachel asked. "The kid was left, no, *tied* out here in the cold and left to die. We have to get her somewhere safe."

"*Eat? Eat, eat? You eat?*"

All eyes fell on the child once again.

Rachel took a knee at the girl's side and rubbed her shoulder. "We'll get you some food, sweetie."

Again, the child looked as lost as ever, Rachel's words eliciting zero response.

"Huh," Tim said.

Michelle looked at Tim. "Huh, what?"

Tim turned to Andy. "Can you go get one of your protein bars from the car?"

Andy frowned. "What for?"

Rachel said, "Those things are gross. She won't eat that."

Tim splayed a hand. "If she's hungry, she'll want it, right?"

Michelle eyed her boyfriend up suspiciously. "What are you up to?"

Tim ignored Michelle and kept his eyes on Andy. "Can you just go get one, please?"

"Whatever." Andy headed towards the car. He returned a few minutes later and handed the protein bar to Tim.

Tim thanked him and began unwrapping the bar.

"She's right, you know," Andy said. "Things *are* gross."

Michelle asked, "So why do you eat them?"

Andy smirked and raised his thick arm, flexing his bicep. The impressive bulge was still evident under the sleeve of his coat.

Michelle looked at Rachel who rolled her eyes.

Tim was oblivious to it all: the protein bar was now unwrapped. He squatted in front of the girl, but did not present her with it right away. He waited until her attention was fixed squarely on him. When their eyes met, he held the bar in front of the child's face and said, "Eat. Eat now."

The child snatched the bar as an animal would, immediately jamming it into her mouth, eating with fevered intent. Except there were no expressions of relief in the act. No satiating moans as she gorged. She was force-feeding herself, like someone bent to win in a contest.

"Jesus," Andy said. "I guess she *was* hungry."

Tim stood. "Doubt it," he said.

Andy continued staring at the little girl, who was stuffing the last of the bar down her throat. "Could have fooled me."

"I don't think she really wanted food," Tim said. "She ate that bar like we had a gun to her head."

"Dude," Andy said, "you're losing us again."

Michelle said, "Why was she asking for something to eat if she wasn't hungry?"

Tim glanced back at the girl, the protein bar now gone, wide eyes back on them. "I don't think she was asking for anything. I think she was trying to communicate with the only words she knows."

IV

Professor Jon had finished his lecture. It hadn't been his best, but he'd be damned if he didn't have a good reason: the mystery student had left halfway through, leaving the professor to wonder if his material on the Windigo had disappointed the man. It was so hard to tell; the man sat like a stone fixture during his stay. When students posed questions to the man's back, he ignored them. When some students tried to get a response via insult, he ignored them still. It was only when Professor Jon asked the mystery student to maybe come to the front and share some background about his Cree culture that the man stood, and then left the auditorium without a word. Some excited chatter and giggles followed his exit, Professor Jon's zeal for his treasured lecture along with it.

Now, as the professor was packing his belongings inside an empty auditorium, a deep voice popped his head up.

"You're not a crackpot."

The professor stared, both startled and exhilarated. "You," was all he said.

The mystery student said, "Kanen."

Professor Jon tried a smile. "Kanen? That's your name?"

"You can call me Kane."

Professor Jon nodded, tried another smile. "Okay… Kane. Did you enjoy my lecture? You left halfway through, and I—"

"You're not a crackpot. You know your stuff."

"Thank you. Coming from someone like you, I take that as a compliment."

Kane frowned. "Someone like me?"

The professor's smile dropped. "I only meant… "

"It's okay, Professor Jon. I know what you meant. I was only joking with you."

The professor exhaled. Kane was a big man. Over six feet and with a powerful physique that did not come from hours in the gym, but from years of physical labor. A physique that gave you forearms like Popeye and a back layers deep. No useless beach muscles here; this was all functional strength.

"Good one," the professor said with a nervous little chuckle. "You had me going for a second."

Kane only nodded.

The professor saw no point in small talk; the roundabout act was almost assuredly foreign to men of Kane's ilk. He went right for it. "You want something from me," he said.

"Yes," Kane replied.

The professor thought it best to stay silent, let the mystery man fill in the gaps. An agonizing pause followed. Professor Jon remained mute, though he doubted how long anxiety would allow it.

"You know your stuff," Kane said. "I have met many who claimed to know about the Windigo."

"And… ?"

"They did not."

Professor Jon's pride swelled. "It is indeed a passion of mine," he said. "Vampires and werewolves—all more fable than folklore, all so done to death. But the Windigo—so close to home, so *seasoned* with culture and tradition. The idea that a man or woman resorting to cannibalism will ultimately transform into an insatiable creature, forever haunting the northern territory in its quest for sustenance … it truly is the stuff of brilliant legend."

"Legend," Kane said, and for the first time the professor saw the man smile: a faint smirk that was gone just as quickly as it had arrived.

The professor was confused. "Yes … legend. This is the twenty-first century, Kane. Surely your people now realize that the Windigo *is* legend."

"You don't believe."

"Oh I believe," the professor said, inserting a deliberate pause for effect—the exuberant teacher in him helpless to melodrama—before adding: "I believe in Windigo *psychosis.*"

Kane said nothing.

The professor, already building a head of steam, would have likely continued even if Kane had started to walk away:

"The mind is exceptionally powerful, yet curiously susceptible to superstition and placebo," he said. "Well over a century ago, many who resorted to cannibalism during periods of famine in the northern territory pleaded guilty to Windigo psychosis. Many psychologists still believe it to be prevalent today, though I doubt their credentials, if not their *own* stability. With all we know about psychology today it seems ludicrous that someone would jump to such an unsubstantiated diagnosis. Shameless people perhaps looking for their fifteen minutes, if you ask me.

"But I'm not a closed-minded fellow," the professor continued. "I'm open to any and all possibilities when it concerns the bizarre behaviors in man. Look at individuals like Albert Fish or Jeffrey Dahmer—men who consumed their victims. Dahmer may have claimed to have done such atrocities to keep his victims with him forever, but how to explain someone like Fish? A horrible man who dined on the flesh of children, the preferred meat of the mythical Windigo itself?

"Of course, individuals like Dahmer and Fish, while undoubtedly sick, never took the form of the monster I showed during my presentation. However, many men—again, over a century ago—believed they ultimately would, and therefore insisted they be executed at once, lest they transform into such beasts. But, of course, the notion was pure fallacy, and factual reports of such fiction at the time were never substantiated." Professor Jon smiled, turned up both palms as though finishing a sermon and said, "The uncanny susceptibility of the superstitious mind." He clasped his hands together. "Windigo psychosis."

The subtle smirk reappeared on Kane's mouth and the professor immediately spotted it. Though he believed he'd said more than enough, the professor felt the need to continue. The subject was his passion, yes, but he also believed anxiety was doing just as he suspected it would moments ago: keeping his trap yapping until someone told him to shut it.

"Did you ever see *The Wolfman* with Lon Chaney, Jr.?" Professor Jon asked.

Kane shook his head.

The professor noted that Kane's smirk was staying this time, and he questioned why. Was he being silently laughed at, or was the smirk a gesture of respect for his knowledge? He continued all the same:

"Okay, well, there's a fantastic scene with Lon Chaney, Jr. and Claude Rains. Chaney plays Larry Talbot, the wolfman, and Rains plays Sir John Talbot, Larry's father. Larry has been bitten by a wolf and worries that he might have been infected with the horrible curse of the werewolf, fearing that he will change into a wolf during a full moon. He asks his father, Sir John, a learned and respected man throughout their hometown in Wales, if he believes that it's possible for a man to transform into a wolf.

"Sir John replies that the notion of a man transforming into a wolf, actually taking on the physical characteristics of an animal, is impossible. *However...*" The inflection in the professor's tone went up a notch, eager to finish his analogy. "Sir John then becomes adamant in emphasizing to his son that most anything can happen to a man... within his own *mind*." Professor Jon smiled and tapped his temple on *mind*.

Kane said nothing, but the smirk was still there. The professor swallowed dry, both from talking too much and unease. Should he continue to speak? Yes, but get back to the original point; you've babbled enough. Why is the man here?

"I've said quite a bit, Kane. It's a weakness of mine when I'm nervous. I apologize."

Kane held up a hand in forgiveness. "It was amusing," he said.

Professor Jon said, "Thank you." And then, "You wanted something from me."

"You know much about legend. More than me, I admit."

Professor Jon said, "Yes—*legend.*"

Kane's dark eyes shimmered. Professor Jon could not tell if the shimmer was one of delight or one of annoyance at his insistence on referring to the Windigo as strictly legend. What he *did* know was that Kane began unbuttoning his flannel shirt.

Professor Jon took a step back. "Uh, Kane, what are you—"

Kane pulled open his shirt.

"*My God...*"

Professor Jon flashed on the film *A Nightmare on Elm Street*. The professor had seen it years back, and was now reminded of the infamous villain Freddy Krueger with his custom-made glove of razor-sharp knives.

Kane, standing bare-chested in front of the professor now, looked as if he'd taken on Krueger and come out second best—four finger-thick scars raked their way across the man's entire torso, each jagged slice a wincing white in olive skin.

"What *are* those?" Professor Jon asked. "What are you showing me?"

"You know more than me," Kane said. "But I would wager you're no tracker."

Professor Jon said, "No ... no, I'm not ... how did you get those—"

"I am the best tracker amongst my people. The best hunter now that my father has passed. I can find the Windigo. I know where to look."

Professor Jon now began to wonder if *Kane* was the aforementioned crackpot. He collected himself, cleared his throat. "Kane, you can't honestly—"

"I know where to look ..." Kane ran a hand over his scars, his dark eyes never leaving the professor. "... and with your help, this time I'll kill it."

V

Andy said, "Trying to communicate?"

Tim faced his friend. "Think about it. All she keeps saying is 'eat' and 'eat now' and 'you eat.' Yet we say 'hungry' and she has no reaction. Rachel says 'food,' and again, no reaction. I offer the protein bar, repeat her own words back at her, and she practically takes my arm off grabbing the thing before shoving it down her throat."

"She didn't look like one for table manners," Andy said.

"No, it wasn't that. I think what we saw was classic conditioning. Like when a dog or cat hurries towards its bowl when it hears the can opener."

Andy shook his head. "That big brain of yours is losing me again, man."

"She's a parrot. She was repeating the only words she ever hears in a bid to communicate. I don't think she was hungry—despite the way she wolfed down the bar—and I don't think she's slow. I think her neglect might be something *way* beyond anything we'd previously assumed."

"And her being overfed is part of that neglect?" Andy said.

Tim nodded. "Ironically, yes."

"Why?"

"No idea."

Michelle stepped forward. "Who cares? This isn't a riddle, Tim. We need to get this child somewhere safe."

Rachel nodded emphatically.

Tim held up a hand. "Just hold on a minute. Don't you want to know exactly what's—"

"No," Michelle said. "Who cares *what* about *what*? We need to help this child. Period."

"I'm well aware of that, Michelle," Tim said with a forced calm. "But I'd also like some answers."

Michelle gestured to the child. "And what? You think you're going to get them from *her*?"

Tim looked at the little girl. "No," he said softly.

Michelle stared at him, waiting for more. "So then *what*?"

Tim said nothing; his mind was churning, trying to make some sense of it all.

"The village," Rachel said.

Michelle looked at her friend. "What?"

"We take the girl to that village on the map."

Andy nodded. "Yeah—we drop the kid there; call the police; boom, we're back on the road in no time."

Rachel slapped him on the chest again.

"What?" Andy said. "Are we supposed to babysit the kid?"

"This isn't just some lost child, *Andy*, it's a kid who was tied up and left for dead."

"I understand that, *Rachel*, but we haven't come across dick for miles. My guess is that whoever left her here is probably *from* that village."

"Exactly," Rachel said. "And you want to just drop her there and leave."

"No—I said drop her there, *call the police*, and *then* leave. For all we know, the whole goddamn village tied her up here. Ever see *The Wicker Man*? I don't know about you, but I'm not keen on hanging out with folks like that when I can be in a cozy cabin gettin' blazed and enjoying a few cocktails."

Rachel threw up her hands and looked at Tim. "What do you think, Tim?"

Tim was still processing it all. Admittedly, helping the girl—an irre-futable priority he was well on board with—didn't interest him as much as finding out *why* the child needed help in the first place.

"Tim?" Rachel said.

Tim's daze broke and he looked at Rachel. "Sorry. Well … I guess we really only have two choices. We can take her to the village, or we can turn around and take her home with us."

"Back to Minneapolis?" Andy said.

Tim nodded.

"Wouldn't we lose the cabin if we headed back home?" Rachel asked.

Andy snorted. "A minute ago you were Mother Theresa. Now you're worried about losing the cabin."

"Fuck you, Andy; that's not what I meant."

Michelle said, "Why not just call the police now? Ask them to meet us here?"

"You know where *here* is?" Andy asked.

"No—but we can give them the address for our cabin; we can't be *that* far from it. Plus they can trace the call to our location or whatever, can't they?" She tugged on Tim's coat. "What do you think? Should we try calling from here?"

"A hundred to one we won't get reception," Andy muttered. "Just like a horror movie."

Michelle glared at him.

"Or maybe we will," Andy continued. "The cop will call us back and tell us, ' … *the calls are coming from inside the tree!*'"

"Would you *please* shut the fuck up?" Michelle all but yelled.

"*Yeah*," Rachel added.

Andy turned his back on them and kicked at a dead tree branch.

Michelle tugged on Tim's coat again. "What do you think?"

Tim said, "I'll go get my phone."

But Andy was already heading toward the car. "I'll get a phone," he called over his shoulder.

"Grab mine too," Tim called after him, "in case one actually doesn't have reception. In fact, grab them all."

Andy was gone awhile—certainly longer than Tim had predicted. But he hadn't vanished; Tim had a decent view of his friend rummaging around throughout the interior of the car. Every few seconds a string of curses would echo back to the group.

"*What's wrong?*" Tim called.

Andy's head appeared over the hood of the car, annoyed. "I can't find them!"

Rachel yelled: "Mine's in my purse!"

Andy's head vanished, appeared again a minute later. "No, it's not!"

Rachel cursed under her breath and headed towards the car. Tim held out a hand to stop her. "Hold on a sec," he said. "Mine's in the glove compartment!" he yelled. "Check there!"

"Already did! …Because that's where I put mine!" Andy splayed his hands. "Nothing!"

Tim turned to Rachel. "All right—can you go help him look?" He would have gone himself, but he didn't feel comfortable leaving the girls by themselves, even a mere twenty feet away.

Rachel headed toward the car.

The couple eventually returned from the car empty handed, Andy looking more than annoyed, Rachel looking scared.

"Our phones are *gone*," Rachel said.

"That can't be," Michelle said. "How could they—"

"Fucking bullshit!" Andy blurted.

Tim held up a hand. "Okay, just relax." He paused, took a breath. "Someone else must be out here."

Michelle wrapped her arms around herself. "Someone else? Like who?"

Tim glanced around the woods. Black in all directions but the road. "I have no idea, but I think our options are now pretty obvious."

"Get the fuck out of here?" Andy said.

"Exactly. We can do the cabin thing another time—but only if there *is* another time."

"You're scaring me," Michelle said.

Tim pulled her close and kissed the top of her head. "It'll be okay. Let's just grab the girl and go. We're heading back."

Andy crouched before the little girl and held out his arms. "Come on," he said.

The girl gawked at Andy, but didn't move.

"Come on!" he said again.

Rachel said, "Stop—don't yell."

"What do you want me to do, just grab her?"

"She doesn't understand you."

Andy stood upright, pulled a face and swept a hand towards the child as if to say: *Be my guest.*

Rachel crouched and held out both hands. "Come on, sweetie." Rachel reached under the girl's arms and pulled her gently forward. The child didn't resist, and soon Rachel had the little girl in her arms. "She's heavy," she grunted, hoisting the child for a better grip. "And … *my God* … " Rachel wrinkled her nose. "The poor thing smells horrible."

"You gonna compliment her hair next?" Andy asked.

"Shut up."

Tim held out his arms. "Here—give her to me."

Rachel passed the child over to Tim. She went willingly, but did not hold on to Tim as a regular child would. She wasn't completely slack either. She felt … awkward, as though she had never been held properly before. And why shouldn't she? Tim thought. She probably hadn't.

"All right, I've got her," Tim said. "Let's move."

They walked a few feet and stopped suddenly. A screech, loud and shrill and impossibly loud, radiated out from the forest beyond and collectively froze them.

"*The fuck was that?!*" Andy yelled.

All four of them circled where they stood, desperate to find the source of the shriek.

"I don't know," Tim said, wide eyes on the distant black of the forest.

They headed towards the car again, and the screech came again, inexplicably louder than before. Michelle, Rachel, Andy, even the child put hands over their ears. Tim did not have the luxury; the screech reverberated in his ears, making him momentarily deaf. When sound returned, he couldn't be sure if the piercing cry was still echoing in his ears or the forest.

Andy asked the obvious again: "What *is* that?!"

Tim kicked his curious nature abruptly to the side and said, "I don't know and I don't care. Let's just go."

They made it to the car. The forest was quiet this time as they piled in. The child was placed and buckled in the middle of the back seat between Michelle and Rachel. Tim put the car into gear,

(*thank God they didn't steal the keys*)

maneuvered it back and forth across the road,

(*why didn't they steal the keys?*)

and before long they were facing the opposite direction, ready to head back the way they'd came.

VI

"I'll go with or without you," Kane said.

The professor, his belongings tucked under one arm as he made his way to the parking lot said: "Kane, please, what you're proposing is shrouded in the very thing I teach. *Myth*."

Kane matched the professor's stride towards the lot, spoke to his profile. "I showed you my wounds. Did I do them to myself?"

"I don't doubt you were injured, Kane. And I'm sorry to hear about your father. But the two of you likely encountered a wolf or a bear ... "

"I know a bear. I know a wolf. It was neither. It took my father. It did not eat him right then and there as an animal would. It *took* him—to dine on at its leisure. That was the last image I can recall before I lost consciousness: my father's body being dragged away by the ankles. What animal does that with its prey?"

"I'm sure plenty do—to avoid unwanted guests ... "

"No," Kane said, his statement not one of dispute when it came to the professor's guess at an animal's feeding habits, but a statement rooted in unmovable belief.

"You're sure it wasn't a man?" the professor said.

Kane placed a hand over the professor's chest, stopping his march cold. The gesture was not a forceful one; it didn't need to be. Kane's gaze was now stronger than anything brute force could manage.

"It was not a man. *No* man is capable of handling my father as deftly as this beast did."

The professor took a step back and swallowed hard. "All right, Kane—suppose I believe you. Suppose I believe a Windigo killed your father and wounded you ... " He shrugged. "I still wouldn't be able to help you. I told you inside; I'm not a medicine man. I can barely cook my own meals, for heaven's sake."

"You have the knowledge, yes?"

"I know the *folklore.*"

"A Windigo cannot be killed by conventional means. My father and I thought this false. Our bravado was too strong. We tried..." Now it was Kane who swallowed hard, his reasons far different.

"All accounts we've discussed of Cree or Ojibwa killing men afflicted with the curse of the Windigo were just men, Kane. Just men. Could you imagine what would happen today if a man shot a schizophrenic and pleaded he was doing the world a service by ridding it of another potential Windigo? My God, he'd be deemed less balanced than the schizophrenic—shipped off to the nearest psych unit, indefinitely."

"So you admit that a Windigo cannot be killed by conventional means."

"That's not what I said; you're twisting my words."

"You said the Windigo was your favorite of all folklore. Your passion. What if I could prove to you it was real?"

"Even if you did; even if the mythology was somehow accurate, I told you, I'm *not* a medicine man. I wouldn't have the ability to stop it."

"But you have the knowledge."

The professor sighed. "Yes—I, along with many other enthusiasts, have the knowledge of how to kill a Windigo. It doesn't mean we are capable though. It would be akin to asking a man to read a recipe for hollandaise then trust he gets it right the first time in the kitchen." He smiled and added, "Trust me; I can give you a firsthand account of how unlikely such a task is. I've never tasted anything so awful."

Kane ignored the quip, undeterred by any attempt at levity. "Your knowledge is all I'm after. I will do all the work. What do you have to lose by accommodating me? If I am wrong, you can cast me off as the crazy you believe I am. But if I am right..."

The professor weighed Kane's words. For years now he had been flirting with the idea for an epic book on the Windigo. Something to earn him the respect of his peers. The students loved his classes on folklore and cryptozoology, but his fellow professors likened such subjects to child's play. He was even made the butt of a joke about leprechauns during a faculty social gathering on St. Patrick's Day:

Now tell us, Russell, is it true they get very aggressive if you go near their gold?

What seemed like endless snickering followed. And although he had smiled and taken the joke in stride, it burned him to his core. The incident occurred six years ago, and it burned just as much now as it did then, more perhaps.

But now, the spark Professor Jon needed to finally bring alight the beginnings of such a book was perhaps revealing itself to him in the guise of this imposing man hell-bent on vengeance. Kane brought an entirely new angle to the venture, and was indeed a character that even fiction would do an injustice; he would make a fantastic addition to the project if it ever came to fruition.

As would a journey. Actual hands-on research with a Cree tracker: member of a tribe historically infamous for their legendary "encounters" with the fabled Windigo. A Cree tracker who would swear on his life that a Windigo killed his father and damn near killed *him*. And let's not forget, the man had the scars to prove it. Be them from bear, wolf, or Windigo, it mattered little as to which beastly lap the guilt fell, the scars would still make for some brilliant and shocking photos.

As for the secret to vanquishing a Windigo? The Internet offered plenty. Plenty that Kane had likely researched and already deemed unsatisfactory, hence his presence. Plenty that Professor Jon could swat aside and replace with the real deal ... as if such a thing really existed.

A book. A good one. A *damn* good one. A book signing with a line out the door a mile long ... on St. Patrick's Day, you bastards.

"All right, Kane," Professor Jon said. "Tell me what you have in mind. I'm not promising anything ... but I'm listening."

VII

Tim wasn't speeding (you couldn't on such a road), but he certainly wasn't the cautious tourist he'd been the first time they'd braved the path. The car bounced and bumped frequently, dips and ruts barely getting a tap of the brakes.

"This is fucking crazy," Andy said. "How the hell could someone sneak into the car without us seeing and steal our phones?"

"They probably did it when we were preoccupied with the girl," Michelle said.

"They *who*?"

"How the hell should I know?"

Tim finally said, "Why didn't they take the keys?"

There was a brief silence. Andy eventually said, "What?"

"Why didn't they take the keys? The car? Anything else? Why just the phones? They went through Rachel and Michelle's bags—why not take their money, wallets … hell, the bags themselves? Would've been a hell of a lot easier than digging around."

"We had the car parked on the side of the road, facing that tree," Andy said. "By the time they started the engine and straightened it out we'd have been on them before they could pull away."

"All right," Tim said. "But why not the keys? Without the keys we'd have been forced to go on foot. They could have easily hid and waited until we were gone—taken the car then."

"You hear that animal screaming its head off out there? I wouldn't want to be playing hide and seek with *that* thing roaming around."

"Chances are this is their turf; they'd know where to go, where to hide. Besides, that animal was probably a bird—they can be loud as all hell."

Andy looked annoyed. "Okay, so what are you saying then?"

Tim shrugged. "I'm not too sure. I'm just asking why they'd take our cell phones and nothing else, that's all."

Michelle said, "They wanted to prevent us from calling for help."

There was another brief silence, Michelle's words like a creak in the attic.

Tim eventually nodded and said, "Yeah … " He then shrugged again. "Except they left the keys."

Andy frowned, turned and looked at the child. "How is she?"

Rachel and Michelle looked at the little girl. Tim stole glances in the rearview. The child appeared over-stimulated, her wide eyes desperately following everything that passed Michelle's window, like a kid being rushed through an endless window display of toys.

"I think she's freaked out," Michelle said.

"Well no shit," Andy said.

"No, asshole, I meant she's freaked out by riding in a car for probably the first time—"

"*Whoa*, what the hell . . . ?" Tim hit the brakes. The car slowed to a stop. Unlike the first time, there was no mystery here; the high beams gave each of them an immediate front row seat. A tree the size of a telephone pole was lying long and high across the narrow road, blocking their path.

Both Michelle and Rachel leaned forward. Rachel said, "Are you *kidding* me?"

"Wait here," Tim said. He exited the car and headed for the tree. They all watched through the windshield as he inspected the scene. When he returned a moment later he said, "The road might as well be closed."

"Fuck!" Andy blurted.

Rachel said, "We *came* this way though, right? I mean, there's no other road? We didn't detour?"

Tim shook his head. "This is the only road." And then, deciding on whether or not he should say it, whether it was wise to stoke the fire of hysteria that was growing just fine by itself, Tim felt a sudden obligation to his friends for full disclosure. Hysteria or not, they needed the truth—if for nothing else than the collective wisdom of four minds instead of one in a situation proving more enigmatic by the second.

"The tree was cut," he eventually said.

"*What?*"

"It was cut. Chopped at the base." Tim made a small axe-chopping motion with his hands.

"Why?" Rachel asked.

"To keep us from leaving!" Andy snapped.

"But *why?*"

No one answered. Anything would have been guesswork, and frightening guesswork at that.

"*Eat? Eat?*"

"Shut up!" Andy hissed, turning in his seat. "This is your damn fault!"

"Dude!" Tim said.

Rachel leaned forward and slapped his arm.

Michelle cradled the little girl and added: "*Asshole.*"

The reprimands, even the one from Tim, seemed to bounce off. "Look, fuck you all—you know I'm the only one here with the balls to say what everyone is thinking."

"No," Rachel said, "you're the only one here acting like a selfish douche bag."

Andy opened his door. "Fine, you know what? I'll climb over the tree and *walk* the fuck back to Minneapolis."

Rachel said, "Fine, go."

Tim said, "Dude, come on—stop."

A big man with olive skin and a shaved head met Andy as he exited the car. The man said, "It's not wise to go wandering out here alone."

VIII

Tim rushed out of the car. The girls stayed put in back, holding onto the child as though she were their own. When Tim approached Andy and the big man they were almost nose to nose.

Andy was big, just under six feet, but heavily muscled. The stranger was taller, and while not as thick as Andy, Tim could spot a powerful man when he saw one. The stranger with the shaved head and olive skin wore jeans, boots, and what Tim quickly processed as some kind of buckskin coat.

"Are you the one that took our phones?!" Andy screamed into the stranger's face.

The stranger was stone in the face of Andy's verbal attack, his reply firm and even. "I did not take anything of yours. Please listen to me—"

"Bull*shit!*" Andy shoved the stranger back a step.

Tim intervened and placed a hand on Andy's chest. Andy blindly pushed it away and stepped forward until he was in the stranger's face again.

Andy pointed at the tree in the road. "You cut that tree down to stop us?" Andy shoved him again. "Bitch, I will stomp you into the fucking ground..."

Still, the stranger remained stone. Not even a flicker of anger. Tim had seen Andy's temper draw him into more than enough scraps during their college days, and maybe a year or two after when the longing for college life might have replaced classes with jobs, but hammered-drunk weekends with... hammered-drunk weekends. Tim had seen his friend fight, and he had seen him emerge, more times than not, with nothing more than a busted hand from hammering the other guy's head in. So in any other situation, Tim's intervening would have been more to save the other guy a beating, and to save Andy a likely night in county, followed by a morning trip to the ER to cast his broken hand.

Except Tim feared this time would be different. And it wasn't the circumstances, harrowing as they were, it was the stranger.

"Andy," Tim said, intervening again, placing a hand on Andy's heaving chest, trying to force him back a step or two without igniting him. "Come on, man, just chill."

"Fuck that..." Andy pushed Tim aside and swung a big right hand at the stranger.

Tim wasn't sure what happened next; he'd never seen anything like it. *Fluid violence* were the first words that popped into his head. *Fluid*, because the stranger's response to Andy's attack seemed effortless; *violence*, because Andy suddenly found himself face down on the road, the stranger pinning him there with one knee in Andy's back and one hand on his head.

Perhaps, Tim quickly thought, fluid *restraint* was more apt; it was obvious the stranger had no intention of hurting Andy, merely controlling him. When the stranger spoke a tick later, it verified Tim's assumption.

"I have no intention of hurting you," he said. "But if you continue to try and harm me, *I will*."

Andy, one cheek mashed against the road, the stranger's hand pressing down on the other, muttered through distorted lips: "Okay, man—I'm cool, I'm cool."

IX

It was an old man with white hair and glasses that offered a hand and a smile to Andy. Andy took it, and the old man helped him to his feet. The stranger with the shaved head stayed a cautious few feet back in case Andy fancied his chances again.

The girls remained in the car with the child, but their window was now down, catching everything.

"Are you all right?" the old man asked Andy.

Andy started brushing himself off. "Fine." He eyed the stranger for a brief moment before focusing all of his attention on the old man. "Who are you?"

The old man smiled and extended his hand for the second time. "Russell Jon. I'm a professor at Bemidji State."

Andy took the professor's hand again. "You lost?"

Professor Jon said, "According to my friend, we are not."

All eyes fell on the stranger with the shaved head.

Andy grunted. "You mean the UFC heavyweight champ over there?"

"My name is Kanen," the stranger said. "You can call me Kane. I apologize for my actions, but you—"

Andy held up a hand, cutting him off. "Forget it."

Tim was shocked at his friend's willingness to yield without issue—not only to the physical encounter (it wasn't like he could dispute such a one-sided result after all), but more importantly, to the aftermath. No pride-dented posturing and finger-pointing from a safe distance after the fact; no empty threats for revenge to quench the ego, to kick-start the guaranteed diatribe he would undoubtedly recite over and over once he was safely back in the car, each telling carrying more venom and sincerity than the last in order to save face in front of Rachel.

Was Tim's *punch first, ask questions later* friend maturing before his eyes? Or was such a swift and sound ass-whooping at the hands of this man who called himself Kane the reason for Andy's sudden willingness to be such a forgiving fellow? Tim wanted to believe the former. His gut was more realistic, wagering on the latter.

"Is it just the two of you out here?" Tim asked.

"Yes," Professor Jon said.

"*No,*" Kane refuted.

"So you saw them?" Tim asked.

Kane stepped forward. His face was as granite as ever, but the inflection in his voice held curiosity. "Them *who*?" he asked. "What did you see?"

Tim said, "We didn't see anyone. But someone *did* steal our cell phones…" He pointed to the tree in the road. "Also cut that tree down to keep us from going anywhere." Tim then paused a moment, Kane's earlier comment coming back to him. He frowned and said, "Wait—you said it's *not* just the two of you out here?"

Kane looked away and said nothing.

Professor Jon said, "No, it is, it is. My friend is looking for someone. He believes they may be out here."

"Wouldn't happen to be a little girl, would it?" Andy asked.

"Come again?" the professor said.

"It's why we're out here," Tim said. "We were on our way to a cabin we rented for the weekend. On the way we spotted a little girl tied to a tree."

The professor's mouth dropped as he put a hand to his chest.

"I know, right? So, of course, we stopped to help her. The poor kid looks ridiculously neglected. She can barely talk." Tim paused as the professor leaned to his left and looked inside the Toyota at the little girl between Michelle and Rachel. "As we were helping her," Tim continued, "someone must have gotten inside our car and stolen our cell phones without us noticing. They left the keys though. In fact, they left everything—everything except the phones."

"But they left the *keys*?"

Tim nodded. "Curious, huh?"

"Very."

Tim said, "Yeah, well, if you told me they were kids just trying to steal something as quick as they could in order to make a few bucks, I might be able to buy it ... "

"Yet you say nothing else was stolen."

"Yup."

"Strange they would risk rummaging around for phones instead of just grabbing whatever they could—if they were only after a quick buck, of course."

"I thought the exact same thing," Tim said. "So we decided whoever it was, didn't want us calling for help." He flicked his chin towards the car. "Maybe because of the child."

"Meaning?"

Tim gave a thin smile. "Still trying to figure that out."

The professor looked at the car again. Kane kept his eyes on the surrounding woods.

Tim continued. "Anyway, we decided to just forget the cabin and head back to the Cities. Of course we were only on the road for a minute or so." He gestured towards the tree.

Andy had wandered over to the base of the fallen tree. He ran a hand over the cut. "Whoever chopped this thing must have been Paul Bunyan on meth," he said. "We couldn't have been with the kid *that* long."

Rachel leaned her head out the window. "Maybe they used a chainsaw."

"We would have heard it," Andy called back.

"Maybe that's what that noise was," she replied.

Andy frowned. "That wasn't a chainsaw, Rach."

Rachel tucked her head back inside the car and mumbled something derogatory.

"Noise?" Professor Jon said.

Andy joined the three of them again. "Yeah—some God-awful screech. Thought my eardrums were gonna burst. You didn't hear it?"

"We did, yes. We figured it for a bird."

"That's what Tim said."

Kane said. "When did you hear this?"

Andy shrugged. "Probably the same time you did."

Kane closed his eyes and shook his head slowly as though irritated. "*When.*"

Andy made a face. "I just told you."

Kane spoke slow and firm. "At which *point* did you hear the animal cry?"

Andy shrugged. "I'm not following you, man. Chances are, you heard it the same time we did. We were carrying the kid to the car—"

Kane turned his back to Andy, cutting him off. He then began wandering towards the woods.

Andy turned to the professor. "What's up with that guy? In fact, what's up with *both* of you? Where the hell'd you come from anyway?"

The professor shot a thumb behind him. "There's a village not far down the road."

"You're from the village?" Tim said.

"Not *from*—staying at. How do you know of it? Have you been already?"

"No," Andy said. "We saw it on the map. We figured whoever did this to that little girl was probably *from* the village. Figured it best to steer clear."

The professor nodded. "Sound thinking—but I can assure you the people at the village are quite friendly. They've been very accommodating."

"Why are you staying there?" Tim asked.

"As I mentioned, my friend is looking for someone nearby."

"How far is that village from here?"

"About a mile down the road."

"You walked a mile? Out here? In the cold? At *night*?"

The professor gave Tim an understanding smile. "My friend is an excellent tracker."

"He an Indian?" Andy blurted.

The professor frowned. "If you choose to use that word for descriptive purposes then I suggest you place his tribe before it. He is *Cree* Indian."

Andy rolled his eyes. "Forgive me."

"Yes, well, I shouldn't have to explain as to why you should show more respect, seeing as how you'll be picking gravel out of your teeth for some time."

Now it was Andy who turned and began wandering away.

Tim said, "I'm sorry if we seem a little worked up—but after all that's happened to us tonight, I'm sure you can understand."

The professor nodded. "Of course. You say you have a wounded child with you?"

"I don't know about wounded, but she's definitely not doing too well. Gotta be chilled to the bone at least. You have a phone on you?"

"Not with me—it's back at the village. In fact, I suggest you stop by—they can tend to the girl."

Andy reappeared. "We appreciate your input, but I suggest we say fuck the village, and keep on driving."

"Past the tree?" the professor asked.

Andy turned a thumb towards Kane in the distance. "What about Tonto? Can't he help us?"

The professor's look of disgust was all but a wad of spit in Andy's face.

Tim stepped in front of Andy and held an apologetic hand up to the professor. "Again, I'm sorry. It's just … we wanna get home. We wanna get this girl some help."

The professor sighed, dropped his head and nodded. "I understand." He lifted his head and faced the woods.

Kane was gone.

"Where'd he go?" Andy asked.

Tim said, "Weren't you watching him?"

Andy threw up his hands.

The professor cupped his hands over his mouth and called for Kane. His own voice echoed back to them, nothing else.

"The hell did he go?" Andy said. He went to the car. "You girls see where that big guy went?"

Both Rachel and Michelle shook their heads.

Andy returned to Tim and the professor. "Dude just vanished."

"If I may suggest *again* … " The professor was facing Tim, but his con- descension wore Andy's name. "We take the child to the village. They seem decent people—a little behind the times, but good and wholesome nonetheless. They can tend to the child while you and your crew rest and regroup. I'm certain someone can help you remove the tree in the morn- ing so you can be on your way."

"But that would be fixing the problem and not the cause," Tim said.

"I'm sorry?"

"Well, we could go to the village. They could help the kid, give us cozy rooms, and make us a good old country breakfast in the morning, but that's still not going to explain anything is it? It's putting a Band-Aid over the fact that we found a child tied to a tree and left to die, and then someone did their best to sabotage our efforts to call for help or leave. You can't just let that drop, Professor."

"I'm not proposing you do." The professor fanned an arm over their surroundings. "But as you can plainly see; it's dark and cold and it will only get darker and colder."

"What about your friend the tracker?"

The professor hesitated. Tim watched his eyes shift like a bad card player's.

Oh good, Tim thought, *we* need *more mystery right about now.*

"He'll be fine," the professor eventually said. "He'll return when he's … satisfied."

Satisfied?

"*Okay*," Tim said, letting an intentional hint of skepticism into his voice. "Will he be returning to the village or … ?"

"Yes—the village. We're *both* staying there."

"And then what?"

The professor did not look at Tim when he said, "I guess I'll have to wait and see."

More puzzles. And the pieces no less ambiguous. Tim sensed the pro- fessor a decent man, but he was hiding something. He was also … scared? No. Nervous? Maybe. Having an imposing guy like Kane sidling up to you would make Mike Tyson nervous. But there was something else, something more. Better still, Tim felt the professor *knew* Tim suspected more. And so Tim, sensing the professor on a back foot the man had neither planned nor expected, decided to nudge—just enough to get the man teetering back over the ledge before Tim would snag his belt and pull him forward to collapse into grateful arms, hopefully blathering the truth.

"All right," Tim said. "You know where the village is, yes?"

"Yes," the professor said, still avoiding eye contact.

He knows that I know.

Except I don't know what I know.

But he doesn't know that.

Seconds from a colossal brain fart, Tim shook it away, refocused, donned his still purposefully wary façade (it was hardly a difficult act), and then waved an arm toward his car as though it were the finest on the lot.

"Well then hop on in, Professor—we'll give you a ride."

X

She watched from her window above. The car emptied. There were four, plus the old man she had already met—and they did indeed have the offering with them.

Although her status in the colony did not privilege a young lady such as herself to firsthand information of this importance, her personal quest superseded such an impudent act as eavesdropping. She therefore heard the earlier news carefully tucked away in a forgotten crawlspace. The clarity had been strong—as though she'd been sitting in on the meeting with the elders themselves.

The offering had been freed. By four outsiders. Outsiders she viewed as hopefuls. She held little comfort in the promises brought by the Cree and the old man. She wanted to be gone—far away from here with her baby before it was too late.

She rubbed her ample belly, due in less than two months' time.

Four hopefuls.

XI

The village was small. Five weathered but sturdy cottages in total, the largest of the five—a white stone building resembling a historic country inn—stood tall in the village center. Professor Jon led them towards it.

"Little pigs, little pigs..." Andy announced after pushing open the heavy wooden door.

Professor Jon looked at Tim. "Can you please control your friend?"

Tim nodded but did nothing. Rachel held the child. Michelle stood at the end of the pack.

"*Hello!?*" Andy yelled.

This time the professor slapped Tim's shoulder in protest for Andy's behavior. Tim was startled by the stranger's swipe, and his instinct was to retaliate, but unlike his friend, common sense was his leash and he simply said, "Andy, shut up. People are probably asleep."

Andy looked at his watch. "It's only eight."

Tim took in the room. It reminded him of a place he and Michelle had visited in Pennsylvania—an old Amish bed and breakfast. The experience had been...an experience—pizza and DVDs and hot showers were happily re-embraced once they'd returned home.

A woman, mid-forties, came down the stairs and approached the group. She wore a beige blouse, buttoned high and tight to the neck, and a beige skirt that may have been an apron in its utilitarian modesty had it not been without a strap for the neck. The woman wore no makeup, long gray hair was pulled tight into a bun. Her expression appeared even, not put out by their arrival.

"Hi," Tim said. "We're having kind of a difficult night to say the least. Is there any chance you could accommodate us?"

The woman's response was curiously immediate. "Of course. How many of you are there?"

Tim turned and looked at the little girl in Rachel's arms, then back at the woman. "Uh, well before we get to that, you should probably take a look at her first."

The woman tilted her head past Tim to get a look at Rachel and the child.

Tim went on: "We found her tied to a tree about a mile up the road. She can hardly speak. We think she's been badly neglected and then basically left for dead. Obviously, we want to get her some help."

The woman put a brief hand to her collared neck. "The poor child." She took her eyes off the little girl and looked at the professor. "Hello again. Did you and your friend enjoy your walk?"

Michelle stepped forward. "Um, *excuse me*? But who gives a shit if they enjoyed their walk? Are you going to get us some help for this little girl?"

The woman dropped her head and drew a cross on her chest immediately following the word *shit*.

Tim put a hand on Michelle's shoulder and squeezed lightly. *Same page, baby—but more flies with honey…* the squeeze said.

Michelle got it immediately and turned her attention to Rachel and the child.

Tim waited for the woman to lift her head. "I'm sorry about that," he said. "As I mentioned; it's been a very difficult night for us."

The woman nodded, looked at Rachel and held out her arms. "If you give the child to me, I can have someone else show you to your rooms."

Rachel shielded the little girl from the woman's outstretched arms with a turn of the shoulder. "If it's all the same to you, I'd like to stay with her," she said.

Another woman came down the stairs, her attire the same as the other. The lack of lines in her face suggested she was younger by perhaps a decade; however her hair, also a tight bun, was just as gray.

The older of the two women said, "I understand." She turned to the younger woman. "Gwendolyn, can you show our guests to a room, please?"

"Wait," Michelle said. "What about a phone? Shouldn't we call someone first?"

The woman said, "We don't have telephones in our colony."

Andy said, "Of course not."

Tim faced the professor. "That's okay, the professor here has a cell." He smiled and added: "Unless you were lying. You weren't lying, were you, Professor?"

The professor had the shifty eyes of the bad card player again. "No ... I wasn't."

But you're about to, aren't ya?

"But I'm afraid I don't get a signal out here. I've tried several times."

"Hard luck," Tim said.

Andy said, "Go get it anyway. I'll go back out and wander around until we get a signal."

"Good idea," Tim said. "Professor?"

Everyone's eyes were on the professor, except Tim's—his held a sly fix on the two women.

"I suppose I could go get it," Professor Jon said.

And then Tim got what he was looking for, only it wasn't exactly what he expected. Tim was waiting for an emotional response from the two women when Professor Jon would undoubtedly agree to retrieve his phone after being put on the spot. He got one, but they weren't the fleeting expressions of concern or maybe even anger he was anticipating. What Tim saw instead was fear.

The puzzle may be starting to come together a little, but the picture could still be anything.

Tim looked at the two women. "Would you mind if we waited here for a moment? For the professor to return with his phone?"

The older of the two women said, "Of course not. Gwendolyn and I will go and start preparing your room."

Tim thanked her, and the group watched the two women head back upstairs.

Andy eventually turned to the professor and said, "Are you gonna go get your phone or what?"

· · ·

The professor took his time climbing the stairs and heading back to his room. How the heck was he going to explain himself? Why didn't he tell them out in the woods that he simply didn't *have* a phone? It would have been a tough one to swallow (who the heck didn't own a cell phone these days?), but it would have gone down a lot easier than claiming you did have one, but *oops!*—forgot to mention you couldn't get a signal. How was he going to explain his phone flashing a full stack of bars?

Should he pop the battery? No—Tim was a clever young man; he would check.

Break it? Should he break his phone? Claim it had mysteriously cracked somehow? It was plausible. Perhaps he had placed the phone in his bag and carelessly tossed it to the floor. It could happen.

Do you really want to break your phone over all this though? he thought. *Kane is getting weird; the villagers, in their naiveté, even weirder. And the child... the poor thing could have pneumonia.*

The professor entered his room and headed towards one of two single beds. Oil lamps on each nightstand gave a soft but sufficient yellow glow. He took a seat on his bed and began digging through his bag.

Your book. Think about your book.

He continued digging, tossing clothes onto the floor...

But the child. Kane doesn't care about the child. She's bait for him, nothing more. Of course no Windigo would show and claim her, but who was to say something else wouldn't? Least of all, and perhaps most assuredly, the elements?

His phone wasn't in his bag. The professor stood and searched the rest of the room, even Kane's belongings. His phone was not there.

.   .   .

"My phone is gone," the professor said the moment he returned.

"Bullshit," Andy said.

The professor's usual pallid complexion began to redden.

He's either lying or scared, Tim thought. *Or both.*

"Please believe me," the professor pleaded. "My phone is *not* in my room—it's gone."

Rachel hoisted the child in her arms in a bid for more comfort. "Maybe—" She stopped, lowered her voice. "Maybe the people who took *our* phones ... " She flicked her eyes towards the stairs.

"So it *was* the people from this village," Michelle said.

"*No*," the professor said. "It wasn't them." He took a deep breath and sighed. "Not exactly."

"What's that supposed to mean?" Tim said.

Andy stepped forward and took hold of the professor's elbow. "Fuck this—he's lying." Andy began leading the professor towards the stairs. "Your Cree buddy isn't here to protect you now, Professor. And I have no problem kicking the shit out of an old man."

Andy began dragging Professor Jon upstairs, the professor pleading along the way. Tim did not interject. The professor had seemed moments from confessing to something. And while ordinarily Tim favored a smooth approach in coaxing out a prospective truth from someone, right now his friend's aggressive method seemed to be doing a sufficient job in expediting the process while simultaneously scaring the shit out of the old man. And a scared man is often a chatty man.

So Tim did not interject. He instead headed towards the stairs and motioned for the girls to follow.

.   .   .

When Tim and the girls arrived, Andy was rifling through the room like a crazed detective looking for evidence. The professor sat on the edge of the bed, still visibly shaken, but resigned to the fact that he was going nowhere and that Andy was going to have his way.

"Andy," Tim said after a minute of his friend's frantic searching. "Andy, stop."

Andy did not. He continued to search—drawers, shelves, under the bed. When Andy hoisted the professor to his feet and began patting him down, Tim physically intervened.

"Okay, that's enough." Tim fronted his friend and put a hand on his shoulder. "That's enough, man."

There was a knock at the door. A sudden silence came over the room, like a secret party being investigated by mom and dad. Tim kicked some of the loose clothing to one side of the room. Michelle pushed in two open drawers.

"Come in?" Tim said.

The door opened. It was the older of the two women they'd previously met. If she had heard the commotion she did not show it. "Your room is ready," she said, a glance around the room, and then at each of them. "Would you like to come with me?"

"Actually," Tim said, "we're going to stay here and chat with Professor Jon for a few minutes first. That okay?"

The woman stepped forward, handed Tim a heavy brass key. "Third room down the hall on your left. Bathroom is the last room on the right." She looked at Rachel who had since wrapped her coat around the child and was now holding the little girl snug to the chest. The child clung silent to Rachel like a koala to a tree, her expression back to vacant. "And the child?" the woman asked.

"We're going to keep her warm for now," Tim said. "If we need anything, we'll let you know."

The woman left without another word.

Andy, his ire no less blazing, still had the common sense to speak in a loud whisper. "*Where is it?*" he asked Professor Jon.

The professor threw up his hands. "Go ahead and search the room some more if it'll make you happy. I'd like to find the bugger just as much as you would."

"Lying piece of—"

"Andy, wait a minute," Tim said. "Professor, you were about to say something downstairs. When Rachel and Michelle accused the people here of taking your phone and ours, you sounded pretty confident it wasn't them. But then you were about to add something. What was it?"

The professor glanced warily at Andy, then at Tim and said, "Will you promise to control your friend if I tell the truth?"

"I can try," Tim said.

The professor swallowed hard. "Fine. The villagers did *not* take your phones. But they know who did."

"Who?" Andy said.

The professor swallowed hard again.

"*You* took them," Tim said. "You and Kane."

The professor exhaled. "Yes."

Michelle blurted: "*What?*"

"Let him explain," Tim said.

The professor ran his hands back and forth over his knees. "Where to begin … "

"Begin with the part about why you took our fucking phones," Andy said.

The professor gave a quick, shameful nod. "A villager spotted your headlights in the distance. He saw that you had discovered the child. He quickly told Kane and me, and it then became imperative that we stop you from calling for help … and then stop you from leaving."

"So you cut down the tree too," Tim said.

"Kane did, yes."

Rachel handed the child off to Michelle and got in the professor's face. "You *knew* about her?" She pointed back at the little girl in Michelle's arms, her eyes staying put on the professor. "You *knew?*"

The professor gave a pathetic nod. "Yes."

Rachel slapped him.

Andy laughed. "Looks like I'm not the one you need to worry about, Professor."

Tim hushed Rachel to one side before bringing his attention back to Professor Jon, who now sported a glowing red cheek and crooked glasses.

"I deserved that," the professor said, fixing his glasses. "But I can assure you, I was never going to let the child come to harm."

"How can you say that?" Michelle asked. She hoisted the child on her hip. "*Look at her.*"

"I only just met the child today. Kane and the villagers had made some kind of prior arrangement before I was even involved."

"Involved in what?" Tim asked.

The professor eyed them one at a time. "Have you ever heard of the legend of the Windigo?"

XII

Their conversations were faint. Not only had they lowered their voices, but the particular crawlspace she now occupied did not afford her the acoustic luxuries the one behind the meeting of the elders had provided. It was also a tighter fit—the wall pressed hard on her pregnant belly as she struggled to listen.

So far she had gotten bits and pieces. Nothing coherent. She would have to take a risk.

XIII

Andy said, "Are you honestly telling us that you're out here with some psycho Indian, hunting a *monster*?"

"There *is* no monster," the professor said.

"Yeah, well I think your buddy Kane disagrees with you on that one."

"I'm well aware of Kane's stance on the issue. His father, his wounds, his hair."

Rachel frowned. "He doesn't *have* any hair."

"He shaves it—in honor of his father. Cutting one's hair is how many Native Americans pay respects to the passing of a loved one. Kane has vowed to keep shaving his head until he kills the Windigo and avenges his father's death."

"Dude's gonna be bald forever," Andy said.

The professor gave Andy a weak smile. Andy did not smile back—no sale.

"So you're going through all this to write a book about something you don't even believe in?" Tim said.

The professor shrugged. "Does one need to be steeped in belief before they can report on the subject?"

"No," Tim said. "No they don't. But putting a child's life at stake?"

"I told you—I didn't even know about the child until after we'd arrived. For all I know, Kane has been keeping the poor thing locked away for God knows how long, waiting for this moment."

"Listen to you," Andy said. "'*The poor thing.*' You knew she was tied up out there."

"But I also knew that a Windigo would never come to claim her. *How could it?*"

"And what about other animals?" Michelle said. "What if they decided to come along and take a bite? Did you ever think about that?"

"Or the weather?" Rachel added. "She could have frozen to death."

"Again, you must understand; this knowledge—a child as bait—was never explained to me in advance. It was thrust upon me *after* my arrival."

"And yet you still went along with it," Tim said. "The villagers too. I thought you said they were good people."

"They are good people. *Simple* people. They truly believe their woods are cursed with a Windigo. Kane promised to rid them of this curse."

"By sacrificing a child."

"The Windigo craves any and all human flesh, but it *prefers* children. The Cree are renowned Windigo hunters. The villagers know this. With my assistance as the so-called medicine man, we formulated sacred tinctures to coat Kane's weaponry. This increased his chances innumerably. My guess is the villagers figured it likely that Kane would kill the creature before the child came to any harm."

"'*Renowned Windigo hunters?*'" Andy said. "'*Sacred tinctures?*' Are you fucking kidding me?"

"I'm speaking in terms of *legend*," the professor said irritably. "I was planning to join Kane as he waited by that tree." He turned and looked at Rachel, then Michelle. "I would have never let anything happen to the child. In fact I was *relieved* when you arrived—it was getting so cold ..."

"Unbelievable," Michelle scoffed.

"Why do you think I kept trying to get you back to the village? Why did I keep suggesting it?"

"Because Kane and the villagers wanted the kid back, and they were afraid we'd take her with us," Andy said.

"*Wrong*," the professor said. "I wanted her out of the cold. I wanted her someplace safe."

"If you wanted her someplace safe then you should have let us take her, dickhead."

"I couldn't stop Kane. Once the villagers told him what was happening he became a man possessed—more so."

Tim said, "Why leave our keys though? The phones I get, but why leave us the keys?"

"The villagers feared for your safety if you made your way to the village on foot. They feared the Windigo would claim *all* of you. It would then turn its attention on the village—payback for botching its sacrifice."

"So you took our phones and left us our keys so we would ultimately return the child to the village in the safety of our car. Had we walked, the big bad Windigo would have gotten us," Tim said.

"Theoretically—yes."

"Wait," Andy said, "where *are* our phones?"

The professor sighed. "Kane has them."

"You're such a fucking douche. You were putting on such an act out there, weren't you? '*Strange they would risk rummaging around for phones instead of just grabbing whatever they could,*'" Andy mocked.

"Again, I was just thinking about the child's—"

Tim said, "What if we just kept driving?"

"Sorry?"

"Well, the tree blocked our way back, but what if we kept going *past* the village? We were headed that way initially."

"The road ends about five miles beyond the village. You would have been stuck."

"So we *were* fucking lost," Andy muttered.

"Okay—well then I guess a 'bravo' is in order for you and Kane," Tim said. "You saw to it that we had nowhere to go but the village. That means they were definitely getting the child back."

"Yes."

"And you were okay with that?"

"Yes and no. Yes, because there is no such thing as a Windigo, and no, because I was worried about the child's health."

"What were they planning to do with us?"

"What do you mean?"

Tim chuckled. "Well, we weren't about to leave tomorrow morning without the kid, you know."

The professor opened his mouth to speak, but then closed it and said nothing.

"Didn't think about that, did you?" Tim said.

"They wouldn't harm you," the professor said. "They're wholesome people. God-fearing people."

"Well that's good to know. What about your buddy Kane?"

Again the professor opened his mouth, only to close it without a word.

"That's why the kid is overweight, isn't it?" Tim said. "It's why the only words she knows are 'eat' and 'eat now.' Kane was force-feeding her to be nice and plump for his Windigo—keeping her locked away like some kind of Christmas goose."

The professor shrugged. "It's possible I suppose."

"I'd say more than possible."

The professor sighed and nodded.

"So what now?" Andy asked the professor. "What do you propose we do?"

"My plan was to call for help in the morning."

"Oh yeah?" Andy said. "You gonna open a window and shout?"

The professor sighed again.

"Kane will never let us leave with that child," Tim said. "Will he?"

"You have to understand; Kane is not a bad man. But he *is* obsessed. Avenging his father consumes him. I'd be lying if I said I didn't question his stability."

"You think *he's* the one who took your phone, don't you?" Tim asked.

"I'd considered it."

"Could also be one of the villagers," Michelle said.

Tim thought of the fleeting expression of fear on the women's faces when the professor said he would retrieve his phone. Could they have ducked in and made a quick grab for the cell on their way to preparing the room down the hall? They would have had to be damn quick about it. Not to mention know where to look. Still, it was possible.

"Could be," Tim said to Michelle.

The professor went to object, but Tim spoke first. "We get it, Professor: they're good people. Wholesome people. But they also believe in monsters."

"Meaning what exactly?"

Tim smiled. "Doctors used to drill holes in a sick man's head to let the evil spirits out, yes?"

The professor nodded.

"Well, whether they believed it would work or not was ultimately irrelevant, wasn't it? At the end of the day you still had a fucking hole in your head."

.   .   .

All five, plus the child had moved to the room prepared down the hall.

"I want to leave now," Rachel said. "I'm not waiting until morning."

"I'll second that," Andy said.

Tim said, "We do still have our keys…"

"And the tree?" Professor Jon asked.

"We'll move it. Somehow, we'll move it."

"What would we tell the villagers?" the professor asked.

"We don't have to tell them anything," Michelle said. She'd since lowered the child to her side and now held her hand. "We just get in our car and go."

"What if they try and stop us?" Rachel asked.

Andy made a face. "It's two women, Rach. I think we'll be all right."

"There are more of course," the professor said. "Men."

"How many?" Tim asked.

"I don't know—twenty, maybe thirty. There are families in the adjacent cottages. Here too—in this one."

"Jesus, they're quiet enough," Andy said.

"You think they'll cause any resistance if we try to leave?" Tim asked the professor.

"No—I don't think so."

"What about Kane?" Andy said.

The professor hesitated. "I don't believe he would hurt us intentionally."

"What kind of weapons does he have?" Andy asked.

"Does it matter?" Michelle said. "He kicked your ass with one finger."

"*A*: fuck you, and *B*: that's not what I was getting at."

"You thinking maybe we could use his weapons against him if he tried to stop us?" Tim asked his friend.

"Exactly." Andy looked at the professor. "Only I didn't see any in your room."

"And I didn't see any when we met him outside earlier," Tim added.

"He had them," the professor said. "He tucked them away before we made contact with you. How do you suppose he cut that tree down?"

"Does he have a gun?" Tim asked.

The professor shook his head. "He has his father's knives. His father's bow and arrows. And of course, a sizeable hatchet."

"All doused in your magical anti-Windigo goop, right?" Andy said.

The professor ignored him.

"Where do you suppose he is now?" Tim asked.

The professor shrugged. "No idea."

"Well then fuck it," Andy said. "Let's just go. The longer we wait … "

"If we all pile out of here now it'll make too much noise," the professor said. "The villagers may not harm us, but I'm sure they'd have no qualms about alerting Kane."

"We sneak out then," Andy said. "One at a time if we have to. There's gotta be a back staircase or a window or—"

"*There is.*"

Everyone's head spun toward the closet. The door was open a crack. A slice of a pretty young girl's face was visible. "There is another way out. I can show you."

Rachel stepped forward. "Have you been in there the whole time?"

The young girl said, "I can show you. But if I do…" She stepped out of the closet and exposed her pregnant belly. "Will you promise to take me with you?"

XIV

"Can this shit get any weirder?"

"Shut up, Andy," Rachel said. Then to the young girl: "Who are you?"

"Elizabeth," she said. "Will you take me with you?"

"Take you where?" Tim said. "Where is it you think we're going?"

"Away from here," Elizabeth said. "Somewhere my baby can be safe." She rubbed her stomach.

"Safe from who?" Michelle asked.

Elizabeth looked at the floor as she spoke. "I know you don't believe. I don't care. I've never seen it either. But others have. The elders have."

"Are you talking about the Windigo, child?" the professor asked.

"Yes."

"How *old* are you?" Rachel asked, her eyes traveling between the girl's porcelain face and plump belly.

"Sixteen."

Michelle's face dropped. "You're so young—to be having a child, I mean."

"It is our duty. On our sixteenth birthday."

"It's your duty to get pregnant?" Andy said.

Rachel elbowed him.

"Our duty to offer our firstborn," she said.

"Who's the father?" Rachel asked.

"One of the elders. The father doesn't matter. The *child* doesn't matter." Tears started down her cheeks, her hands clutching her belly. "Firstborn is an offering."

"Jesus Christ." Tim looked at the professor. "Am I hearing this right?"

The professor, his expression no less horrified, nodded. "I think so."

"Please help me," Elizabeth said. "Help me save my baby." She gestured to the little girl next to Michelle. "Help me save them all."

"Oh, don't worry," Michelle said, petting the little girl's head, "she's coming with us."

Elizabeth shook her head. "You're not seeing the whole picture just yet. Please follow me. Stay close and be as quiet as you can."

XV

A man with a long black beard approached the main door and knocked. He was granted permission to enter. The room was filled. Six elders—three men and three women. The man with the long black beard held a look of panic on his face.

XVI

They had made their way down the back staircase. A route easy enough to travel, yet tricky to find. Elizabeth had used it countless times.

Before long they were outside, their car in sight. Tim squeezed his keys tight in his palm, the metal biting into his skin a queer reassurance. All six headed for the Toyota. Elizabeth did not. She stayed put by one of the cottages flanking the main one they'd occupied.

Michelle, balancing the child on her hip, frantically waved Elizabeth toward them with her free hand. Elizabeth shook her head, waved them to *her*.

A trap, Tim thought. *We're being led to a trap.*

But before he could voice his suspicions, Michelle, Rachel, and the child were heading toward Elizabeth.

Shit.

Tim followed, Andy and Professor Jon close behind. All three men crouched and scurried forward in the moonlight like thieves.

When they were all together by one of the smaller cottages, Elizabeth brought them to the building's rear where two cellar doors protruded from the ground on an angle. The doors were padlocked.

Elizabeth pulled a key from her pocket and dropped to one knee with a grunt, her full belly making the simple task laborious. She stuck the key in the padlock, unlocked the double doors, and stepped back.

Andy took the initiative, stepped forward and pulled one of the double doors open. They descended into the cool earth. Tim found a light switch on the stone wall and hit it. Their eyes were rewarded with light and then punished with atrocity.

XVII

Mesh cages lined the cellar walls. Each cage housed a plump infant, some already too big for their housing—their plentiful bodies pressing against the wire casing, flesh pushing its way through the patterned mesh like cubes of pink dough. The smallest lay slack on their sides, eyes far away, like neglected animals.

But to Tim, this wasn't the worst of it.

The worst was that some of the infants weren't crying or cooing like infants should. They were mewling—like calves, like sheep.

The five of them stood in shock-horror, taking it all in. There were six cages in all. The oldest occupant appeared maybe three, the youngest barely one. The smell was a jolt of human feces, the task of feeding seemingly more a priority than discarding their leavings.

Elizabeth, perhaps fearful that her intent on shock had not been forewarned, and was thus *too* effective, pulled a stunned Tim by the arm towards the nearest cage.

"Help me," she said. "We have to free them all."

Elizabeth's words, like a starting pistol, shot everyone into action, each heading for a cage.

They pried, pulled, and ripped with desperate urgency. When all six kids plus the first child were safe in their arms, they hurried back towards the cellar door … where Kane and two villagers were waiting.

XVIII

Kane stepped forward but said nothing; his presence alone was enough to collectively freeze them all. One of the villagers was the first to speak—a man to Kane's right, seemingly in his thirties, short black hair in contrast to a long black beard, his attire the male equivalent of the female villagers they had met earlier: utilitarian, nothing more.

The man said, "Please put them back. You have no right."

Michelle, who held one of the babies in her arms as though it were a football she would sooner die with than fumble, breathed, "You're crazy. You're all fucking crazy."

Kane took another step forward. Both Tim and Andy blocked his path, each holding a child of their own, each holding in the same protective manner as Michelle.

Kane locked eyes with both of them, each gaze brief in duration but forever in intensity. "You know what I'm capable of," he said. "Please don't make me hurt you."

Tim knew they were no physical match for Kane. The villagers on his side made it even more lopsided. "Kane, please," Tim said. "We know all about your father. We know all about the Windigo. We understand your cause. But this is *not* the way to go about it. My God, man, look around you ... "

As though on cue, one of the children began its calf-like cry. Another followed. And then another, each one spurring on the next like some horrific Pavlovian chorus hoping for sustenance—the only thing they knew.

"Do you *hear* that!?" Tim yelled. "It's like a goddamn farm! These are *children*!"

The second villager, a near mirror image of the other, replied, "They are offerings. They are not blessed by our priest when born. They have no souls. They are meat, nothing more."

Andy and Tim looked on in disbelief. Rachel had since backed up towards the end of the cellar, two babies in her arms. Elizabeth was next to her, one baby in her arms, the original child by her leg. The professor stayed quiet in one corner of the room.

"I don't want any unnecessary hurt," Kane said to Tim. "Give me the original child. When the Windigo comes for her, I will kill it." He waved an arm around the cellar. "Once I do, all of these children can be saved."

And then Tim asked, "What if it kills *you*?"

Before Tim could regret—or wonder—why he would ask such a thing, it was too late: Kane had reacted. He'd snatched Michelle in a blur and had pulled her to him, a blade pressed to her throat.

"Bring me the child," Kane said. "I don't want any unnecessary hurt, but I *will* slice your friend's throat unless you bring me the child."

"The baby," Tim said to Kane, motioning towards the infant in Michelle's arms. "She's going to drop the baby."

Kane flicked his head downward, indicating Tim should take it. He did. And now Tim held two children.

"Bring me the child," Kane said again.

Nobody moved.

Kane looked at one of the villagers. "Get her," he said.

The villager hurried forward, scooped up the child and brought her back. Rachel and Elizabeth stayed still and mute, the blade to Michelle's throat a blade to their own.

"Take her above," Kane said.

Both villagers paused.

Kane said, "What is it?"

The villagers were focused on the back of the cellar—where Elizabeth stood. "She is one of ours," one of them said.

Kane locked eyes with Elizabeth. "Go," he said.

Without protest, Elizabeth placed the infant in her arms back into its cage, hurried forward and up the cellar stairs with the two villagers.

Kane, his knife still to Michelle's throat, spoke with what sounded like rueful scorn. "This is your own doing. I offered you a peaceful way." He shifted his gaze towards one corner of the room. "Professor, we need to go."

The professor crept forward.

Andy locked eyes with him. "You pathetic motherfucker."

"What's going to happen to us?" Tim said.

Kane shoved Michelle into the corner where she fell on all fours. Tim flinched, but did nothing.

"Well," Kane said, taking the professor by the arm, ready to climb the cellar stairs, "I suppose if the Windigo kills me—as you proposed he might—then I would say you should start getting used to your new quarters."

Kane slammed the cellar doors and the world went black. The sound of the padlock came immediately after.

.   .   .

Kane took the child in his arms and began carrying her to the tree. The two villagers ran to their homes. Professor Jon followed Kane. Elizabeth hung back.

"Kane," Professor Jon said. "Please, you have to let those young men and women out of that cellar."

Kane marched on, the child on his hip. "When this is done."

The professor fronted Kane, stopping him. "When *what* is done? Kane, for God's sake, *please* listen to me. There is no damn Windigo. It simply isn't real!"

Kane shoved the professor aside and continued his march.

Professor Jon hollered to Kane's back. "*I'm using you!*"

Kane stopped, turned slowly, a curious expression on his face. "You're using *me*?" He gave a slight smirk. "Perhaps you have that backwards, Professor Jon."

"Do I? You're nothing more than a *character* for me, Kane. Pages in my book. My stupid, *stupid* book that is now jeopardizing lives because of my fragile ego. I took your proposal to give my project merit." He threw his head back and laughed. "*Merit!* It all sounds so laughable when spoken aloud. *Merit for monsters!*" Professor Jon made a sardonic gesture towards the weapons fastened to Kane's back. "I made no silly 'magic tincture' to coat those. Pungent herbs at my corner market mixed in ethanol is all it was!"

Kane glanced over the shoulder where his weapons hung. Glanced back at Professor Jon. "You were sending me to battle with tainted weaponry?"

"I was sending you to battle *nothing*, Kane! There's *nothing* out there! Good Christ, I must be insane to go as far as I did with this nonsense.

Truly, *I* am the monster here. The discovery of those poor children may be my only salvation."

Kane set the child to the ground, walked calmly towards Professor Jon, drew his blade, and sliced the professor's throat with one effortless swipe.

Wide-eyed, clutching his throat and sputtering red, the professor dropped to his knees. A look of disbelief was his final expression before pitching into the earth.

"If you are the monster," Kane said, wiping his blade on the arm of his coat, "then I believe your silly tinctures work rather well."

A small cry. Kane looked up. Elizabeth stared from behind a tree.

"You have nothing to fear, child," Kane said. "You know the truth."

Elizabeth gave a frightened nod.

"I *will* kill it," Kane said.

Elizabeth chanced emerging from the safety of the tree. "How? The professor claimed your weaponry was—"

Kane held up a hand, silencing her. The expression that fell over his face was an odd blend of purpose and sorrow. "Perhaps it takes evil to destroy evil." Kane bent and sliced into Professor Jon's face, removing a sizeable hunk of his cheek. He stood and brought the flesh to his lips. Elizabeth's scream paused him. He glanced at her, the flesh of Professor Jon inches from his mouth.

"Who will kill *you*?" Elizabeth asked.

Sorrow masked purpose entirely for a brief moment. When the moment passed, purpose back on equal ground, Kane said: "I will take my own life before the curse gathers strength."

Kane swallowed the chunk of Professor Jon's cheek whole.

Elizabeth gave another frightened yelp, backed up towards the safety of the tree again.

Kane shot her a sidelong glance. "I *will* kill it."

Elizabeth said nothing.

Kane scooped up the child and headed off into the woods.

XIX

A metallic rattle. A thump. The cellar doors opening. Elizabeth standing there in the moonlight.

·   ·   ·

"So what do we do?" Michelle asked. "We need help." She cradled one of the babies in her arms.

Elizabeth dug into her apron, pulled out a phone.

"Is that a cell phone?" Tim asked.

"I think so," Elizabeth said.

"Where did you get it?"

"I took it from the old man earlier. It was not the Cree, it was me. I thought it might be useful if you agreed to help me. I took it. It was not the Cree. Please don't think me bad."

Rachel stepped forward and kissed Elizabeth hard on the cheek. "Bad? I *love* you."

Elizabeth blushed, but the response was brief. "We need to hurry," she said.

Tim glanced down at Professor Jon's body. "Jesus, he really ate him?"

Elizabeth nodded. "And he has the child."

Rachel motioned towards the cell in Elizabeth's hand, and then looked at Tim. "Well, call the police!"

Elizabeth handed the phone to Tim. He was prepared to dial when an agonizing scream echoed its way out of the woods and caused him to fumble the cell. It was not the inhuman screech they had heard earlier. It was the scream of man.

"What the hell was that?" Michelle said.

"Was that Kane?" Andy asked.

Tim stuffed the phone into his pocket and started towards the woods.

"Tim!" Michelle called.

"*The kid!*" Tim yelled over his shoulder.

They all followed.

XX

Everyone came to a sudden halt behind Tim, as if the ground had suddenly crumbled away and they found themselves teetering on the edge of a cliff. If Tim sensed the group's arrival, he did not show it; his manner was trance-like, his blinkless eyes stuck on the football-shaped object lying on the ground. Kane's head.

"*Jesus Christ …*" Andy muttered.

Rachel turned away and vomited.

"What the hell happened?" Michelle asked in a breathless whisper.

"It's close," Elizabeth said.

Everyone looked at her. The consistent looks of skepticism they'd shared since the moment the girl had voiced her beliefs about the Windigo were gone. Fear and self-preservation were paramount now, the catalyst—however outlandish—irrelevant.

"I say we bolt," Andy said.

Michelle turned to him. "Without the girl?"

Andy pointed down at Kane's head. "Something did that to *Kane*. You think she did any better?"

Tim headed deeper into the woods.

"*Tim!*" Andy called in a loud whisper.

Tim ignored his friend and kept going. Rachel wiped her mouth. She looked terribly pale. Michelle put an arm around her. Again, they all followed Tim's lead, eyes straight ahead, refusing to acknowledge Kane's head at their feet as they shuffled past.

Ignoring the next find was impossible. Kane's body, next to it his discarded weaponry, next to that, the little girl, very much alive, sitting next to Kane's mutilated torso, her plump face smeared with red, her little hand digging into Kane's chest cavity, withdrawing whatever it could, shoving the find into her mouth, chewing and swallowing, and then digging for more. When the child became aware of the group's presence, she looked up and acknowledged them with a proud and bloodied smile. "*Eat? Eat? You eat?*"

Rachel vomited again.

Andy looked away as though angry with his own eyes.

Michelle attended to Rachel, the diversion welcome.

Tim was watching Elizabeth. Watching her sidling towards Kane's discarded hatchet. Watching her try and mask intentions of bending for it, her cumbersome belly betraying all attempts at subtlety. Watching her give up the act and deciding to drop and snatch the hatchet quickly. Watching her running towards the child with the hatchet raised, her murderous scream splitting the air.

Tim dove and the hatchet hit him in the arm, sinking deep, the pain dulled with adrenaline, but still intense enough to pause him, give Elizabeth time to raise the hatchet again, to *throw* it at the child, the weapon hitting the little girl in the chest, knocking her onto her back. Andy involved now, wrestling a screaming Elizabeth to the ground without care for her pregnancy, pinning her down and holding her as she thrashed and begged for the cursed child to be destroyed. Tim rolling onto all fours and crawling towards the little girl, checking her torso, finding the sizeable gash where the hatchet hit home, blood pumping pitilessly from the wound and Tim putting pressure on it with both hands, turning to Michelle and Rachel and screaming at them to call for help ...

XXI

Tim, Andy, Rachel, and Michelle stood by one of the many flashing squad cars on the scene. An EMT attended to Tim's arm as they spoke to the local sheriff.

"Got men from Saint Paul on their way," the sheriff said. "Major Crimes Division. Something like this ... Christ, I'm betting even they won't know where to begin."

Michelle pulled hard on a cigarette she'd bummed from one of the deputies. "Putting those crazy villagers in jail for life would be a good start," she said.

Tim winced a moment as the EMT tended to his arm, then glanced back at the sheriff. "You've never been here before? Never heard of these people?"

The sheriff nodded. "Sure—we knew they were here. *Knew what they were up to?*" He made a face that said hell no.

"How long have they been doing this?" Rachel asked, taking the cigarette from Michelle and taking a drag herself.

The sheriff shrugged. "Won't know until there's a proper investigation. But judging by what I saw in that cellar … " The sheriff removed his hat and glanced away, visibly disturbed. "Ah hell, I'd rather not guess. I just thank the good Lord we were able to save the ones we did."

"How could someone not know sooner?" Andy asked. "I mean, we spotted the kid on that tree at *night*."

The sheriff waved an arm over their wooded surroundings. "You see what it's like out here. You kids were lost; not many venture this far out, especially on a road that dead-ends. Freak luck you spotted the child before whatever's been taking those kids did."

Tim frowned. "'*Whatever's been taking those kids*'?"

The sheriff smiled a little. "I'm not talking Windigo nonsense, of course. Real wildlife finds a food source and they keep on coming back to it like a dog to its bowl, hoping it'll be filled. My guess would be a regular pack of wolves came sniffing around that spot periodically to see if the bowl was full." The sheriff made the sign of the cross on his chest. "God almighty when it was."

"You saying wolves did that to Kane?" Andy asked.

"Doubtful," the sheriff said.

"Well then what did?"

"*A Windigo*," a skinny deputy said with a grin, appearing out of nowhere by the sheriff's side.

The sheriff turned and scowled at the deputy. "You find this whole scene amusing, do you, Starnes?"

The deputy's smile vanished and he dropped his head. "No, Sheriff."

The sheriff kept his scowl on the deputy for a few more seconds before turning back to Andy. "My guess would be a bear, son."

"A bear can rip a man's head off?"

"Good-sized one, sure. One good swipe is all it would take."

"Do bears eat people?" Michelle asked.

"Typically, no," the sheriff said. "But you claim the Cree went into the woods, hell-bent on killing a Windigo, right?"

Tim and Michelle nodded.

"Well, my guess is the Cree came upon the bear and tried to kill it. A bear usually won't bother you and me, but it's still an exceptionally deadly animal. Provoke it and you're asking for trouble. Probably took the Cree's head off with a swipe, then ripped into his chest a bit before it lost interest."

"Why didn't it harm the little girl?" Michelle asked.

"Who can say? Probably because the little girl wasn't a threat."

Tim shook his head in disgust, eyes on the ground. "And after all that, it's the fucking pregnant girl who puts the little kid at death's door. Crazy superstitious bitch."

The sheriff waved a hand at Tim. "Ah, she's gonna be fine, son. A scratch is all it was."

"What?"

"The child's fine. Just a little cut on her chest." He threw a thumb towards an ambulance in the distance. An EMT was holding the child in his arms as if it were his own. The child had a lollipop in her mouth. She appeared fine.

"How is that possible?" Tim asked. "Her chest was *gushing* blood. I saw it; I had to put *both* hands on it to try and stem the bleeding."

The sheriff put a hand on Tim's shoulder. "You were scared, son. It was dark. Point is, the child's gonna be fine."

Tim shrugged the sheriff's hand off. "I was scared, and it was dark, but I'm *telling* you, that little girl had a hatchet wound in her chest this big." Tim held his hands six inches apart.

The sheriff sighed, decided to placate Tim. He looked at Andy. "You get a good look at the wound, son?"

Andy shook his head. "I was holding down pregnant Lizzie Borden."

The deputy snorted.

The sheriff looked at Rachel and then Michelle. "Ladies?"

"We headed back towards the village to find a signal to call you."

The deputy broke in. "You say the little girl was eating the remains of that Cree?"

Tim squinted at the deputy, annoyed and confused; he saw no relevance in the question. He grunted a yes anyway.

"Well, there you go," the deputy said with another grin. "Windigos can *regenerate*."

The sheriff spun his deputy by the shoulders and shoved him away. "See if I don't have you cleaning the head when we get back to the station." The sheriff turned back to the group. "Sorry about that, kids. I think it's safe to say we've all heard enough Windigo bullshit for one night, yeah?"

FISH AND BISCUITS IN A BARREL

Benny worked at a fish market. He worked at a fish market, and he hated cats. And while his unavoidably pungent occupation may have guaranteed Benny a private seat on the train, it regrettably turned him into a feline rock star on the walk home from the station—he must have cursed and shooed away ten furry fans a night.

The fish job was recent, and what Benny convinced himself to be temporary—an interim position that would provide some stability until he could get back on his feet. If Benny was honest with himself, he would accept the fact that *every* job he had held in his uneventful 41 years had been an interim position—a collection of mundane rides that spun him in the same fruitless circle while the impressive roller coaster fueled by initiative stood in the background, its power and prestige far too daunting for the likes of Benny.

Now, with the fish job only a week old on his resume, the past seven nights were producing an unusual after-hours routine that seemed to run like clockwork:

Benny would come home late, reeking of fish, and carrying the market's latest catch bundled in newsprint under one arm. His only friend, a three-legged yellow Labrador named Moby, would greet him at the door with an enthusiastic wag of his tail and incessant whines for the biscuits Benny kept on the kitchen counter. Benny would head for the biscuits, give Moby only one, and then unwrap the day's catch and place it in the refrigerator to be cooked later.

And that's when the meowing, or more appropriately, the *wailing* would start.

Every night since Benny had gotten the job at the fish market, the same black cat with its glowing yellow eyes would appear on the fence outside his kitchen window. And every night as Benny placed the day's

catch inside his fridge, the same black cat would begin his wail—an incessant, ear-bending yowl that was only abated when Benny would turn
to Moby and repeat the same mantra he had composed since day one of
this annoying ritual.

"*Come on, Moby! Let's go, boy! Go get him!*"

Benny would run to his front door—the three-legged Moby doing
his hurried best to stay close behind—and yank the door open, allowing
Moby to hobble past him into the night with Benny emphatically cheer-
ing on his charge. "*Get him, boy! Go get that stupid cat!*"

The wailing would eventually stop, and, like clockwork, Moby would
reappear, limping his way back to the front door a short time later. He
would receive a pat on the head, a '*Good boy,*' and only one biscuit from
the kitchen counter.

.   .   .

Two weeks passed of the same routine.

It was *always* the same.

A pungent Benny coming home late and miserable; one biscuit for
Moby; catch of the day in the fridge; wailing outside the kitchen win-
dow; Benny opening the front door for Moby to chase the cat away;
Moby returning shortly after to get his one-biscuit reward.

.   .   .

A change in the routine finally occurred one evening when Benny noticed a red welt around the nose of his yellow Lab. He immediately
dropped into a catcher's stance and took hold of Moby's face with both
hands.

"Who did this to you, boy? Was it that stupid cat? Did he scratch
you?"

The dog looked back at his owner, black eyes wide and innocent.

"Well that's it," Benny said. "We'll deal with this furry bastard *together*."

Benny stomped towards his coat closet, opened it, and withdrew his
rifle. He gripped the weapon tight with both hands, pumping it into the
air. "We'll get him, boy. We'll get that stupid cat once and for all."

Benny knew what to do next, knew how to set the bait.

He leaned the rifle against the wall, unwrapped the catch of the day, opened his fridge and placed the fish inside. He even opened the kitchen window, and then the refrigerator door again—wafting it back and forth in hopes that the smell from the fish therein would soon float its way out that open window.

"Any minute now, boy," he said to Moby, his eyes never leaving the window. The view outside gave him nothing but night and the dim outline of an empty fence. "*Any* minute now . . . "

The dog whined at Benny's feet. Benny looked down.

"What? What's the matter, boy?"

The dog whined harder.

"You want a treat?"

Moby wagged his tail.

Benny took his eyes off the window and went to the kitchen counter. He took one biscuit from the container and gave it to Moby who immediately gulped it down. The dog whined again.

"No, boy—that's enough."

Benny picked up the rifle again and waited. It was a good five minutes before the wailing began, but boy was it ever there—as clear and as shrill as a passing siren.

Benny looked hard out his kitchen window, eyes wide with intensity, rifle aimed into the dark. He saw nothing.

"Where is it?" he asked himself, the dog, and finally the cat: "*Where are you?*"

The wailing was louder now, rising from somewhere below the window.

Benny leaned forward, his ample belly pressing into the kitchen counter's edge. He looked down onto his lawn. Nothing.

The wailing continued—climbing louder still, certain to break glass if it rose a pitch higher.

"Aw to hell with this," Benny said. "Come on, boy! We're going outside!"

Benny tore out his front door with Moby close behind. He turned the corner of his house, paused, and squinted into the dark.

"*Here kitty, kitty, kitty…*"

Silence.

"*Come on out, stupid little kitty…*"

He waited, rifle pointed at nothing. A minute passed. Two minutes. Five. He was impatient now.

"*Moby!*" He turned to the dog at his side. "Go get him for me, boy! Flush him out so I can draw a bead on him!"

The dog gave an eager wag of his tail and then limped off out of sight. Benny remained fixed where he was, certain his dog would force the cat in his direction. The second he spotted that black fur and those beady yellow eyes round the house's corner he would not hesitate. He would fire and shoot it dead.

Benny expected the echo of a hiss to follow. Or maybe the woman-like scream a threatened cat can make. What he didn't expect was a cry of pain from his own dog.

Benny sprinted blindly towards the noise, the rifle rocking from left to right in his hands. Moby's cry rose louder. Benny ran faster.

"I'm coming, boy!"

Benny turned the corner of his house and his feet caught something, tangling them up into one another. The rifle that took up both his hands impeded his balance. Benny found himself falling forward, the tip of the gun's barrel pressing beneath his chin during his descent. There was a thud and an explosion.

.   .   .

The man who smelled like fish, and only gave out one biscuit at a time lay face down on the lawn—the top of his head now missing and resembling a red fountain.

The black furry obstacle with yellow eyes that had caught his feet was now taking cautious steps forward to sniff and inspect the aftermath. It was soon joined at its side by Moby who sniffed and inspected just the same.

Content, the dog and cat sauntered side by side, around the corner of the house, and towards the open front door that had been left ajar in the one-biscuit-fish-man's haste.

Upon entry, the black cat with yellow eyes wasted little time hopping up onto the kitchen counter where it knocked the jar of biscuits to the floor, spilling dozens of them before a delighted Moby.

Moby, in kind, made his way to the refrigerator. He nudged the door open (wincing slightly from the red welt that repeated late-night-fridge-opening practice had given his nose) and then took a few hobbled steps back to allow the black cat with the yellow eyes to hop off the counter, approach the open fridge, and seize the catch of the day between his teeth where he proceeded to drag it to the floor, beside the scattered biscuits.

Very content now, the cat and dog sat side by side, eating—Moby with as many biscuits as he wanted, and the black cat with the catch of the day that had been taunting him for weeks.

At one point both animals looked up from their meals and glanced at one another. The cat purred. Moby wagged his tail.

Stupid humans. Like fish and biscuits in a barrel.

SUGAR DADDY

I
NOW

1

The auditorium is packed. I should be flattered, but I'm not. Not today. Today every fan is going to get the answer—or the result?—to the question I have been avoiding since I published my first bestseller twenty years ago.

Are you ever going to write horror, Mr. Kale?

"Maybe one day."

That's what I usually tell them. I'll tell them I prefer to write about things I believe in; things that are real. Serial killers; psychopaths; terrorists—*that's* what scares me. I'll then crack some lame joke about how I stopped believing in ghosts and goblins when I was ten, and I'll get a unanimous laugh, obligatory only because of my literary status, of that I'm sure.

It's not the truth though.

The truth, if they knew it, would scare the shit out of them. Like it does me—even some twenty years later.

So here I am, veins flooded with Lexapro and Abilify, stoned on enough Xanax to drop an elephant, and in front of a podium ready to deliver what everyone wants to hear: a *horror* story written by someone who writes under the pseudonym of Adam Kale.

I roll up both sleeves and look at the old scars on my wrists—thick lines that wrap all the way around like a child had a go at me with a white Crayola.

I look at Emma's name tattooed on the inside of my left forearm and touch it.

I rub my always-aching right hand; the one with three pins in it, the one I can't tighten completely.

And then I rub the shoulders that still insist on popping out just as I think they're getting better.

"Okay…" I sigh. "Shall we begin?"

II
THEN

1

Emma and I were a half hour late when we joined Kevin and Tony in the booth. There were six empty beer bottles on the table already—the waitress at our dive never daring to remove your glass trophies until elbow room became impossible.

"Where you guys been?" Tony asked.

We were late for no good reason other than being late. I decided a quick apology would end it. "Sorry."

He frowned, shook his head and dove right in. "Okay, listen to this—"

"Whoa, whoa—can we get a drink first, please?" I was not about to open my ears to someone like Tony before I had a drink in front of me. I looked at Emma. "What do you want, baby?"

"Red Bull and vodka."

Kevin grimaced. "How do you drink that shit?"

Emma wiped her ink-black hair out of her face with a middle finger, her blue eyes rimmed with what I always felt was too much eyeliner batting playfully at Kevin to underline her gesture.

"Such a classy girl you've got," Kevin said to me.

I grunted and looked around. It was pretty empty for a Thursday night. The big oval bar in the center of the place held a few scattered locals around its perimeter—grumpy old men with mushy red noses mumbling complaints into their whiskey and beer. Was I looking at myself in thirty years? Likely, unless I grew a pair and stepped out of my safe little pond to make some changes.

I am—and please forgive how arrogant this will sound—the smartest of all three I'm hanging out with right now. That even includes my girl Emma who, while sweet as a blueberry, is the type to buy a newspaper, pull out the comics, and toss the remainder in the trash.

I love to read and write. Always have. And I suppose this love provides me with a learned way of thinking that's different than theirs, if they do much thinking at all. I can remember one time when I told Tony about this book on giant squids I'd just read. Told him what amazing and mysterious creatures they were. He looked at me as though he'd just smelled a wicked fart, and his response was along the lines of: "Who gives a shit about a *squid*?"

I'd say that one comment there summed Tony up pretty well.

I continued surveying the bar. "Where's Carol?"

Tony snorted. "Chain-smoking bitch is probably outside again; it takes forever to get a drink from her since the smoking ban."

I held my tongue. Both Tony and Kevin were heavy smokers. Emma too, and she was constantly promising she was going to quit. That promise began our senior year in high school when we started getting serious. Now, seven years later, she was still promising.

Carol appeared almost on cue a second later. She stunk of smoke.

"Another round?" she asked.

Tony and Kevin nodded.

She looked at Emma, then at me. "How about you guys?"

Carol was close to fifty. She was tall and painfully thin, her scrawny arms wrapped in thick blue veins that raised the skin. Her hair was shoulder-length and unhealthy, straw-like. She'd make a perfect scarecrow. Hell, she could scare sharks. I thought about the old men at the bar being me in thirty years. Would this town inevitably turn Emma into Carol? My penis made an instant threat of eternal impotence if I continued with that line of thinking and I squashed the thought immediately.

"Vodka and Red Bull, and a shot of Jack and a lager," I said.

Carol left with our orders.

Tony leaned forward. "Okay? Can I start now?"

"You see a drink in front of us yet?" I said.

He sat back hard in the booth, his constant frown etching deeper. He nudged Emma. "Can you get up? I'm gonna go out for a smoke."

Emma stood and said, "I'll join you."

Kevin turned and looked at me. He was short, bald, and stocky. The guy started losing his hair when we were sixteen and by now he had next to nothing left. Fortunately for him, the bald head suited his round stumpy features quite well, and the goatee that he sported—like his idol, Tony—only added to his wannabe tough-guy image.

Unlike Tony, however, whose temper threw his punches for him before his common sense did, Kevin was a jellyfish. He'd even started crying during a confrontation once. He denied it vehemently after the fact, but we all saw it. And we all let it go. Even Tony, who loves busting balls almost as much as busting a nut, never made a fuss over it. If you ask me, I think Tony is just grateful to have someone look up to him other than a cockroach.

"You want me to get up?" I said to Kevin.

"Yeah, you mind?"

I knew it was killing him that Tony was outside having a smoke without him. I stood and let him scooch past me towards the exit.

I sat back down, alone. Carol returned with our drinks.

"Should I clear some of these?" she said, motioning to the empty bottles.

I shrugged. "If you want." As I mentioned from the start; in a place like this, where your status as a fledgling alcoholic was important for some reason, empty beer bottles were symbols of your prowess. To clear them away before absolutely necessary was taboo.

But I couldn't give a shit. Yeah, I loved to drink as much as the next guy, but unlike the majority of these clowns, I felt shame when I overindulged. It made me feel weak; for every night I got wasted and acted the fool, I knew I was taking one step closer to becoming a permanent fixture in this shit town. A permanent fixture that would end up craving those self-medicating nights of defilement as a means of quieting the shame and disgust that would inevitably haunt me forever.

I shuddered, gulped my Jack, and then followed it with a sip of lager just as the three of them walked back in.

Emma sat next to me this time, leaving Kevin and Tony on the other side. This didn't seem to bother them now, but would have appeared far too "gay" had they sat next to one another before we arrived.

"Cheers," Emma said as she raised her drink. We all clinked glasses and bottles and took a sip.

I leaned back in the booth, savoring the warmth of the Jack in my belly. "Okay, Tony, you may enlighten us now."

He was too anxious to return fire at my sarcasm. He just started. "I found a way to make a shitload of cash."

I had suspected this was about money, and kept from rolling my eyes. Tony was always playing the get-rich-quick angle. He even spent his meager earnings from his job at the gas station on lottery tickets each and every week.

"How?" Emma asked.

I glanced over at her to see if she was humoring Tony or actually interested. Sadly, I saw the latter.

Kevin spoke next. "Tony's banging this new Russian chick."

They stopped there for a moment, and despite two predictable tools like them, I had to confess I had no clue where they were going with this.

"Okay … " I said. "Has she agreed to let us pimp her out or something?"

Emma laughed. Tony did not.

Kevin continued. "She cleans houses."

"And?" I said.

"She cleans *big* houses—all the places on Elmwood."

I sighed. "Are we gonna keep doing the twenty questions thing or are you gonna start making sense?"

Tony leaned in. "We got wasted together the other night. We're lying in bed just after I tapped that ass, and she starts babbling about her crappy job. I don't know, maybe she was trying to hint that she would love some American guy to marry her so she didn't have to work anymore."

"Did you tell her you pumped gas for a living?"

He ignored me. "So, she starts telling me about what she does, and I'm kind of half-listening and half-dozing. She's going on and on about these 'rich bitches' and how it's not fair that they've got money and she doesn't"—he then made the hand gesture for talking too much, mouth opening and closing with— "blah-fucking-blah-blah ... "

"Maybe she's hoping one of the husbands she cleans for will leave his wife and marry her," Emma joked.

And that's when Tony said: "Nah—they're all single."

"What?" I said.

"All the women on Elmwood are single."

"How can that be?"

"How can what be?"

"How can all the residents on Elmwood be single women?"

"So what?"

"Elmwood stinks with money," I said. "You can't convince me that every castle in that development is owned by a single woman. There has to be *some* husbands."

Emma elbowed me. "You're being sexist."

"I'm being reasonable."

Tony looked constipated. "Whatever—I'm only telling you what she told me." He leaned in, dropped his voice. "The ones who *leave the keys* are all single women."

"Leave the keys?" Emma asked.

"Yeah, some of the women aren't there to let them in. It's a safe suburb; how else would Nadia and her crew get in to clean?"

"They do the 'Hide-A-Key' thing for them," I said.

Tony pointed at me. "Bingo. Like I said, Nadia was completely wasted. And just after mentioning the keys she starts babbling something else about locked rooms filled with antiques and shit. I pushed her on it, and she said all of the homes on Elmwood have these huge security doors in their basements, almost like bank vaults or something. She said they're *always* locked up tight."

I knew where this was going now. I might be miserable and pining for a kick in the ass towards a fresh start, but I'm no thief.

"Please tell me you and Nadia aren't planning on robbing the place," I said.

Tony scowled, patted the air and whispered: "*You wanna keep your voice down?*"

"You are, aren't you?"

"Nadia? No way. She'd be the first to get blamed if anything went missing; she'd never go along with it. Fortunately, she was so drunk that night she doesn't remember telling me shit."

"So then...what? You're gonna do it on your own and frame your girlfriend?"

He snorted. "She's not my girlfriend. Who gives a shit about some Russian bitch?"

Who gives a shit about a squid? I thought.

"So what *are* you suggesting?" I asked.

"I'm suggesting we *all* go."

"You're high," I said.

"I'm *not* high. It's almost too easy. I mean the key is *right there* for us. We take it, stroll casually into the place—"

"And what? Empty it? Don't you think it will arouse just a *tiny* bit of suspicion if neighbors see the four of us going in and out of the place carrying televisions and stereos?"

"Who said anything about televisions and stereos? I'm talking about the fucking *antiques*. *That's* what we go for. If we all go and grab something it can be one quick trip—in and out."

"You said Nadia claimed they were locked in a fucking vault. You been studying how to crack safes in between pumping gas, Tony?"

"She said it was *like* a vault, not an actual bank vault. Who the fuck would have one of those in their home, Alex?"

"I don't know, *Tony*, but neither do you. Until you've actually seen the thing, you'd be going in blind."

"We'll get it open," he said.

I looked at Kevin; he was hanging on Tony's every word. No ethical support there. I looked at Emma. She seemed interested in Tony's plan. I really hoped I was reading her wrong.

"Okay, suppose you do get it open," I said. "What then?"

"Isn't it obvious?"

"Well, let's just skip over the whole morality issue of *stealing* for a second, but do you even know what you'll do with these antiques once you've got them?"

"I'd sell 'em, stupid."

"To *who*, stupid? You made any recent connections with underground antique dealers you haven't told us about?"

I expected a giggle from Emma but got nothing. Shit—she *was* considering this.

"Well, it just so happens that I *do* know someone," he said.

"Who?"

"You don't know him."

"Oh, well now I'm really convinced."

Tony's frown hardened. "I'm doing you a favor by telling you this, Alex. I didn't have to include you."

"They're probably panic rooms," I said.

Both Tony and Kevin said: "Huh?"

"These vaults full of 'treasures' you're talking about are probably just panic rooms. Lots of rich homes have them in case of intruders. You lock yourself in and call the police. Remember that Jodie Foster movie? Your Russian girl probably just assumed something valuable was insid—"

"Oh yeah?" Tony's frown dissolved into an arrogant smirk. "Did I forget to mention that one of her employers on Elmwood actually *told* Nadia that what was inside her particular vault was *priceless*? Told Nadia it was worth more than anyone could ever imagine? The other houses on Elmwood may have your weird little panic rooms, but I couldn't give two shits—we'd only be focusing on the one Nadia mentioned." Tony's frown returned, a righteous snort along with it when he added: "Lady shouldn't have blabbed to a stranger like Nadia to begin with. Stupid bitch practically *deserves* to get robbed."

"You know exactly which house it is, huh? Nadia told you the number?"

The arrogant smirk returned with relish. "1507 Elmwood," Tony happily said. "Jumped out of bed and wrote it down in the other room the second she slipped up. I guess *this* Russian couldn't hold her vodka."

Kevin laughed.

Tony continued. "Now, just take a moment and *think* about how set we'd be if we helped ourselves to just a few of those priceless goodies." He chugged the remainder of his beer to underline the conclusion to come. "And I'm telling you that this guy who'll buy the antiques is legit. My Uncle Fred has used him before, and you know what Fred's like. He's always 'finding' things to sell. Says this guy never asks any questions. Just looks it over and quotes a price—take it or leave it."

I studied all three of them. Their minds were made up. Even Emma's. Mine was not. Like I said; I'm no thief.

"Okay then," I said. "*If* we went along with this, there's still a shit-ton of obstacles."

"Such as?"

"Well, the vault for one. If these are 'priceless goodies' then I imagine the locks are heavy duty."

"I got someone who can handle it."

"Oh yeah? Who's that?"

He looked away for a second.

I looked at Emma. "Oh, Jesus Christ, he's talking about his Uncle Fred." I turned back to Tony. "*Please* tell me I'm wrong."

Tony just stared at me. He didn't have to say anything.

"All right then," I said. "So Honest Uncle Fred joins the party and we manage to open the locks. We're still gonna be four, no, *five* misfits looting a rich suburban home in broad daylight."

"We play it careful," he said.

"That's your advice? *We play it careful?*"

Again, he just stared.

I looked at Emma. "I think we're done here. You ready to go, Em?"

Emma looked at Tony and Kevin first; then at me. "I ... okay."

"So I take it you're out?" Tony asked as we slid out of the booth.

"You are correct," I said.

"Shame—I was counting on you."

"Yeah, well maybe you should have thought it through a little more."

We were past the table when Tony said something that stopped me like a shove.

"You're better than this place, Alex. Why you stick around here is a mystery to me. I was thinking this money—this one little score—could be the kick in the ass you needed to get you the hell out of here and moving towards something better."

I had no words. He'd even used the "kick in the ass" expression I'd thought to myself only moments ago. Was Tony really this insightful? Or was my wasted potential really that sad and obvious.

I turned and looked down at him. He afforded me only a quick glance, then looked straight ahead at the empty booth and said: "Just think about it and call me later."

2

Susan Roberts whistled cheerfully while she prepared the marinade in her giant kitchen on 1507 Elmwood Drive.

The rest of the house was equally huge—fit for ten families and show-casing an extravagant décor that hinted only royalty would suffice.

And yet Susan Roberts lived alone and rarely entertained.

Of course, tomorrow would be different. She had big plans for tomorrow. Plans she had been making for some time now.

He was coming.

She left the wooden spoon in the big bowl of dark marinade and walked towards the calendar hanging on her fridge. The square holding tomorrow's date was circled in blue, the time of one o'clock followed by a hand-drawn smiley face written inside the blue-circled square. She caressed the time with a finger as though it were silk.

One o'clock. That was the time she was assigned, and that was the time she needed to be ready. Her belly swirled hot with anticipation.

Susan spun to return to her marinade when the doorbell stopped her midway. It was a neighbor from three houses down. She too wore an anxious smile. She asked Susan for the marinade recipe they were using this time. Susan gave it to her and then asked what her scheduled time was. The woman told her she was scheduled for three o'clock. They shared an excited giggle then parted company.

Susan returned to the kitchen, tied her apron, picked up the big bowl of marinade, and headed for the basement.

The finished basement was almost as vast and as grand as the home's first floor. A multitude of baroque cabinets, elaborate étagères, and rich doors lined its endless walls.

Only one door stood out, and it was not for its décor. It was twice the width of any other and it was made of steel. Susan stood before it now.

The giant door had two locks: one flat to the door, and one a protruding latch that used a padlock. She set the bowl of marinade down and fished a set of keys from her pocket.

Unlocked, Susan now pulled on the heavy door, its weight making her grunt as she peeled it open.

The door did not lead directly into another room, but to a second set of stairs further down into the earth. Susan hit a switch on the wall and fluorescent bulbs flickered and exploded with buzzing light.

At the bottom of the stairs, a concrete pathway twenty feet long lay ahead. The path was as wide as a school's hallway, the walls white and as bare as an asylum's.

At the end of the path Susan paused and shifted the big bowl of marinade to one arm. To her left was another steel door, to her right a giant cage. Behind the thick vertical bars of the cage a man was bound, gagged, and hanging by both wrists. He was stark naked, his body recently shaved, appearing as bare as a newborn child.

The man began to whimper when he saw Susan unlock the cage door and enter. She smiled at him and told him to hush the way a loving parent might tell their child to stem their tears.

Taking a large paintbrush from her apron, Susan began to paint the man from the bowl of marinade. The man whimpered some more, and

Susan hushed him some more, still smiling, still coating him in the thick dark sauce until no pink remained.

Finished now, Susan locked the cage again, and before leaving for the stairs could not resist pressing her ear to the steel door in front of her. She could hear slight chirps and scurrying sounds from within. She made kissing noises at the door, and the scurrying and chirping grew louder.

She suddenly became so giddy with anticipation she dropped the empty marinade bowl to the floor and hurried upstairs to pee.

3

Emma and I lay in bed together later that night. We'd started to have sex, but I lost my hard-on halfway through. And no, it wasn't on account of the threat my penis had made earlier about Emma turning into Carol.

It was about what Tony had said. It consumed me, and even held the distinctive honor of making sex impossible.

Emma was upright on both elbows, the blankets just over her stomach, both breasts exposed. Usually a glimpse like that was enough to make me go from six to midnight in seconds, but tonight it just wasn't happening. I could think of nothing else to say but: "Sorry."

"It's okay. To tell you the truth, I wasn't really feeling it either."

"I was that bad, huh?"

She smiled. "No, no—it was about what Tony said."

A pretty fucking apt example of coincidence, I must say.

"You don't actually think that was a good idea, do you?"

"No, not that … about you … being too good for this town."

"Em, he was just trying to convince me—that's all."

"But it's true. You *should* be somewhere else."

"Oh yeah? Like where?"

"I don't know. College? Somewhere where you can pursue your writing?"

I didn't share my writing with Emma. In fact, I shared it with no one.

"What are you talking about?" I said.

"I found some of your stuff," she said. "I wasn't snooping, I promise. But I found one of your stories. It was really, really good."

I was flattered and annoyed. A part of me felt she *was* snooping. Emma still lived at home, and when she would come to my place I often suspected she dug around when I was temporarily engaged (toilet; shower; you choose). I'm not sure what she thought she was going to find; after seven years we had very few secrets between us. Maybe it was something like *this* she was looking for. Some tangible evidence of my creativity that meant I was considering leaving her behind.

I didn't bother to ask her what story she'd read. I just thanked her for the compliment and said, "I'm not going anywhere, Em."

"But you should. You *should* go."

"What about us?" I asked.

"You could take me with you … if you wanted."

I thought about her comment. Would I? I was admittedly still with Emma for the same reason I was still in this town. She was safe and simple. But I'd be lying if I said I didn't care deeply for her. Still, Emma was insecure and didn't even *try* to better herself; she seemed content with mediocrity. And I'm sure if we did move on to bigger and better things there may come that awkward time when I felt her inability to expand would hold me back. But I knew I liked having her by my side. And I knew that she would support me in anything I did. Sometimes that's all you need. It's enough to get you through anything, especially the scary transition she was suggesting. Emma was loyal and loving, and contrary to how she felt about herself—or the unfair picture I may have painted earlier about her intelligence—she wasn't dumb.

Kevin and Tony? Dumb.

Emma? She just didn't believe in herself. Maybe what she needed was that kick in the ass I needed.

But the means? The means for this possible transition towards a new start? It was illegal. Theft. And call me crazy, but something orchestrated by Tony and his crazy uncle didn't necessarily make me think this was the sure thing Tony was preaching it to be.

I squeezed her leg gently. "I'd take you with me."

"So what does this mean?" she asked.

I rolled away from her and stared at my ceiling. "It would be great to have the money. We could, and *would* leave. But come on … are you honestly going to tell me this doesn't sound like a huge risk?"

"Life's a risk."

"That's *weak*, Em. We're talking about breaking the law. *Big time.*"

"Yeah, big time. But it would only be the *one* time … "

I sighed. "If it was a sure thing then *maybe* I'd consider it, but … "

"Let's call Tony and tell him we're in. You and I can have our *own* agenda. If it looks shady, we leave. If anyone acts funny, we leave. And if we see it to the end, and we get our money, *we leave*. You and me. We give this town the finger and drive off without ever looking back."

I was seeing a side of her I hadn't seen before. An ambitious side. And I'd be lying if I said it wasn't reeling me in.

I repeated her words. "You and me. A new start."

"A new start, baby."

I leaned over and kissed her. She kissed me back, and suddenly everything below my navel started working again.

She reached down to confirm it. "Oh, well, *hello* there … "

.   .   .

There were five of us standing around Uncle Fred's van the following morning: the original four, and of course, Uncle Fred. The van was a pathetic offering—one or two good whacks away from being beaten into submission. I couldn't even tell what make it was. What I *did* know, however, was that if we drove this thing into Elmwood we might as well attach a siren onto it.

"We can't go in this thing," I said to Tony.

Fred stepped in front of Tony. "Why's that, son?"

"Because it's a piece of shit, sir."

Fred took a step closer to me.

"Uncle Fred, chill," Tony said.

Picture a rat. Not the kind you see in a pet store that's actually cute, but the kind you'd see near a sewer or a dumpster. Now imagine a human version of that rat. That's Uncle Fred. The big pointy nose, the narrow black eyes, the protruding front teeth, all encased in a slicked head of greasy black hair.

"What's the problem, Alex?" Tony said.

"The problem is that van looks like Fred Flintstone drove it. It's gonna stick out like a hard-on in Elmwood."

"It's the only thing we've got that can carry the five of us, *and* the stuff we're gonna be taking."

"You said last night that we wouldn't be taking much," I said. "Only a few valuables."

"Yeah, but who knows how big they're gonna be?"

I shook my head.

"So don't come then, hotshot," Fred said. "More for us."

I looked at Emma. Her eyes were wide and innocent. She looked nervous.

I sighed. "How big is the driveway?"

Tony had gone and gotten a good look at the house last night after he'd left the bar.

"Huge," he said. "We'd be hidden off the main road."

"What about neighbors?"

"The houses are far apart," he said. "Besides, they'll probably just think the van is Nadia and her crew."

Fred stepped forward again. "Yeah, you see, hotshot? Quit whining."

"Okay, whatever. But if we're gonna drive through that neighborhood in this shitbox then we need to do it in a hurry."

Fred sneered at my comment, his rat-teeth jutting forward.

"Fine," Tony said. "Then can we go, please?"

I looked at my watch. It was eleven.

"What time does Nadia get there to clean?" I asked.

"She's already been."

"*What?* So then how the hell do we get the fucking *key?*"

"She puts it back in the same spot she took it from, dumbass. It sits there until the lady comes home and takes it back."

"And when does the lady come home?"

Fred moaned. "What's with all these fucking questions?"

I ignored him and kept my eyes on Tony.

"Around dinner time, I think," Tony said.

"You think?"

"I'm almost positive that's what Nadia said."

I turned and stared down Uncle Fred. "You're confident you can get through those locks?"

He grinned—a sinister, almost pornographic leer. "Haven't met a cherry I couldn't pop yet."

4

Susan Roberts left early that morning in preparation for the big day. *All of the women* on Elmwood left early that morning in preparation for the big day.

They talked about the marinade they had prepared the night before while they sat in rows of salon chairs having their hair cut and colored.

They chatted quietly to one another about their preferred methods of disposal when it came to the offerings they served for *Him* and *Them* as they sat close together while their freshly painted fingernails dried.

They asked one another if they found it painful or erotic when He penetrated them as they sat in the sauna and massaged cocoa butter on their stomachs for what was about to play host there.

And they all giggled and agreed that while what they were doing was unholy, the compensations of endless luxury coupled with His intoxicating charm and affection more than eased any misgivings they had.

5

Uncle Frank pulled the van deep into the driveway of 1507 Elmwood.

"Should we go in one at a time?" I asked.

"No, we all go at once," Tony said.

I took a second to marvel at the house. I referred to it as a castle earlier. It *was* a castle—a far cry from the sad dwellings that littered my neighborhood back home, that's for sure. I seldom ventured out this way for the simple reason a poor, starving man doesn't walk into a bakery and start sniffing.

"Yeah, hotshot, let's go," Fred said to me.

I looked at Tony. "He calls me 'hotshot' one more time, and I'm gonna crack that beak he calls a nose."

"Yeah, keep talking, hotshot," Fred said with a grin.

.   .   .

The key was exactly where Nadia had told Tony it would be on that drunken night she would undoubtedly regret if we pulled this off. It wasn't a tough find. It was under the welcome mat by the front door.

We quickly filed inside, then collectively froze as we stood in the foyer.

"Jesus Christ," Kevin said.

"Anyone bring a map?" I asked.

"Let's just find the fucking basement," Tony said. "Don't touch anything else."

Fred was eyeing up a lamp that looked as though it was worth more than both his van (which isn't saying much, I suppose) and his house. Tony spotted him.

"Leave that shit, Uncle Fred." He then turned to the rest of us. "Spread out; holler if you find the basement door. Move fast and don't touch or *take*"—he eyed up Fred again—"anything while you're looking."

It was about five minutes of quietly opening and closing doors until it was Emma that announced: "I think I found it."

We were all at her side in seconds. Tony pushed to the front and looked down the carpeted steps.

"Yeah, this has got to be it," he said. He turned to Fred. "You got your shit with you?"

Fred reached into his back pocket and pulled out something that resembled a big wallet. He flipped it open revealing all types of skinny metal instruments that looked like something a sadistic dentist might use.

"What if there's a padlock?" Tony asked.

Fred pulled a six-inch bolt cutter from his front pocket.

"Isn't that kind of small?" I asked.

Fred looked at Emma and winked. "Ain't the size, but what you do with it that counts, right, honey?"

God, I wanted to hit this fucking guy.

We hurried down those carpeted stairs and soon found ourselves standing and gaping just as we had done in the foyer. It was gigantic and beautiful. I had been in a furnished basement once—a small room with wall-to-wall carpeting that I thought was nirvana—but this place? You could have a game of hide and seek down here and never find each other.

"Jesus Christ," Kevin said again.

Tony said, "Fan out and find the door."

"There's a million doors down here," I said.

"Then find the one that looks like it doesn't want to be opened."

.   .   .

Once again it was Emma who found the door. It was twice the width of every other door and made of steel. It was only the basement's size that kept us from spotting it immediately.

"Look at the size of that thing," Tony said.

Fred rapped his knuckles on the metal then looked it up and down.

"Something wrong?" I asked.

He didn't answer me, just dropped into a catcher's stance to study the locks.

"How does it look, Uncle Fred?" Tony asked.

He answered without taking his eyes off the locks. "The padlock will be a quick snip. But this gal … " He fingered the lock flat to the door above the handle. " … she may need a few drinks before opening her legs to me."

Emma looked at me in disgust and I shook my head at her in agreement.

"Okay, stand back, kids … " Fred smirked, still in his catcher's stance, still fingering the flat lock. "Uncle Freddy's gonna show you how it's done."

6

Susan frowned when she spotted the van in her driveway. Nadia and her crew should have been long gone by now.

She looked at the clock on her dashboard. It was nearly one. She felt panic. Would He skip her appointment if He found someone else in the house? Oh God, she hoped not. She had spent so much time preparing. So much time *yearning*.

She didn't bother pulling her car into the garage. Instead she parked it halfway up her driveway and ran to the front door. She checked under the mat. The key was gone. It *must* be Nadia and her crew.

She opened the front door and immediately called for Nadia.

7

I had already mentioned that Kevin was a dim bulb. But I have to confess that the simple choice of words he spoke when we finally broke through the door and descended deeper into an unexpected second basement were as profound and as appropriate as anything I'd ever heard come from his mouth.

He said: "What kind of sick shit is this?"

The five us stared—no, gawked—at a naked man in a cage who was bound and dangling from both wrists. The man was coated in some kind of dark slime and had what looked like a small billiard ball jammed into his mouth, tied tight around his head.

Fred turned away from the spectacle and poked Tony in the chest. "*What the hell is this?*"

Tony couldn't take his eyes off the dangling man.

"Where are the fucking antiques?" Fred demanded. "You brought us into a house to see some sick shit out of *Pulp Fiction?*"

Tony shook his head. "No ... I ... "

Emma spoke up. "Wait, look ... "

There was another steel door directly across from the cage. I think it was safe to say that none of us even *remotely* acknowledged it once we'd

117

spotted the naked man. But there it was, and it was the only other door within the subterranean lair we'd found ourselves in.

Fred brought his attention off of Tony and spun around to look at the door. "That's gotta be it," he said.

"Fred," I said, "we can't go in there."

His eyes bulged. "*What?*"

I was adamant; I pointed at the dangling man in the cage. "Something is *very* wrong here." I pointed back to the door. "Who knows what's behind *that* door? I say we get the fuck out of here now."

"*Fuck* no!" he yelled. "I didn't come this far to go away with an eyeful of some naked freak hanging in a cage. Whatever these rich bitches do in their private time is their problem. I'm going through this door and I'm leaving with *something*. You don't like it, you can fucking leave."

The man in the cage began to whimper through his gag. All five of us spun and gawked again.

"*Look at that guy*," I said. "You tellin' me he's here on his own accord? There's some freaky shit happening here and we have to—"

The voice at the top of the stairs cut me off and froze us all in an instant. It was a woman's voice, and she was calling for Nadia.

8

Susan was furious. How *dare* Nadia and her crew break into this room? They were going to ruin everything.

Susan stomped her way down her secret stairs. He was going to be here any minute and she prayed He wouldn't be angry. Prayed He would understand that none of this was her fault.

Her anger was at a fever pitch by the time she reached the bottom step.

9

We heard the footsteps coming down the stairs, and by their speed and force it was a safe guess that whoever they belonged to was *pissed off.*

We all looked at one another in a panic.

A woman hit the bottom step and marched right towards us, seemingly unafraid. She stopped a few feet from our group, her angry eyes ping-ponging between us, and then *behind* us, searching.

"Where's Nadia?" she demanded.

I guessed the woman at around forty. She was attractive and looked as though she was fighting off Father Time rather well. Her crow's feet and jowls were still smooth and tight to her silken skin and her blonde hair was thick and healthy. Her clothing, however, was modest. Jeans and a sweater.

"I haven't had a chance to dress for Him yet, dammit," she said. "*Where's Nadia?*"

Uncle Fred stepped forward. "Nadia's not here." He drew a knife from behind his shirt. "And you might want to call your date and tell him you've got to cancel."

"What are you doing, man?" I asked.

Fred kept the knife stuck on the woman when he answered me. "Shut up."

He then addressed her. "There's two ways this can happen, lady. You are going to open this door for us, and we are going to leave with something…" He took a step towards the woman and pushed the tip of the knife to her throat. "…or things are gonna get messy, and we're *still* gonna leave with something. Your choice."

"What's with the man in the cage?" I asked the lady.

Fred turned and shot me an angry look. "Who cares, Goddammit!" He turned back to the woman. "Lady, did you hear what I said?"

The woman started to cry. Heavy tears rolled down her cheeks and dripped onto her sweater. "You're going to ruin *everything*," she sobbed. "He'll never want to see me again after this."

A male voice, smooth and soft, yet somehow loud enough to capture our attention said, "Nonsense, sweetheart. Of course I will."

The woman spun towards the voice. All twelve of our eyes were now fixed on a man who seemed to materialize out of nowhere.

He sauntered down the white hallway towards us, the florescent glow overhead illuminating his brilliant features. And when I say brilliant, I don't mean handsome—even though he was—I mean, well, brilliant.

The man was over six feet tall with a slender build and dressed immaculately in black. His face was chiseled and his lips were smooth, delicate and red like a woman's. His hair was jet-black and slicked back tight against his head, eyes as dark as his hair and shone like black marbles.

But this is the description of a handsome man, and I already told you he was handsome. I also said he looked brilliant. The thing is I can't really explain *why* he looked brilliant. No, wait—yes I can. It was his eyes. I just told you they were black, but they're not. They were a second ago … but then they turned green. And then they turned red. And then silver. And then black again. The changes were rapid fire and brief, but they were there.

This wasn't a man. It couldn't be.

The woman ran into his arms and hugged him as though he were a relative long thought dead. He allowed her embrace, then nudged her back and took hold of her face with both hands. He looked into her eyes (I saw them change four different colors as he did) and leaned in, giving her a gentle kiss on the lips.

"I know what's going on here, sweetheart. I know it's not your fault," he said.

"Thank you," she replied, looking into his eyes as though her whole world resided within them. "I prayed you'd understand."

He chuckled at her choice of words and then gently pulled her behind him so he could face the five of us.

Fred still held the knife out in front; it was now pointing at the man in black.

"Listen pal, I'll tell *you* what I told *her*. We are not leaving here without—"

The man didn't move at all. Even his expression of mild interest never changed. But his eyes did. They went from black to red. And that was when Uncle Fred stabbed himself in the neck.

Blood shot in pulsating spurts from the wound and streaked the white walls. Emma screamed. Both Tony and Kevin took several steps back, their mouths open and useless from shock. I grabbed Emma and pulled her back towards the rear of the cage.

Fred fell to his knees, paused there a second—his eyes wide and unbelieving—then finally fell forward onto his face, a rich pool of red soon encircling his head.

Now it was Kevin's turn. And it was painfully fitting that he left this earth spouting the kind of moronic comment as only Kevin was capable of. His last words were: "Fred, why did you stab yourself in the neck?"

The man smirked at Kevin, and then pointed his index finger at him. The finger grew five times its own length and pierced Kevin's forehead between the eyes. The impact was quick and sudden—in and out like an air-powered cattle gun. A small trickle of blood began to leak down the hole in Kevin's head, and instead of falling forward onto his knees as Fred had done, he fell backwards like a plank, his head ricocheting off the cement floor with a hollow thud.

Tony was not keen on being number three. He bolted past the man and ran for the stairs. He made it up two steps when I heard a sound like tree branches cracking in a storm ... the sound of Tony's legs breaking. Each leg splintered and snapped in directions they were never meant to go. Their red and white shards pierced the cloth of Tony's pants causing him to tumble backwards and cry out in a scream that was higher than something I believe even Emma was capable of.

The man smiled towards us (never once glancing back in Tony's direction) and with a final shimmer in his eyes (a quick flash of yellow this time), Tony's head exploded.

Emma screamed again, and if Tony's legs still worked I would imagine they'd have twitched involuntarily once his brain popped.

I tried taking my eyes away from the gelatinous clumps of red that was once Tony's head, but found the gore both shocking and mesmerizing. Surreal. I so badly wanted this to be a dream. A dream right after the discussion Emma and I had that night about whether or not we should go through with this. About pushing away our better judgment and going through with it for the better of *us* so we could have a fresh start together. I knew now that would never happen. There would be no fresh start. No new beginning. Only an end. A horrific one.

"Come on out from behind there, you two." The man spoke to us like he was coaxing children out from their hiding place.

I turned to Emma. Her eyes were wide and glazed. I shook her by the shoulders but the fog didn't clear.

The man said, "*Hellooooo…?*"

I decided to leave Emma where she was and step out on my own. She didn't try to hold me back; she was frozen.

"Please don't hurt her," I said.

The man tilted his head and studied me. His expression was almost pleasant, his eyes stuck on yellow.

"And what about you?" he asked.

"I have no idea," I said. "But after what I just saw I would guess you could manage most anything you wanted."

He straightened his head, his eyes gray now.

"I may have something in mind," he said, "but it won't be immediate."

"I don't know what you mean." My voice cracked with fear.

"*Immediate,*" the man said. "As in: *right now.*"

"Okay, fine, whatever. But you'll let her go?"

He smiled and shook his head, pointing his finger past my shoulder. I turned and followed it.

Emma was sprawled out behind me. At least I think it was Emma. Whatever it was, it was wearing Emma's clothes. Inside her clothes was just skin. Like a suit of flesh dressed in clothes. Her fluids, her bones, *everything* looked as though it had been sucked out by some industrial vacuum. The only thing that remained—and I believe this was intentional—were her eyes. They stared up at me lifelessly—blue and glistening wet—within the wrinkled fleshy sockets that were still rimmed with what I used to think was too much eyeliner.

I cried out and put a hand to my mouth—something I thought only women did in the movies. I whirled back around and launched a right hand towards my assailant. He caught my fist with little effort, squeezed it and turned the bones in my hand into an excruciating mess. He then reached out with his other hand, touched me on the forehead and said: "*Boop!*"

And I was out.

.   .   .

I wasn't sure if my eyes were open or if I was in that weird dream stage where you *think* you're awake, but you're really not.

I felt pain in my wrists, especially my right hand, and a ball was in my mouth. A rubber ball.

I smelled something. Something like … piss? Did I piss myself? No, it's animal piss. Like a cat's piss.

My vision was coming back. Fuzzy and shaky, but getting better. Someone was in front of me. No—*two* people were in front of me. I blinked hard several times and my vision finally cleared.

I was in the cage. My wrists hurt because I was hanging by them next to the naked man. My right hand throbbed like a rotten tooth because all the bones were crushed. I bit down on the ball in my mouth and attempted to struggle free, but this only made my shoulders scream and threaten to pop.

The man in black was in front of the cage with the woman. Both naked. His body was smooth and white, lacking all detail: no pectorals; no nipples; no belly button; no buttocks—a hypocritical conception by its creator who opted for the shell, yet seemed almost offended by the anatomical intricacies of man … if not for the penis—for a moment I thought it was a tail; it was over a foot long and pointed at the tip.

He reached down and gripped it with one hand, stroking it until it stood upright like a large dagger.

I expected the woman to lay on her back for him, but instead she remained on her feet. The man held his pointed penis in the one hand and caressed the woman's soft belly with the other. He then asked her if she was ready and she nodded eagerly.

He pierced her navel with the tip of his member and inserted it about halfway. A trickle of blood began leaking down the woman's belly and I expected her to cry out, but instead she appeared to be on the threshold of an orgasm.

The penis began to undulate like a giant worm as it pumped something deep into the woman's stomach.

When finished, the man pulled the penis from her navel and hung his head just as any man might do after an intense climax.

The man eventually lifted his head, and began to caress the woman's belly a second time, the pierced wound on her navel gone, somehow healed. She smiled up at him adoringly—a teen worshipping a celebrity.

"I'm hungry now," he said to her.

He entered the cage, still naked, his giant penis now flaccid and hanging between his legs like an inconvenience. He ignored me completely.

He went right for the man covered in brown. And that's when I noticed his teeth. He looked to have thousands, all of them razor sharp and serrated like a shark's.

The man—if that's what we still want to call him—bit down onto the neck of the man covered in brown and began a ravenous feed. I flashed on hyenas pulling flesh from a carcass.

I looked at the woman in the background. She was still naked, rubbing her stomach, watching her mate feed on the man next to me. I glanced away and suddenly realized that there were no traces of Tony, Kevin, Fred, or Emma.

Done feeding, the man pulled his head away and wiped his bloodied mouth with the back of his arm. There was not much left of the hanging man's neck; his lifeless head dangled to one side like a tetherball.

The man left the cage and stroked the woman's cheek before heading over to the infamous steel door. He gave it a playful knock and smiled. Eager scratches from the other side intensified his smile.

"*My babies,*" he whispered.

He opened the steel door, and for a moment I only saw black.

Several seconds passed before I heard a chirping sound—something between a bird and a cricket.

A white monkey was the first to appear at the door. It was hunched over, behaving primitive like a monkey, but I eventually saw it had the features of a child—the exception being its many serrated teeth, smooth white body, and multi-colored eyes that were changing rapidly in its excitement.

One by one they appeared at the door. Four in all.

The man bent over and stroked the tops of their bald white heads.

"So big," the man said to himself, and then, turning excitedly towards their host, "They've gotten so big."

He squatted down and spoke to them.

"This is your final offering. After this I can take you with me."

The chirping intensified, their hungry razor mouths opening and closing, eyes twinkling and changing color by the nanosecond.

"I've sprayed the man on the left," the man said. "You're to stay away from him for now. But please help yourselves to the one on the right. I'd be very pleased if you picked it clean. It leaves less of a mess for our lovely host." He turned to the woman and winked.

All four things leapt through the cage door, attaching themselves to various areas of the dead man, his body swaying from the impact like a punching bag. The sounds of chirping and ripped flesh managed to drown out everything. I closed my eyes and looked away.

I never thought I'd be grateful to be covered in piss—and I was now fairly certain it was *his* piss and no cat's—but I was because not *one* of those things touched me.

·　　　　·　　　　·

The frenzied chirping and chewing stopped after roughly five minutes. I turned my head expecting to see a badly wounded corpse. Instead, I saw a red skeleton with hair, nearly picked clean. Only the odd bit of viscera dangled here and there.

The man had dressed himself during the feeding, and was now writing something in what looked like a checkbook. He spoke to the woman while he wrote.

"Of course I'll be back soon for the birth and the initial offering for the new ones—" He caressed her stomach again and then returned to the checkbook. "Six months later I'll return for the final offering and to take them with me."

She closed her eyes and nodded to him as if he'd just told her something she's heard before.

The man tore off the check and handed it to her. I poked my head forward and squinted to make out the sum of one million dollars.

The woman took the check, stood on her toes, kissed him and said: "Thank you, my sugar daddy."

He laughed at her comment and patted her on her still-bare bottom.

"I need to get to my three o'clock," he said, looking at his watch. "This little incident almost put me behind."

She apologized again, and he consoled her again.

The man called to the four white things (like children, their recent meal was still evident on the corners of their mouths and down their fronts—red stains and flecks of meat) and they scurried up the stairs after him, their chirps piercing the air like blasts from a whistle.

Once gone the woman sighed deep, and I'm sure I saw sadness in her eyes.

"I miss him already."

I could only stare at her incredulously.

"I'm going to shave you now," she said to me as she entered the cage, still nude and seemingly indifferent to the fact. "I have to clean up the offering's remains, so I might as well give you your first shaving."

I struggled against the shackles, but an explosion of pain in my hand and shoulders stopped me. I tried to holler through my gag but only snot and moans escaped.

"Don't worry," she said. "The first offering won't be for a while; it'll be a month before I deliver."

She lifted up my shirt and examined my chest. "Good. Smooth."

She unbuttoned my pants, pulling them down to my ankles. She felt my pubic hair. "I'll need to shave you a few times so your skin gets used to it. I know they don't like razor bumps."

She turned her back to me, and began to pull the man's bones free from their shackles. She continued speaking as she worked

"Eventually, you'll have to tell me what you like to eat—I need to keep you well fed. Oh, and of course then there's the marinade. I'll have to talk that over with the girls. Maybe teriyaki next time?" She was in her own little world now—eyes wide, unblinking, somewhere pleasant. Then the dream faded and the look of sorrow returned again. "I miss him already."

III
NOW

1

I stop reading, turn my manuscript over, and look up at my audience. There is a sea of wrinkled brows. I know they want more; their eyes are begging, almost demanding for more. But they're not going to get it.

A brief silence passes before the first hand goes up.

"Are you finished?" she asks.

I smile and nod.

Another hand shoots up.

"What happens to Alex?"

All questions I expected. And I give them the responses I have prepared.

"Well, that's up to you, isn't it?" I say.

Another hand. "Does he die?"

"Maybe." I look in the front row. *He* is standing in the center aisle, grinning at me. He looks exactly the same as I remember those twenty-odd years ago. Still handsome, still the same black attire, eyes still changing from one color to the next. He is impossible to miss, but no one else glances in his direction.

I know that only *I* can see him.

"I think it's inevitable he dies," someone declares. "How could he not? I mean, even if he managed to escape you'd think a demon like that would be able to find him whenever he wanted."

I look at Him again. He is laughing now, and I see the infamous rows of razor teeth that I see every night when I close my eyes. The student's statement is so spot-on that I find it hard not to laugh myself.

"I suppose you're right," I say. "That's one way of looking at it."

Another hand. "What would be the other?"

I shrug and wish aloud: "The demon lets him go."

Lots of frowns and chatter. Obviously not a popular choice. Except for one girl. "I think the demon *does* let him go," she says. All heads in the auditorium turn towards her. "When you think about it, all the demon was doing was protecting his children. The women he impregnated on Elmwood weren't forced against their will. I mean, they even *liked* it. Not to mention they were paid shitloads of cash too." Everyone laughs. When it eventually fades she adds: "Plus, the people who were killed were in the wrong. They broke into someone's home. They were trying to steal. I say the demon is nothing more than a lion defending his cubs."

"And the offerings?" a man asks. "The one who was already in the cage with Alex? And the ones that were apparently in the other homes? Were they criminals? I think we can hardly call this demon thing a do-gooder who was just protecting his kids."

The girl shrugs. "Who knows? But a lion doesn't check the references of a gazelle before killing and feeding its family." Some more laughs. "It's all about survival of your species. A primitive urge refined through evolution."

The man smirks and says, "Yeah, I guess shaving a guy's balls before you eat him *is* pretty refined."

Big laughs that last a solid minute.

But I'm stuck on the girl's words. They're hardly a revelation for me, yet they still hurt, and only serve to scratch a twenty-year-old wound of stupidity that will never heal.

The laughter is gone and I realize I've been quiet for a while and quickly clear my throat. "Great insight," I tell them. "Let's do a show of hands. Who thinks Alex lives?"

A few hands go up.

"Who thinks Alex dies?"

A mass of hands go up.

I don't need to look at Him again to know He's loving this.

"Well there you go," I say. "You've got your ending. Poor Alex."

They laugh, and the laughter is even *more* obligatory than my earlier joke about ghosts and goblins; they are pissed about the ambiguous ending. But I don't care. I hardly wrote it for them.

A woman's hand in the second row: "Why did you switch back and forth between first person and third person when telling your story?"

Ah! A question I *hadn't* expected. A good one too. I tell her that and she beams.

"I had no way of knowing the specifics of what Susan was up to during the interim of the whole ordeal we went through, but I could certainly *imagine* given what I eventually experienced. It's a risky technique—switching perspective back and forth like that—but if you're careful, it can be a nifty little tool in your toolbox."

And just as the next hand shoots up, I realize what I've just said. Not so much *what* I've said, but *how* I said it.

"When you say, 'the ordeal *we* went through,' and, 'what *I* experienced,' is that an inadvertent way of describing how emotionally involved you become with your characters?" a man asks.

Bless this bastard for giving me a fantastic response to my stupidity.

I smile, almost gasp, and say: "*Yes.* Yes, that's exactly right."

An excited chatter builds as they digest my response.

I glance over at Him. He lifts up his left arm and taps the back of wrist, indicating time is almost up. I nod.

"Okay. Shall we call it a day?" I ask.

The audience, likely hoping for more of a discussion, is hesitant, but like the infamous golf clap, applause slowly builds to a rousing one. I thank them, and then explain that I have a prior engagement that will hopefully deter those looking to approach the podium.

It does the trick, and before long the empty auditorium would echo the sound of two mice fucking.

It's just me and Him.

"What did you think?" I ask.

He approaches the podium with the charm and confidence of ten … *whatever* the hell He is. He climbs the small stairs and is now on stage with me. We face one another. His eyes are yellow.

"I enjoyed it. You're quite talented," He says.

"Thank you." I have no conviction in my voice.

"You're not proud of it."

"No."

"They seemed to like it."

"I didn't write it for them. Besides, I could probably take a dump on stage and they would love it."

He laughs and his razor-teeth freeze my spine.

"One of them brought up a good point," I say. "You could have gotten to me whenever you wanted."

"Yes."

"My pseudonym was feeble."

"To avoid me? Yes. But I imagine necessary to pursue your profession after the … unpleasantness. You were kept under suspicion for quite a while, weren't you?"

I nod.

"Hard to shake such a stigma."

I grunt in agreement.

"And yet you never told the truth."

"Who would have believed it?"

His eyes turn green and He smirks. "You want to know why I waited so long to call on you."

"Yes."

"The story."

"What about it?"

"I wanted to hear it."

"That's it?"

"What were you expecting?"

"Retribution."

"For what?"

"Freeing myself."

He points to Emma's name on my forearm. "I would think *you* would be the one who wanted retribution."

"I may chase prescription meds with booze on an hourly basis, but I'm not crazy. I'd have a better chance of fending off a tiger with a plastic spoon."

He studies me. "You *knew* I would show if you wrote this."

"I suspected. I can't live in fear anymore. I need to end it."

"But I've already told you I'm not here seeking vengeance. You did no harm in your escape. You hurt no one. I was actually impressed you managed such a feat. No one else ever has."

"Thanks to you. If my hand wasn't as mashed and as numb as it was I couldn't have slipped it free from the shackle."

He smiles. His eyes are blue.

"I robbed your newborns of their offering," I add.

"We found another."

"So then ... what? You're here to cover your tracks?"

He smiles and shakes His head. "You said it yourself. No one would believe you anyway."

I wanna cry. "You're *fucking* with me. Please—I've kept this shit inside for so long."

He goes to speak but I continue.

"I'm an emotional fucking recluse. A walking pharmacy. A fucking alcoholic. Christ, I haven't even been able to have *sex* since Emma. That's *twenty years!* Please ... if you have any mercy in your body ... just end it now."

He steps forward and caresses my cheek with those long white fingers. His touch is like the fur of a mink. "I just want the story."

I can't fight the tears now; they're flowing big-time. "That can't be it. That can't be all you want."

"But it is. I really did enjoy it, and your female student was quite perceptive in her assumptions. Besides, would I be wrong in presuming you don't intend to have it published?"

I shake my head.

He takes His hand off my face and opens his palm. It looks like a large white crab flipped onto its belly. "May I have it?"

I'm crying still, but I don't care; a twenty-year dam of repressed fear has just exploded. I take the manuscript, roll it into a tube, and hand it to Him.

He takes it, nods, and says: "Thank you. You won't see me again."

I believe Him. Somehow, I know He is telling the truth, but I cry harder.

A blast from a whistle jerks me out of my sobbing and I look towards the entrance of the auditorium. I know what it is before my swollen eyes can settle. It's one of His children—waiting.

"Must go," he says to me. "Will you write more horror?"

I wipe away snot and tears. "I'm not sure I'll be able to write *anything* anymore."

He frowns. His eyes are black. "Why?"

"I think my constant fear was what kept me going. If I ever stopped writing I'm not sure what I would have done."

He smiles. "Well, now elation will be your stimulus. You will write for the love of it—like you did before you encountered me."

He turns and walks down the small stairs, the manuscript rolled tight in his hand. He reaches the entrance and his child jumps into his arms like a chimpanzee. He kisses it on the cheek and looks back in my direction.

"Take some time off before getting back to it, *Adam*." He smirks after speaking my pseudonym. And then with a gesture that is pure theatrics, He pretends to cover his child's ears, grins and says: "Go get laid."

2

My stuff's packed up and I'm heading to the auditorium exit.

I was certain that once my story was told I would want many, many drinks, but now I'm not so sure.

His arrival felt cathartic.

I'm not especially proud of the way I broke down and cried like a little girl, but hell, twenty years of intense fear was finally confronted. I'm surprised, and delighted, tears were the *only* thing my body leaked.

Cathartic.

As in: I don't need to numb myself anymore.

Still, a drink—celebratory or medicinal—*would* be nice right about now. Just don't get hammered. Everything in moderation from now on.

And your precious benzos, Alex? Your Xanax? Your Klonopin? Will they be moderated too?

I pull a Xanax bottle from my coat pocket and pop one out of spite.

You stop showing me Emma's corpse in my sleep every fucking night, and I'll lay off the benzos, dick.

The pill is crazy bitter, but I chew it anyway. Placebo effect, no doubt, but I can feel it working instantly.

I get to the exit and someone is waiting for me. It's a man, and he appears slovenly: faded t-shirt (image of an alien giving the peace sign); the gym-virgin combo of a big belly and skinny arms; heavy five o'clock shadow; thinning, greasy hair; and frayed jeans hanging down far enough below his tire to give the occasional glimpse of crack to any unfortunates.

I'm praying this guy didn't stay behind to show me a manuscript.

"Hi," I say. "Can I help you with something?" I give my watch a glance on purpose and hoist my briefcase as though it's cumbersome, even though there's fuck-all in there except more pills and a turkey sandwich that's been in there since yesterday.

The guy *does* hand me something, but it's not a manuscript—it's a business card.

"Some of us do believe," he says.

I look at the card. It's all black save for a phone number in white lettering across the middle.

"What's this?" I ask.

"Others have seen Him," the guy says. "I know the truth about your story."

I glance at the card again, then back at him. "Were you at my reading?"

"Yes."

"And did you see this *Him* you're talking about?"

The man's face comes alive. "No—why? Was He here?"

Oh, He was here, pal.

I shrug. "I really don't know what you're talking about. Sorry." I go to move past him, but he blocks my way.

"When you're ready, call that number," he says, scruffy fat face gravely serious. The only thing that keeps me from laughing—the catalyst being his comical appearance blatantly contradicting his assertive and serious manner—is the content of *what* he's pitching. Apparently, my late friends and I weren't the only ones who'd encountered Him.

My friends and the women back on Elmwood, of course.

I wonder if those women are still there, giving birth and feeding poor schmucks to His kids? It's *been* twenty years. That would make most of them 50 or 60 by now, I guess. Still, who knows? After seeing what I've seen, my expectations of life and reason are up there with winning Powerball. Not to mention; He didn't necessarily impregnate those women back on Elmwood via standard method: a foot-long penis, pointed sharp at the tip like some kind of flesh sword, plunging then pumping His seed into the belly button?

I'll be very dead before I forget that image.

Still, this guy in front of me believes, *despite* his apparent inability to see Him at my reading. Huh.

I brush him off all the same. "You got it, pal," I say. "Thanks for coming."

I stuff the card in my pocket and move past him. There's some unavoidable anxiety in my gait, and I only hope he's not spotting it as I hurry towards my car.

.   .   .

I slide into my Lexus and toss my briefcase on the passenger seat. It lands on His lap.

"I see you had a visitor."

I nearly shit myself. "*Jesus Christ.*"

He makes the sound of a game show buzzer. "Wrong." His eyes are yellow.

"How did you get in here?"

"I wanted in."

"Just what the hell *are* you, anyway? A demon?"

"No."

"Ghost?"

"No."

"Vampire?"

"*Please.*"

"Well, then *what?*"

His eyes change colors rapidly now, too fast to keep track. "Let's go with that. *What.*"

I sigh. "I thought you told me to go get laid."

"I did."

"You coming with me?"

He smirks. "Perhaps I will. You're out of practice, and I can be very persuasive with the fairer sex."

I give him a look. "Yes, I'm well aware of your charm."

"Well, thank you."

"Wasn't a compliment." I shift in my seat. "Besides, I may be out of practice, but the idea of putting my sex life into the hands of someone like you … you'll forgive me if I respectfully decline."

"Spoken like a boy who stamps his disgust on a culinary unknown before sampling."

"Clever, but I think I'll just soldier on with my head in the sand if it's all the same to you."

"Well, then I'll just leave my offer on the table, shall I?"

"Whatever."

He places my briefcase on the floor. "Your turkey sandwich smells a bit off."

"You can smell it?"

He grins at me—endless rows of what I'll always liken to sharks teeth in a man's mouth. His eyes are ink black. No pupils, no whites. All black. As if He knows I flashed on a shark and is trying His damnedest to em-ulate one.

I struggle to keep my face from coming apart, glance over at my brief-case and decide to address said turkey sandwich. "Yeah—I thought it might be a little ripe by now. You can have it if you want."

"Thank you, no."

"Oh right," I say, "you prefer naked people soaked in marinade. I was supposed to be teriyaki, if I recall."

"Very witty," He says before repeating: "You had a visitor."

"Yeah, so … ?"

"What did he tell you?"

"Something tells me you already know."

He steeples long white fingers beneath His chin as though looking for the right response. "I have an idea," He eventually says. "Would you mind sharing all the same?"

I'm hesitant. If He *does* know what the guy told me, perhaps He'll now see me as a liability, that my story wasn't so harmless after all.

I tell the truth, consequences be damned.

"He said he knows about you," I say. "Says *people* know about you."

"People *do.*"

"No, not the women you … *work* with—*other* people."

"Yes—I know."

I lean forward and plunk my forehead onto the steering wheel. I keep it there as I say, "Well, if you know, then why are you here? I thought you said you were done with me."

"I thought I was."

My head still on the wheel, I say: "You decided to kill me after all?"

"Not you," He says. "Your mother."

I sit bolt upright. "*What?*"

"Your mother."

"I *heard* what you said. Why the hell would you include my mother in this? What the hell did she ever do to you?"

"Nothing that I can recall," He says matter-of-factly.

I begin to panic. "I was right—you *were* fucking with me inside the auditorium. You didn't just want the story … "

He makes the game show buzzer sound again. "Wrong. I *did* just want the story. I *did* intend on leaving you alone. But then I spotted your friend. I'm surprised I missed him at your reading. Either he was hiding quite well, or I'm losing my touch."

"What friend? The fat guy who handed me a card?"

He nods.

"I don't even know the guy!"

"But he knows me."

"He couldn't even *see* you!"

"I'm sorry—I should say he knows *about* me."

"Well, so what? Let him tell the world. Who's going to believe him?"

His eyes change to a pleasant blue for some reason.

"There are those who *can* see me," He says. "Those that *have*. Ordinarily, I can choose when I do and do *not* want to be seen. However, there are a select few that possess the ability, *despite* my choosing."

"But this guy *couldn't* see you."

Eyes still blue, He says, "No—he couldn't. But his affiliates … "

"*Affiliates?*"

"Four in total. One that can see; three that take him at his word."

My brain feels like a water balloon being filled. Every word that comes out of His mouth stretches it a bit more. A part of me is hoping the damn thing would just pop already so I could finally transcend sanity and just flat-out not give a fuck about anything anymore. Especially if He is planning to kill my mother—the only person I still care about in this world.

"I'll say it again," I start. "If there's only one who can see you, then who *fucking cares* who these guys tell? *Nobody* will believe them."

He smirks. Thank God no teeth. "They don't aim to tell," He says. "They aim to kill."

"Kill *you?*" I bark out a laugh. "How the hell would they do that? Did you *see* that guy? The only things he's killing are some kittens followed by a crate of Hot Pockets in his parents' basement."

He seems amused by my quip. "Kittens?"

"It's just an expression," I say. "Every time you uh … touch it, God kills a kitten?"

He stares at me.

I then elaborate by trying: "Uh … a guy like this would say something like: '*Dude, I totally killed a few kittens thinking about Scully from 'X-Files' last night.*'"

He still just stares.

"It means *jerking off*," I blurt. "You know—" I mime the gesture on myself.

He laughs, and my mime slows to an embarrassing stop.

Asshole.

I straighten my posture, clear my throat. "Anyway … all I was saying is that a guy like that posing a threat to you is downright laughable."

"That's true—the ones who cannot see are incapable of harming me. But the ones who can … "

Wait, does that mean … ?

I blink and He's gone.

I blink and He's back.

"I *choose* to let you see me, Alex," He says.

I swallow what feels like sand. "I wasn't thinking … "

"Of course you weren't."

The inside of my left forearm starts to burn. I immediately roll up my sleeve. The tattoo of Emma's name is no longer inked in black: it's a blistering red, the lettering raised as though I've been scorched by a branding iron.

The pain grows instantly, horribly intense.

I clamp my right hand down over the tattoo in a desperate bid to stem the hurt, yet it only seems to heighten it.

I turn and cast Him a desperate look, His eyes now a blazing red, glowing like embers.

I can hear sizzling, actually *smell* my flesh cooking. The smell is smoky sweet, like a barbecue, and the sudden correlation makes it impossibly worse.

"*Stop!*" I yell, gripping my forearm tighter. "*Please, I'm sorry!*"

The pain grows deeper still. I haven't felt anything this excruciating since ...

(*my hand*)

(*my shoulders*)

(*Emma*)

(*because of Him*)

"*MOTHERFUCKER, I SAID STOP!!!*"

And he does.

And the pain is instantly gone.

Emma's tattoo is back to its original black, the lettering no longer raised like a branding. For a split second there's a part of me, the part of my mind that feels like the water balloon being filled, that wonders if I'd imagined it all, if the balloon had mercifully popped and I had well and truly lost my shit.

But I only need turn and look at Him again to know that line of thinking holds no merit. Unless, of course, it's all been imagined. *All of it.* I'd been batshit crazy this whole time, the last twenty-plus years a warped dream. I am still a ripe twenty-four; Emma and my friends are alive and well, perhaps watching me in a padded cell through one-way glass, Emma crying, my mother consoling her. Wait ... my mother—

"Tell me what any of this has to do with my mother," I say, trying to control my breathing, my pulse, everything. "Why do you want to kill her?"

His eyes are no longer a fire-red. They're orange, as if the fire inside had mellowed, but was far from dead.

"I don't *want* to kill her," He says. "But my hand may be forced."

"How's that?"

"If you fail to do what I ask of you."

"And that is?"

He gives me a quizzical look, as if the answer is self-evident. "Isn't it obvious?"

"No."

"I want you to kill the one."

"*What?*"

"The one who can see me. The one who is capable of killing—"

"I know what you meant, but…I mean…*are you fucking kidding me?*"

A harsh rap on my car window turns my head fast enough to wrench it. It's one of Villanova's professors who attended my reading. I roll down the window.

"You okay in there, Mr. Kale?" he asks.

I nod, perhaps too eagerly. "Yes, I'm fine. Why?"

"Looked like you were talking to yourself in there."

Before I even glance over at the passenger seat, I can *feel* the fucker grinning at me. Of course I look anyway. And, of course, He is. Eyes changing color by the second, every razor tooth baring, the works.

I am suddenly very aware of my face. It feels like it's cracking. I want to touch it, smooth out the cracks with both hands.

I think I'm smiling when I turn back to the professor and say: "Just reciting a few notes out loud; that's all."

The professor nods and says, "I see. Well, everyone seemed to love the reading. I wonder if you would ever consider taking the time to look over *my*—"

"I'm sorry to interrupt," I say, "but I'd like to get these notes onto my recorder while they're fresh in my head."

The professor looks around inside my car for a recorder that isn't there. I don't explain myself, only smile

(*I think*)

again.

"I see," he says again, although much more wary this time, perhaps aware that I'm basically telling him to piss off; no, I don't want to read your manuscript. "Enjoy the rest of your day."

I say goodbye and roll up my window.

"You loved that, didn't you?" I say to Him.

He says nothing in return, but He's still grinning, eyes now locked on gray.

"What makes you think I'm capable of killing anyone?" I ask.

The grin fades and He shrugs. "Your mother. She's dead if you don't. And I'll take my time with her. I'll make you watch."

Whatever nerve I had summoned moments ago feels as if it's going down a dark drain. In just over a whisper I say, "I'm not capable of killing anyone."

"You'd kill me, if you had the chance."

"You're not just anyone."

He shrugs. "True—but I believe you *are* capable of the act itself. You've managed to escape me once before; and just moments ago you summoned the strength to challenge me."

"Number one: I didn't escape you; I escaped the crazy bitch who was keeping me locked up for you. And number two: I stood up to you because my forearm felt like it was roasting over a fucking spit."

"You don't give yourself enough credit."

I say nothing.

"Think of it as a sequel to your story," he says.

"Sequels suck."

"Not entirely."

"Would you stop with this bullshit banter like you're only asking me to look after your dog for the weekend?" I say.

"I rather enjoy our banter."

The dark drain begins to slow its rapid swirl of diminishing nerve, frustration producing a small clog that allows me to scoop a handful of spirit.

"Dude—*fuck you.* You're incapable of any camaraderie. You can barely see beyond the tip of your own exceptionally disturbing dick."

He smiles. "Ouch."

"Why can't *you* just kill him?" I ask. "You don't think I remember how effortlessly you obliterated my friends? Why would you risk it and use a nobody like me?"

"A fair question," He says. "And believe me, I've thought about it … " He sighs. "But I just can't bring myself to kill my own child."

3

He's gone. Or maybe He's not—who knows? For all I know, He's still sitting next to me in the car as I sit here listening to my stomach acid churn.

I go into my coat pocket and pop another Xanax. The crazy bitter taste is almost welcome now—like a buddy you can only tolerate when you're wasted.

I lean back in my car seat, close my eyes, and play the rest of our conversation back in my head…

.   .   .

"*Child?*" I said. "You mean like one of those fucked-up little white monkey things?"

He did not look amused. And I guess I didn't blame Him. As crazy as it may sound, I suppose those *are* His kids, and standard rules felt like they still applied; you don't talk shit on someone's kids, no matter who or *what* they happened to be.

"Sorry," I said. "I just meant… is the kid you're referring to just like the ones I saw twenty years ago? Like the one that jumped into your arms at the end of my reading today?"

"Yes and no," He said.

"Meaning?"

"Yes, he originated from one of my litters—initially different than no other. No, he no longer resembles the ones you saw years ago; the one you saw today."

I tried to wrap my head around it. "Wait, the ones I saw… they grow up?"

He gave me an odd look. "Of course they do."

"No—that's not what I meant. I'm sure they age, but do they ever, like… *physically* grow? End up looking like you?"

"The majority? The *vast* majority? No."

"But there are some that *do* end up like you," I said.

"No—not like me. More like you."

"Say what?"

"Shall I give you the simple version?" He asked.

"That would be nice."

"It happens rarely. So rarely that it has been a non-issue for the majority of time I've existed."

"Which is how long?"

He gave me a sly look. "Long—but I'm not eternal. I *will* have my day."

And I'll dance and piss on your fucking grave if I'm still around to see it, I thought before suddenly becoming aware that He was capable of reading me like a book.

"You know what I was thinking just now, don't you?" I said.

"Yes."

"Are you going to hurt me again?"

"Would you like me to?"

"No."

"May I continue now?"

"Yes."

"I've existed for some time. As a result, my seed no longer carries the potency it once did. In the past couple of decades there have been two anomalies within my brood."

"Okay …"

"Those anomalies carry my genes, *and* the genes of my host."

"Don't they all?"

He closed His eyes and shook His head as though annoyed, as if I should have known better. "No. The hosts I choose are just that—hosts; nothing more."

I was starting to get it. "Okay. But *now* you're saying that in the past two decades, some of your offspring *have* shared the DNA of your hosts."

"Yes."

"Didn't you spot this the moment they were born? Didn't the host? I'd imagine they'd look … different."

"They looked no different than the remaining litter—at first. But their rate of growth, *despite* their refusal for human sustenance … "

"They wouldn't eat?" I asked.

"Correct," He said. "The first time this happened—fifteen years ago, I believe—the host suspected problems. She assumed he was a reject; product of certain unavoidable truths when birthing so many at once. She slaughtered him before he grew much larger. She then fed him to the others.

"I admired her fortitude and willingness to take matters into her own hands. But he was still my child, and she acted without my approval. I broke open her skull and ate her brain. The rest of her body was given to my children."

I tried to will the image away: Him, face buried deep into the top of the woman's skull, ravenously devouring her brain like a man in a pie-eating contest, but the second he spoke it stuck.

Curse of being a writer, I tried to kid myself.

And then Mr. Water Balloon Brain expanded a little more and had his say: *Curse of actually having seen him and his kiddies in all their gory action. Nice try, Señor Suppression—I don't envy your nightmares tonight.*

I eventually found my voice and asked: "What about the other one? The other anomaly?"

"Recent—a little over a year ago. This host also suspected something wrong. But at the risk of upsetting me—I suppose rumor might have gotten around about the status of the last host who had encountered such an ordeal—she secretly compensated for his lack of appetite. She gave him food she herself would eat."

"You mean *real* food?"

He raised an eyebrow at me. "Semantics."

"Fair enough."

He continued. "When I arrived to check in on the host for my litter's final offering, I found her very dead." He lowered His head for a moment, sighed and added: "My children too."

"So then how did you find out what happened?" I asked.

"Funnily enough, the offering was still alive—shackled and gagged inside his cage. *He* told me what had happened."

"How many of your children were killed?"

"Eight."

"How was only *one* of your children able to kill so many? *Including* the host? You said this was only a year ago, right? Wouldn't he be … I don't know how it works, but wouldn't he be considered an infant or something?"

"According to the offering, the half-breed grew by the *day*. By the time he had slaughtered the host and my children he was the size of a grown man."

"And the host didn't find this unbelievably odd? Or downright *scary?*"

"Perhaps rumors of the prior host kept her discreet. Usually the women I work with gossip exclusively amongst themselves. This woman never said a word. Besides, according to the offering, the half-breed hardly moved. Just ate what he was given … and waited."

"What does he look like?"

He didn't answer.

I tried to envision some mutated result of a human and one of His children.

His children: the things that continue to gather at the foot of my bed. The dark corners of my room. Crawl across my ceiling in the dead of night. Pale white skin glowing in the surrounding black of either my room or mind. Their small bodies contorted, behavior primitive like a monkey's, their actual features anything *but* a monkey's—the hundreds of serrated teeth, so small and razor sharp; the eyes changing colors uncontrollably, product of their youthful vigor, lack of control. Their calls to one another strangely nature-like—a cross between a bird and a cricket … unless extreme arousal took hold; and then any similarities to something natural ceased: anticipation of their excesses producing something like chirping blasts from a smoke detector—frightening and alarming.

A half-breed.

More human, or more … His?

The size of a man...

One of *His* the size of a man...

The prospect was paralyzing.

"You call him a half-breed," I said. "You say he murdered your children. So then why are you claiming loyalty to him? Why the conflict over killing him yourself?"

"It's still my child."

"A child you claim wants you dead."

He only nodded.

"I don't get it."

"You don't need to. My motives are my own. You need only worry about one thing."

"How do you know he's capable of killing you?" I asked.

"We share the same bloodline. My kind are only susceptible to each other."

"*There's more of you?*"

"Did you think I was the only one?"

"I think I was too terrified to even consider it."

He smirked.

"How do you know he's trying to kill you?" I said. "Better still: *why* would he try and kill you?"

"I suspect he's more human than me—" He then rolled His eyes in disgust. "*Cursed* with innate morals perhaps."

"Okay fine—but once again: how do you *know* he's trying to kill you?"

"The man that came to see you after your reading...?" He said.

"Yeah?"

"There are two others."

"So you said."

He leered, eyes blood red, a slight smirk itching to be a grin. "There used to be more."

I looked away. "Gotcha."

There was a pause.

I eventually said, "I still don't understand a few things."

He started to look annoyed, His eyes shifting back and forth between black and red. "As I've said, your absolute knowledge on this matter is superfluous."

"You've made that very clear. But you're asking me to do something I *still* don't believe I'm capable of doing. You can't indulge me?"

He gave a frustrated sigh.

I took this as an invite to continue. "Okay—what I'm not totally grasping here is … well, there's a lot of shit I'm not grasping … "

"Please make it quick."

"How did guys like that geek who approached me ever get in contact with the half-breed to begin with? In fact, *why* did a geek approach me? You implied that you killed off a bunch of them already. Why was *that* guy still alive? Why didn't you kill him too?"

"As to how the 'geeks'—as you call them—contacted the half-breed, it is the other way around. The half-breed contacted *them*. The geeks were more than willing to believe: their desperately hopeful nature in all things other-worldly, coupled with a demonstration of ability from the half-breed was more than enough to have them all collectively … *killing kittens?*" He smirked, eyes flashing a zillion colors like a slot machine.

Apparently, my previous envisioning of this half-breed merely being a giant version of His children was way off. It was beginning to sound more like they resembled *Him*. Which of course raised more questions. Not the least one being the question that has plagued me from the moment I had encountered Him and His supernatural brood: why did His kids look and act nothing like Him? I mean, even in the movie *Alien*, the queen alien gave birth to those giant spider things, but at least the spider things laid eggs in people's stomachs and produced *more aliens*. What's this guy's grand scheme? How does *He* procreate? What's the advantage of producing and feeding a zillion little ravenous freaks that apparently never amount to anything but … a zillion little ravenous freaks?

"Wait a minute," I said. "Are you saying this thing can do what *you* can do? It can … fuck people up without even touching them?"

"*Exactly* like me?" He said. "No. Of course, he shares my blood, and is therefore gifted with certain capabilities, but his strength is diluted."

"*How* diluted?"

"Enough to make him vulnerable to the likes of you."

"*How* vulnerable? If this thing possesses even *one-tenth* of the abilities you possess, then that's still a million times more than anything *I've* got." I waved a hand over my torso. "I may look reasonably slim and fit, but that's only because my diet is mostly ethanol and pills. I probably couldn't even manage five minutes on a treadmill."

"You needn't worry—I'll help you incapacitate him. But the final deed? That's you."

Hooray.

"So he's not invincible when it comes to humans," I said. "The way you are."

"Correct."

"And he's the one who's capable of seeing you, whether you want to or not—the one you alluded to earlier."

"Correct."

"I'm assuming you got all of this information—the half-breed hanging with the geeks; their plan to kill you—from the geeks you killed?"

"Correct. Are you finished now?"

"Almost. You never answered me as to why you didn't kill *all* the geeks."

"They're devoted fools," He said. "Always best to have a few around to lead you in the right direction."

"Last question."

He sighed again. "Who would have thought that it would be *you* making *me* suffer?"

"Why me?" I asked. "You've got legions of hosts who would be willing to die for you at the drop of a hat. One of them even took it upon herself to dispose of a half-breed without any provocation whatsoever. Granted, things didn't turn out too well for her, but still, now you *want* the half-breeds dead. Why not use one of the hosts to do the deed? Why not leave me alone like you *promised*?"

He appeared undeterred by my *promise* comment and said, "They would never trust a woman—they are more than privy to my legion of hosts."

"So get a smokin' hot host to help you! *Guarantee* at least one of those three guys is a virgin. UFOs, aliens, Bigfoot ... I don't care how devoted they are; none of that stuff can compete with first-time pussy."

"I'd have to agree with you. But the issue is not finding a way to eliminate the geeks; the half-breed is our target—he would have no interest in procreating with a woman."

"You sure? Maybe its *human* side would."

He gave me a look. "Quite sure."

"Okay, fine ... but still, why me—?"

But I stopped right there. It was suddenly all too obvious.

They had contacted me. Likely expecting me to contact *them*. I was the perfect

(*idiot*)

candidate for what He was demanding. I was a public figure; a celebrity of sorts; a guy who was given the metaphorical key to the front door of Castle Half-Breed and The Geeks. I was as unassuming as unassuming gets.

I gave him a defeated glance.

He returned a thin, unapologetic smile. He knew I got it now. The son of a bitch knew. Always knows.

"If I help you, my mother is safe?" I said.

"Yes."

"At this point, I'm not sure it means anything; but do I have your word?"

"Yes."

"So then what now?"

"Go visit your mother," He said. "In case you get second thoughts once I'm gone. I'll find you when it's time."

.   .   .

I dig into my coat and pop a Klonopin this time. Unlike Xanax—which kicks in damn fast, but wears off pretty damn fast—Klonopin takes its time before having an effect. And that effect isn't in a hurry to leave like Xanax's is. I tend to use Klonopin when I anticipate a stressful situation (like having to visit my mother after being told she might be killed unless *I* kill), and I tend to use Xanax when my anxiety feels as though an anvil has suddenly dropped onto my chest (like right after a visit from Him).

I start the car and head towards my mother's house.

4

My mother and I didn't have much of a rapport until *after* the incident. It wasn't for her lack of trying though. She did. I was just too much of an asshole kid who, like most asshole kids, thought he knew everything by the time he was eighteen.

My mother had me when she was just a kid herself. Seventeen. I resented this for some reason. Looking back, she could have easily given me away like the majority did in the shit-hole town I grew up in, but she didn't. She kept me. And with my 'father' (still don't know who the prick is) doing an Usain Bolt the moment he got news about the impending me, Mom had to work two jobs to support us; sometimes three if the opportunity came about.

And yet I still refused to warm to her. And I now hate myself for it. *Despise* myself for it. Hindsight now, sure, but I guess if I can rationalize my line of thinking at the time, my mother represented everything I was desperate to escape from in my miserable little world. Had my stubborn idiocy not been so strong, I might have seen that she too was desperately trying to transcend the norm of our shit life in that shit town. But really, what chance did she have? She had to drop out of school to raise me, and no matter how hard you scrubbed floors and waited tables, the prospects in promotion for a high school dropout were akin to getting your allowance raised from a dollar a week, to a dollar twenty-five.

But she kept at it. Kept scrubbing, kept waiting in dives. She'd come home at all hours, her clothes stinking of stale smoke, stale beer, and rotten God-knows-what. And I'd turn my nose up at it all and cringe. Even at fourteen I can remember creeping into her room at 8 A.M., her sprawled out on the bed, facedown, on top of the blankets, too exhausted to even crawl under them, and I can remember feeling revulsion for what I *thought* she was.

Want another reason to think me an even bigger douche? My mother was one of maybe two percent in our town who didn't drink. She didn't even smoke—because that was money that could have been better spent elsewhere. Christ, with the life she had to live, you'd think she'd almost be justified in pickling her liver whenever she pleased, going through two packs a day.

Nope. No booze, no drugs, no cigarettes—she barely even ate; it was all for me. Yet still the *idiot glasses* I wore kept her fixed in time. What do I mean by that? Ever notice how people in your life often become fixed at a certain age? No matter how grown your cousin might be—college graduate, engaged, maybe married with a kid on the way—you'll always see him as that Ritalin-*now!!!* kid who fell from the monkey bars and broke his arm when he was six.

Or how about the friend you see maybe once a year? He'll always be that buddy you raised hell with back in the day: full head of wild hair; constant exuberant and optimistic shimmer to his eye; fit and full of life.

And then, on one of your yearly get-togethers, the timeless filter vanishes without warning, and you're looking at a stranger: thinning hair with more than a mild peppering of gray; the shimmer in the eye, long since dwindled to a dull, lethargic flame; the once fit body now a flabby gut and sunken chest.

It took me awhile to peel the timeless filter off and look at my mother for the wonderful woman she was. And like I said; it was only after "the incident." You'd think with what a dick I'd been to her my whole life that she might have dropped by the hospital after I had escaped the crazy bitch on Elmwood and given me a simple pat and a "get better," but no, she stayed bedside the entire time. Even insisted on holding my hand (the one that wasn't broken into eight million pieces, of course) when they had trouble popping my shoulders back in.

When the police came? She backed my lie without pause. I never told her it was a lie, but I suspected she knew something was amiss. Four people just don't vanish after a supposed late night "mugging," never to be seen from again. And while the police couldn't necessarily corroborate my story—I claimed I was knocked unconscious by the marauding group of thugs, and when I awoke, everyone was gone—they couldn't necessarily *disprove* it either: my injuries, the doctor confirmed, could *not* have been self-inflicted; I was most assuredly attacked.

The public had not been so kind. The families of my friends especially. They held me under a deeper suspicion than the police. For a while it had been a good old witch hunt. People stood outside my mother's house—in a town like that, there are no secrets; everyone knew where I was—hollering, picketing, occasionally throwing things at the house. One fucker even shattered my mother's window with a brick.

When the police had officially called off the investigation, you'd have thought things would have died down, but no. My mother and I remained pariahs. I think it was a good year before I even chanced venturing past the mailbox. And even then it was only to Wendy's. The drive-thru window. Hat, sunglasses, even a trench coat with the collar turned up. The lady at the window probably wondered if I was planning to pay for my meal or flash her.

Why didn't we just move? Simple. With what? And to where? We could barely afford our lives now.

So I started to write. Many things spurred me on, the financial and social status of my mother and me only being one of them. I was doing it for Emma, and I was doing it for therapeutic reasons. My mind was a constant mess. Writing would be the intangible drug (in addition to the many other prescription meds I was growing hooked on) that would keep my head from spiraling out of control.

I developed a pseudonym—Adam Kale—for obvious reasons, and I dove in. Rejections were aplenty at first, but with a little luck, and long, long hours honing my craft and knocking on cyber doors, I eventually landed an agent, and I think you know the rest after that.

Ironically, I think it was being such the pariah that allowed me to make it in the industry sooner rather than later: I had fuck-all to do each day except write and read. If I was an aspiring author who worked nine to five and had a family, writing on the weekends? I'd probably still be on my first query letter to an agent.

I'm nearly done … just one more reason to respect my mom, if you please:

She never wanted a dime from me. When I became a successful writer and offered her everything and anything, she wanted none of it. The only thing she *would* let me do is relocate us. And that was just fucking fine by me.

I moved her far away—and right next to me. Five miles from me to be exact. I had relocated us to a beautiful suburb in Chester County, Pennsylvania, twenty minutes or so from Philadelphia. I wanted to move her into a palace, but it seemed her limit for gratuity peaked at relocation. The pleasant surroundings were enough; she would take a small modest home, nothing else. According to her, I worked hard for my money and she would *not* mooch it from me. I tried to explain my gratitude for the years she provided for me, working horrible jobs for horrible pay, but she only closed her eyes and shook her head. "*That was my job,*" she'd said. "*You're my son; I'm your mother.*"

Christ, thinking about it now, I want to cry. I mean really cry.

My mother still works. She waitresses at a lovely restaurant in a swanky little town called Wayne, and she makes a decent income for someone with only a GED. With her house paid for, the only thing she has to worry about are minor bills. Even her car is paid for. Nice car? I'd call it modest. She paid for it out of her own pocket, insisted of course, and the thing gets her "… *from point A to point B; that's all that matters,*" she'd tell you.

Suddenly, Villanova University seems a million miles from Berwyn, where Mom lives. I want to see her now. And as soon as I do, I'm going to wrap my arms around her, squeeze for all I'm worth, and tell her how much I love her.

I won't tell her that I have to kill some fucked-up half-breed in order to keep her from dying a horrible death.

5

My mother is waiting for me by her front door. I had phoned on the way and she sounded eager.

I give her the hug I had been pining for, then tell her how much I love her.

She wiggles out of my arms and looks up at me, concerned. "What's wrong?"

"Nothing's wrong," I say. "Just telling you how much I love you."

She continues to eye me curiously. I think it's harder to lie to *her* than it is to *Him*.

She eventually shrugs it off, but I know it's not gone; she's logged it away for a later date, when my guard is down. She's sneaky like that.

"So tell me about your reading," she says. She then looks at the clock; it's almost four. "You want tea?"

I don't tell her that I'd prefer a martini served in a fish bowl—she knows I drink too much, and doesn't approve—so I say: "Sure. You have any Lapsang?"

She wrinkles her nose. "Only what you leave here. I don't like it."

"I know you don't, Mom. You tell me that every time."

Lapsang souchong tea is probably the only thing I drink more than water or alcohol. It's an acquired taste, very smoky, but I freaking love the stuff. My mother can't even bear to smell it, says it's like burnt fire-wood. She also mentions her distaste for the stuff every single time we have tea together.

She smacks my arm. "You saying I'm getting senile?"

I make a sad face. "Awww … Mommy's projecting."

"Your shrink talk is as welcome here as your father."

My face pops with playful surprise. "Wow—right out of the gate with the serious stuff. Calling him 'father' and everything. What happened to *The Sperm Donor*? Or my own personal favorite—" I do a lame Arnold Schwarzenegger accent and say: "*The Inseminator.*"

She's fighting a smile. "I figured 'father' might shut you up faster."

"Well played."

She yields to the smile and I marvel at how beautiful she still is. A year past her 60th birthday and my mother still has people guessing her in her mid-forties. You'd think that with the kind of life she'd led, the years would have accumulated everywhere and without remorse.

Nope.

Sure she has some grays and some lines, perhaps a few pounds where they didn't use to be—but they're only *some* grays; *some* lines; a *few* pounds.

And today she looks especially radiant. More so than only just yesterday, though I'm certain I can thank *Him* for affecting my perspective.

Why my mother is still single is a mystery to me. I know she's lonely and would like to meet someone, despite her expressing indifference on the matter. I think the truth is that she's shy when it comes to men. Yeah … despite her fearless nature in all other aspects of life, when it comes to men I think it boils down to good old fashioned shyness. When you have a child at seventeen and work dozens of jobs to feed the thing while keeping the heat and electricity on, your social life doesn't just take a back seat, it ends up in the trunk. While others were spreading their dating wings in college and beyond, Mom had no choice but to keep hers flat to her back. And as the saying goes: use it or lose it. After so many years without, I think Mom, despite any desires, has resigned to … well … going without. Of course she'll always have me by her side, but as a certain Oedipal caretaker for The Bates Motel once said, a son is a poor substitute for a lover.

"So are you saying you *do* or do *not* have any Lapsang in the cupboard?"

"If you didn't take it home with you last time, then it's still there."

"Awesome. Well, then how about I spare your nostrils from my burnt wood leaves, and *I* go make the tea."

She gives me that headstrong look of hers. "You will not. Son or stranger, you're still my guest. Sit your butt down."

I smile and flop on the sofa. She leaves for the kitchen and my smile fades.

.   .   .

When I left my mom's I gave her another extra-long squeeze, and an "I love you" that was unavoidably too heartfelt for just a hello and a cup of tea.

Again, I got the curious look, and while the meaning behind my affection was no different than it had been when I arrived, there was also something else; something that hit suddenly and painfully mid-hug.

155

I might never see her again.

Yes, I was going to go through with His proposal, but some major *what-ifs* had flashed all at once:

What if the half-breed killed *me* before I could kill *him*?

What if I failed, the half-breed fled, and He punished me for my failures by killing my mother?

And what if I didn't fail? What if I succeeded, killed the half-breed, and He *still* killed my mother? He gave me His word He wouldn't, but big-fucking-hairy deal. This is *Him* we're talking about here.

Bottom line? Anyway you rearranged the above scenarios, the final outcome proposed a likelihood that I might never see my mother again.

Unless I successfully kill this thing. And He keeps His word.

And that's why I squeezed Mom harder on my exit than I did on my arrival.

6

I'm mixing my third vodka martini. The sound of ice and vodka swishing and clanking inside the metal tumbler holds a shameless comfort. After I pour, my glass will predictably frost then shine; and this too will bring a shameless comfort, as though I'm being given something pristine. And in a way I suppose I am. I am also unabashedly and systematically defiling this pristine gift. With each sip I am removing an article of its clothing, whispering sweet nothings in its ear, promising eternal love afterwards if you just keep it coming, please; let me have my way.

The next morning? Christ, the analogy I'm playing with here is so obvious it's insulting to even elaborate. Onward.

I pour; I watch the frost, the shine; and then I pick it up and sip—perhaps I'm unhitching the bra with drink number three here.

"I'm not sure you should be drinking."

He's behind me, lips at my ear. Somehow I didn't drop the glass, but my drink stood no chance; it was all over my clothes the second He spoke.

"*Jesus Christ!*"

"Again with your insistence on calling me that," He says.

"Again with your insistence on trying to give me a coronary."

"Oh, if I wanted to … " He extends one of his freakishly long fingers and touches my chest. I immediately feel an uncomfortable tingle down my left arm. My chest starts to tighten, breath leaving me.

Now I drop the glass. I'm not sure if it broke when it hit the floor because I don't care; the pain in my chest is everything. I drop to one knee, struggling to breathe. I place a hand down on the floor to steady myself and a glass shard pierces my palm. I guess it did break.

I'm getting tunnel vision, the circle of light at the end going farther and farther away. My sternum feels as if it's being crushed, each labored breath shorter than the last.

Yet somehow, amongst all the pain and fear, I know …

I know He won't kill me.

The fucker is simply amusing Himself.

And that makes me fight on.

I begin frantically patting at the floor of broken shards, cutting my already-bloodied hand some more. I'm hoping I can find it. I'm also hoping He's now looking at me, confused, wondering why I would do such a thing. When I finally find it, the long stem to the broken martini glass, palm the circular base, and then ram it for all I'm worth into the top of His foot, I know He doesn't feel a thing, but it's the closest my dying body can come to saying: *Fuck you, bitch—you can't kill me and you know it.*

And then, just like He'd done with the burning tattoo in my car, He makes everything stop. The pain in my chest is gone, my breath is back, and my vision is no longer a constricting tunnel.

The glass stem is no longer sticking out of His foot—He's spinning it between His thumb and index finger like it's a flower, not a trace of blood (or *whatever's* inside Him) on it. How it went from His foot to His fingers, I don't have a clue; I never saw Him move, even after I jammed the damn thing in.

I get to my feet. He's smiling at me, eyes yellow, still spinning the glass stem in His thumb and index finger.

"You really don't give yourself enough credit," He says. "That was remarkably impressive. First your verbal defiance in the car and now a *physical* response? I believe this evening will run smoother than I'd hoped."

"You didn't have to do that," I say, rubbing my chest even though all traces of pain are incredulously gone. "There was no fucking reason for you to do that."

"Oh, but there was."

"Such as?"

"Testing your resolve."

"Fuck you. I told you I would do it. You didn't need to test anything."

He smiles then flicks the glass stem away. "Shall I give you a free one?"

"What?"

He sticks out his chin and taps it. "A free one."

"Hit you?"

"You don't want to?"

"I'd fucking *come* if you let me."

"I *am* letting you."

I shake my head. "No way."

He sticks His chin out farther. "Yes way. No games, no repercussions. Just swing away."

I don't think, just throw. Punch after punch, smashing into his face. My right hand is still—and will always be—a mess, and I've had enough fights back in the day to know that if you punch someone in the head long enough, you're probably going to bust your hands.

I feel none of that here.

Each punch cracks then *sinks* into His face, sparing my hands, like I'm hitting a head made of rubber. With each punch His face caves, only to instantly pop back until the next punch caves it again.

His cheekbone collapses, pops back.

Nose flattens, pops back.

Eye socket caves, pop.

And He's just standing there, letting me, none of it fazing Him—He may even be smiling…yeah, He's smiling—but I don't give a shit.

I'm sure it all looks comical, surreal, grotesque; a fool's exercise in futility—His face sinking then popping then smiling, sinking then popping then smiling; me punching and punching and punching and punching—but again, I don't give a shit.

It feels so damn good; I may just come after all.

My wind, not my desire, eventually stops me. I'm pitched over in front of Him, hands on my knees, catching my breath.

"Feel better?" He asks.

I look up at Him, hands still on my knees, still breathing hard. "Only if you don't retaliate."

He looks down at me, not a mark on His face, eyes…green, I think? Can't really tell. "Wouldn't dream of it," He says.

I eventually stand upright. "Why'd you let me do that?"

"I wanted to see if you would."

"More *resolve* bullshit?"

He points to my cell phone on the kitchen counter. "Don't you have a call to make?"

7

I snap my phone shut and look at Him. "They gave me an address." I show Him a piece of paper I scribbled on during the call. "I'm to be here in an hour."

His long white fingers pluck the paper from my hand.

"I know the neighborhood," I say. "Town called Broomall. Should take us twenty minutes or so."

Eyes on the paper He asks: "Do they suspect anything?"

I shrug. "Doubt it. The guy I spoke to sounded excited."

He smiles and hands the paper back to me. "Excellent. Shall we?"

I take the paper on reflex, my mind elsewhere. "Uh, don't we need…don't *I* need…?"

He looks annoyed. "What?"

Two martinis have numbed my apprehension, so I blurt: "Something to kill your child with."

He closes His eyes and softly says, "When the time comes…"

8

An hour later.

I'm standing at the front door of an impressive two-story colonial. Not at all what I expected. I ring the doorbell and it's answered immediately. Same guy who was at my reading. He's still wearing the alien with the peace sign shirt, and he still looks as if bathing and grooming and exercise were things you only did after losing a bet.

"Are you alone?"

I look behind me. "Far as I know."

"Were you followed?"

I look behind me again. "Don't think so."

He waves me in quickly. I step into the foyer and he locks the door behind me.

I'm lead through a tastefully furnished living room, through a modern and immaculate kitchen (no way this guy lives here), and then to a basement door.

"Down here," he whispers quickly.

Ah—mom and dad's place. Wonder if they know what Junior's got hiding in his man cave…assuming the thing is even down there.

He opens the door and waves an anxious hand for me to go first. I go down a few steps and he shuts the door behind us. I hear a heavy bolt sliding. It doesn't sound right given the home's décor. Surely mom and dad didn't have something like that installed just so Junior could have his priv—

Something jabs into my back. I don't turn around, just look over my shoulder. Junior's got a gun on me.

"Sorry about this, Mr. Kale."

9

I'm tied to a chair in a finished basement. I normally avoid basements as much as I do sobriety (fifty bucks if you can guess why), and though I feel I can handle it without flashing back twenty years ago, the gag they have stuffed into my mouth is starting to make me panic, hitting on too many memories. At least the thing is cloth and not a rubber ball. If it had been the latter I'm quite sure it would feel like the anvil was on my chest.

The basement is nice. Not elaborate—certainly not like the one on Elmwood—but not humble either. Perhaps the only thing it's got beat on the Elmwood mansion is a very impressive computer station in the distance that looks as if it communicates with NASA.

Take away my binds, and you'd think I was the guest of honor. I'm sitting in the middle of the room. Three men face me, seated on the rug in a semicircle, looking up at me like kids about to hear a campfire tale. And who knows, maybe they are. Maybe He was wrong. Maybe these guys just wanted to hear more of "the truth."

They didn't have a half-breed.

They didn't know about Him.

They just got some wild idea about kidnapping an author so he would spin more yarns for their desperate-to-believe ears.

I think about the great Stephen King and his brilliant novel *Misery.*

Mr. King's character, Paul Sheldon, is a best-selling author being held captive by Annie Wilkes, a crazed nurse and "number one fan" who insists Sheldon writes Annie her very own sequel to his best-selling *Misery* series.

Of course shit got way crazy during Mr. Sheldon's stay. And why not, Ms. Wilkes was pretty fucking crazy. I still giggle when I think of specific lines, long since memorized, long since giving me comfort every time I crack the book, which is usually once a year, if not just to read my favorite bits. I don't know if Mr. King meant for certain parts to be funny, though I'd wager a foot and a thumb

(*ha!*)

that he did, and the dark side in all of us giggled devilishly with him.

It's funny; even now I feel a small giggle could escape. I probably shouldn't—for all I know, the three geeks could be three male Annie Wilkeses. But I think Señor Suppression may have given up, and Mr. Water Balloon Brain is getting fatter and fatter.

However, perhaps what's stifling the giggle for now is that a *third* candidate appears to have launched a campaign in my warped little head, and his voice seems fairly strong.

Let's call him *Mr. Holy Shit That's Fucking Ironic As Hell.*

Why? Because Mr. Holy Shit That's Fucking Ironic As Hell has just gotten to the podium and pointed out that after twenty years of dreading His arrival, I am now hoping for it.

10

I've named them. And the names are very original. Geek One, Geek Two, and Geek Three.

Geek One is the guy who met me at my reading. The faded t-shirt of an alien giving the peace sign; the oxymoron exclusive to slothful males known as *skinny-fat* (huge gut with chicken legs, pipe cleaner arms, and no ass); the heavy five o'clock shadow (heavier now); thinning, greasy hair (greasier now); and frayed jeans hanging down the crack of his (no) ass.

Geek Two is tall and skinny and has long dirty-blond hair. He's wearing rimless glasses and has a pathetic goatee that needs to go. His shirt is a faded *Futurama* tee of a robot drinking a beer and smoking a joint.

I remember that show.

Geek Three looks a lot like One. Maybe an inch taller and a few pounds lighter. His hair is dark and thinning and greasy too. No heavy five o'clock shadow though. His shirt is a standard button down, wrinkled and untucked.

Geek One gets up from the rug and approaches. He removes my gag.

"Again, I'm sorry about the deception, Mr. Kale, but I'm afraid we didn't have a choice," he says.

"No worries," I say pleasantly. "This happens all the time. I'm assuming you guys weren't happy with the ending of the story? You want to hear more?"

They all exchange curious glances.

"Autographs?" I say.

"Mr. Kale, this is serious," Geek Two says from the rug.

"The ending really bothered you, huh?"

Geek Three: "Mr. Kale, please."

I say nothing. I know why they've got me, but I intend to play dumb until He shows. *If* He shows.

"Do you know why you're here?" Geek One asks, taking his seat back on the rug.

"Not a clue."

"We know your story wasn't just a story."

"Yeah—you alluded to that at Villanova."

"So ... ?" Geek Two says.

"So what?"

Geek Three: "We want to hear it from *you*."

"So this *is* story time," I say.

"You wouldn't be so flippant if you knew what was in store," Geek One says.

I'm bait, I want to say. *You've kidnapped me, hoping He will follow, show up, and then your half-breed buddy can do its thing. Pretty ballsy if you truly believe He exists and know what He's capable of.*

"What's in store?" I ask, my eyes going all over the basement, spotting three doors, perhaps potential hiding spots for the half-breed. Will it make an appearance before He shows?

"I'm afraid we've tricked you," Geek Two says. "We needed to draw Him out of hiding."

"Him who?"

"Why do you insist on playing dumb?"

"Fellas ... I really don't have the slightest clue as to what you're talking about."

They all exchange glances again.

"Your story," Geek Three says. "Him from your story."

I sigh. "It's just a fucking story, guys. Jesus, you really need to get outside once in a while."

More glances at one another. Geek One nods at the other two as if they're communicating telepathically.

They all rise and head over to one of the closets, the one furthest from me at the far end of the basement.

They're going to show me.

My "flippant" persona—part-façade and part-real—plummets, and fear grips me instantly. I don't want to see it. Earlier, I tried to imagine what it would look like. Now I'm terrified I'm going to find out.

Geek One opens the closet door.

I want to look away. Close my eyes. Yell for help. Yell for His

(*Mr. Holy Shit That's Fucking Ironic As Hell is climbing the polls big time…*)

help.

But I don't. I don't want to give the game away. I keep my eyes on the open door. Adrenaline has started to bounce my feet. I feel like I might piss myself. My pulse is thumping everywhere. Señor Suppression has officially dropped out of the race. I want Mr. Water Balloon Brain to win. *To pop!* Give me that insane ignorance with a side order of who gives a crazy man's fuck.

My eyes are on the open door. Black inside … like the first time I saw His kids twenty years ago. I think it might have been easier then; I didn't know what to expect. Now I have an idea. A debilitating one.

"All clear," Geek One calls into the closet.

Still nothing. Still just a dark open doorway.

I hear something. A voice. It sounds human. I can't make it out.

Geek One repeats: "It's clear."

I want to yell, "*How the fuck would YOU know! He could be right next to you, stupid!*"

(*And you* want *Him to be more than anything*)

(*Ladies and gentlemen, Mr. Holy Shit That's Fucking Ironic As Hell is on fire!*)

I can't help myself—I close my eyes.

I hear something.

The shuffling of feet on carpet.

The closet door closing.

People approaching me.

"Mr. Kale?" one of them says.

My eyes stay closed. I can feel them standing around me. I can sense a fourth presence.

"Mr. Kale?" he says again.

Open your eyes, you pussy.

And then a woman's voice: "Mr. Kale?"

My eyes snap open, and I'm looking up at one of the most beautiful women I've ever seen.

11

Without thinking, I blurt: "Who is *this?*"

The beautiful woman stands in front of me, the geeks behind her.

"You can call me Anna," she says.

Relief for what I'm seeing is short-lived. Confusion is now everything.

"Anna?" is all I manage.

She reaches forward and strokes my face. Her touch is like a bubble bath. The rest of her is ridiculously hot. Like supermodel hot.

She's wearing a light blue sundress. Her lips are full and pouty. Eyes pale blue in a flawless face of smooth white skin, a striking and appealing contrast to hair long and dark and full.

This ... this is all wrong.

"Who is this?" I say again.

"I think you know," she says.

I don't have time to catch myself, because I say, "But you're ... "

She cocks her head, gives me a coquettish, inquisitive look.

"You're a woman," I finish.

She smiles, and her pale blue eyes go from green to yellow to red to black and then to pale blue again.

"Still want to play dumb, Mr. Kale?" Geek One asks.

Yes. Because I am.

12

He lied to me.

His half-breed is a *she*, not a *he*.

Why? Why lie?

The confusion on my face is anything but subtle. Anna steps to one side and Geek One approaches.

"He thinks Anna's a male," he says as though reading my mind. "We wouldn't stand a chance without deception on our side."

The game is well and truly up, so I don't even try to make excuses. "So, you expect Him to show up, looking for a male, and instead He finds...?"

"He finds Anna," Geek Two says. "He'll ignore her, think she can't see Him. Continue searching for a male. Then when His guard is down..."

"How can you be sure He doesn't know?" I ask.

All three geeks exchange smiles, Anna too. "What did He tell *you*?"

"Fair enough," I say. "But He could have been lying to me. The guy fucks with me constantly."

Geek One puffs his flabby chest proudly. "You may think we need to get out more, Mr. Kale, but we've taken precautions. Put in tireless efforts. Made arrangements. Trust us; He thinks Anna's a male."

You guys don't have the slightest clue who you're fucking with.

"So is that the plan then?" I ask. "I sit here like bait, while you guys wait for Him to show? Wait for Him to slip up?"

They all nod.

"Sounds too easy. For all you know, He could be here now—listening."

A look of worry hits two of the geeks' faces.

Geek One looks more confident. "Anna would be able to see him," he says.

I feel breath on my ear. Then: "*Think she does?*"

It's Him. He's here. Standing next to me.

I look at Anna. Her eyes are on me; not Him.

She doesn't see Him.

Oh dear. You folks are about to get a serious, serious *ass whoopin'.*

"And if she can't?" I say. "What then?"

All three look at Anna.

She turns to them. "I can," she says. "I *have.*"

All three turn back to me with confident smiles.

"There, you see?" Geek Two says.

And then suddenly it all clicks:

He said: "*Think she does?*"

She said: "*I can—I* have."

I *have.*

As in: I'm looking at Him *now.*

She *can* see Him. *Does* see Him.

(*Mr. Water Balloon Brain is not out of the running yet, people*)

13

He appears. Not just to me, but to the geeks.

I know this because their faces are a sudden line of horror masks as they stumble backwards.

Geek One screams: "*I can see Him! I can see Him!*"

Geek Two screams: "*Anna! Anna!*"

Geek Three just screams.

Anna winks at me, eyes red, and steps aside.

He steps forward. "Evening, gentlemen."

All three gawk back in frozen terror.

He points to Geek One's feet. The sharp crack of bone is brief. Geek One cries out and collapses, writhing in agony. I can see blood and bone protruding from one of his socks, each foot twisted backwards, heels for toes.

Geek Two turns to run. To where, I have no idea. The closet maybe. He gets a few feet before the sharp crack of bone is heard again. He collapses too, even though his feet appear fine. His spine? Not so good. His torso is folded backward, stomach protruding as though he's been impaled by a spear. Geek Two does *not* writhe in agony on the ground like his friend—paralysis has allowed only his face to contort, eyes wide, mouth opening and closing without words like a dying fish.

Geek Three drops to his knees and starts to beg.

"*Anything,*" he stutters, "*anything…*"

He approaches the kneeling man and places His large white hand over his forehead. "Are you begging me?" He asks.

Geek Three nods desperately. "Yes, yes, I am. Please…*please…*"

He looks over His shoulder at Anna and smirks. She smirks back. "I must be getting soft in my old age," He says, taking His hand off Geek Three's head and turning to walk away.

Geek Three's eyes widen in disbelief. "*Oh thank you…! Thank you!*"

Anna lunges forward and kicks Geek Three in the face, taking his head clean off the shoulders where it rockets into the far wall, leaving a blotch of red before it hits the rug and lulls to one side, eyes open, one of them twitching involuntarily. The headless corpse remains on its knees for a tick, periodic pumps of blood rising and falling like a geyser before falling to one side in a convulsing heap.

Anna laughs.

Mr. Water Balloon Brain is almost there. I can feel it. *Come on, man, pop. Pop!*

He and Anna both turn towards me.

"What do you think?" He asks Anna.

She caresses my cheek again. I don't flinch. I'm quite sure that inherent response is gone.

"Beautiful," she says.

"I agree," He says. "His spirit is strong. And he's been prepared."

I giggle. Don't know why.

(*almost there…*)

They exchange a curious glance.

"Alex?" He says.

(*almost there…*)

I giggle some more.

(*pop… PLEASE pop*)

"Alex, are you ready?"

"Sure," I find myself saying.

Anna kneels in front of me and begins to unbutton my pants, pulls them to my ankles. I look down and for some reason I have the biggest hard-on I've ever had in my life.

She strokes it a few times, then gets to her feet and takes a step back. She unhitches the straps to her sundress and lets it fall to the floor.

She has breasts but no nipples. No belly button. No vagina.

I flash on when I saw Him naked: no anatomical features of a man's body, except for his foot-long penis pointed at the tip like a devil's tail.

What would be her trick?

I don't have to wait long. Small doors of skin where her vagina should be open like a puzzle box. Something the size of a fist begins extending towards me. It stops after a few inches, the fist opening. It looks like a mouth. The lips

(*labia?*)

drip with desire as it creeps further like a python slithering in on its meal.

The mouth engulfs my penis, slides down the shaft.

I want to look away, want it to stop, but it feels…

The mouth squeezes tighter. I can feel something inside tickling the head of my cock. I feel an orgasm—brutally intense—building from the base of my spine.

I look up. Her head is tilted back in the throes of ecstasy, her body quivering.

My orgasm builds. I'm nearly there. By the looks of her, so is she.

For some reason I glance over at Him. He's watching, smiling, approving.

I come and it's the whole world. My body begins to shake uncontrollably and I actually cry out.

My head drops and I'm light-headed, feel as if I'm going to pass out.

When I look up again, she's back in the blue sundress, standing off to one side, her flawless face content, eyes changing colors with each breath.

I look down and my penis is flaccid, shriveled. I still don't understand how it got as hard as it did. Even when jerking off—a forced act my body occasionally seemed to insist upon over the years—the most I could usually manage was half-mast, ending with a dribbling orgasm that was more pain than pleasure.

I look up and He's standing over me. "Good?"

I nod, dumbfounded, dazed.

"Looks like I got you laid after all," He says with a smile.

I go to say something, but Geek One cries out, cutting me off.

He looks furious at the intrusion on our conversation, snaps His fingers, and suddenly there's a dripping red tongue in His hand. Geek One begins to moan and sputter. I look past Him and see blood pouring from the geek's mouth. He rolls onto his stomach to keep from choking on his own blood. He vomits.

"What … ?" is the only thing I can think of.

"So many questions, yes?" He asks.

I nod, still dazed.

"I'll be happy to answer them. But first I'm afraid I'm late for a prior engagement."

I give Him a curious look.

"Mom," He says.

The daze breaks, Mr. Water Balloon Brain leaks, and I snap to. "*What?*"

"Your mother," He says.

"*No … no, you said … you said if I …*" I'm stuttering, panicking—nothing, *nothing* makes sense.

Anna comes over and kisses my cheek. My flinch response is back, and I pull away from her. She only smiles and begins heading up the basement stairs.

"What the fuck? *What the fuck?!*"

He watches Anna leave, turns to me, leans in. His eyes are glowing red. He grins and says, "Why not sleep on it awhile ... "

He touches my forehead and ...

14

...

15

Mom ...

16

"*Mom ...* "

A hand petting my brow ...

"*Mom ... ?*"

The hand running gentle fingers through my hair ...

"Alex."

Faint recognition that the dream world is receding ...

"Alex, wake up."

I open my eyes.

My mother is leaning over me, smiling, more radiant than ever.

"Mom?"

She pets my brow again. "It's okay, sweetheart."

Can't be. Can't all be a dream. The writer in me would positively *refuse* such an awful cliché no matter how fucked up my state of mind.

I ask anyway. "A dream?"

She continues to pet my brow, her smile broadening. "It's okay now."

"A dream?" I ask again.

And then His face joins my mother's, smiling with her, eyes yellow.

I jerk upright and scoot back against what I now realize is a bed. "*What the fuck!?*"

"*Alex,*" my mother scolds.

"This is a big moment, son—no need for profanity," He says.

Son?

"Hi, darling," a voice behind them says.

It's Anna, standing to one side, a white sundress this time. Her belly has a bump.

I scoot further back on the bed, the corner of the wall stopping me.

Soft laughter from my mother and Him. My mother then joins Anna's side and rubs her own belly. And that's when I notice my mother has a bump too.

I open my mouth but nothing comes out.

"Questions…" He says.

I say nothing.

He looks at my mother but still addresses me. "Look how happy she is."

I look at Mom. Her smile is … radiant.

Radiant. Like the day I visited just before recent events. She'd looked especially radiant. And why not? He'd just paid her a visit. What was it I'd thought about her radiance that day? That I could thank *Him* for affecting my perspective? Even *Mr. Holy Shit That's Fucking Ironic As Hell* would be humbled at such an exquisite example.

"Happy," I mumble.

Mom joins His side again. He puts His arm around her.

"You're going to be a father," He says to me.

"I'm sorry about your tea, sweetheart," Mom says to me. "But He told me I needed to prepare you."

My tea?

He looks at Anna, beaming. "Anna will be having a *special* birth. My time is almost up. Towards the end I begin to produce females, and I need a male—a *human* male—to offer his seed in order to carry on my legacy." He looks back at me. "I'm sorry I lied to you about that silly 'half-breed' nonsense, Alex. Lots of hoops jumped through, I know, but I needed to be sure of your spirit. How far you were willing to go. You didn't disappoint. Your seed is more than worthy."

Mr. Water Balloon Brain is now at full capacity.

"Anna … " I stutter. "Anna will give birth to … ?"

"To me," He says with a smile. "One of me." He sidles up to Anna and now it's He who rubs her belly. "Congratulations, daddy."

I turn and gawk at my mother. "Why … ?"

"I was becoming so worried about you, sweetheart," she says. "The pills, the booze. He assured me you wouldn't need them anymore. Wouldn't *want* them. Everything is different now." She approaches and soothes my brow again. "I would do anything for you, honey."

"And she doesn't even want any money," He says with a hearty laugh.

Mom looks back at Him. "That's right, mister. I make my own money."

He laughs some more. "I see where you get your resolve, Alex. You two are perfect."

"Mom … the offerings … *the offerings …* "

"I know all about them, Alex. I'm okay with it. I'm more than okay with it. It all feels so right. *I* feel so right."

(*almost there …*)

Anna walks over to the bed and extends her hand to me. I take it, and she guides me out of bed. I look around. I don't know where we are, but it's the most extravagant place I've ever seen. Puts the homes on Elmwood to shame.

Anna walks me to the far end of the room, Mom and Him following.

There are cages, three of them, like the ones in the hidden basement on Elmwood. Geeks One and Two are shackled, hanging by the wrists in their respective cages—shaved clean, gagged, moaning, weeping.

Cage three is empty.

"The third one was already spoiled. We need to keep them fresh, don't we?" He says, casting Anna a naughty glance.

Anna shrugged playfully. "Got carried away."

Spoiled? How long ... ?

"How long was I out?"

"A week," Mom says. "The rest did you good, sweetheart."

(*almost there ...*)

All four of us are standing in a row, looking at the cages. Anna still has my hand. My mother's head is resting on His shoulder, His arm around her.

"We're going to be a very happy family," He says.

(*POP!*)

I turn and look at Anna. She kisses me and I kiss her back.

My mother comes over and gives me a huge hug, tears in her eyes. "I love you, Alex."

I hug her back. "I love you too, Mom."

She pulls away and I look at Him. He grins.

I'm going to be a daddy.

FIVE CARD — DRAW!

He hated her. And guess what? She hated him. The hatred was strong enough for murder. But why risk murder if there's no money involved? So the policies were taken out—each one a considerable sum and kept secret from the other…for a little while. The secrets were leaked from supposed confidants and ultimately revealed the silent truth—last one standing was getting mucho bucks.

The paranoia in the house was palpable; each of them lead on as if they were ignorant to the other's intentions. When would the moment come? How would he do it? How would *she* do it? And most intriguingly: How would they make it look like an accident?

Each creek of a floorboard turned a head fast enough to wrench it. Sleep was something done with one eye open and one leg on the floor. Meals were carefully inspected to ensure they didn't contain any 'surprise' ingredients. It was maddening.

A decision was made between the two—ironically, a mutual decision; the first one shared in a decade. They both confessed, not to the intentions of murder, of course, but to the policies. The intended murders *needed* no confession; they were as good as pasted on one another's foreheads like a game of Indian Poker. And as incredulous as it sounds, it was the game of poker that would decide their fate.

They were both very good at the game. They had hosted parties for years, each of them matching the other's abilities, each of them silently spewing venom in the opposite direction when one would best the other on any given night. They didn't mind losing to their friends, but he couldn't bear to lose to *her*, and she to *him*.

So a game of poker was decided. One hand. Five Card Draw.

It was brought up one evening when the tension in the house had no room left to grow.

"We know what's going on here," he said to her. He stood in the doorway of the den. She was on the sofa reading a book with one eye.

She set the book on her lap, and placed both eyes on him now.

"Yes, I think I do," she said.

"I haven't been able to sleep," he said.

"Neither have I."

"I have a way to settle it."

He explained his intentions. One hand to decide who would 'stay' and who would 'go.'

She told him he was crazy. He called her a heartless bitch. She told him that he would *lose* anyway. He laughed at her, told her she was suffering from delusions of grandeur; he was always the better player. She asked him what would occur when the game was done. He told her that the loser (and he assured her it would *not* be him) would accept defeat gracefully, and allow themselves to 'retire'—as long as it looked like an accident.

She told him he was crazy again. He called her a coward and a lousy player. Her temper agreed, made her get to her feet to retrieve a deck of cards. He put a hand up and told her not to bother, reached into his back pocket and tossed a packaged deck at her.

"You can deal," he said. Then tried not to laugh when he added, "I trust you."

.   .   .

They sat across from one another. A small folding table usually reserved for eating in front of the television was their platform. To the left of the deck of cards was a revolver. When the loser was dealt with, the trick was to make it look like a robbery gone bad, otherwise there could be no claim. Phone calls to someone trusted (not the spineless confidants who leaked news of the policies) were made, and alibis were established. All that remained now was the game.

She dealt—each of them receiving five precious cards that held their fate. He snatched his quickly from the table as though she may have the ability to see through them. She scoffed at his behavior, then slowly peeled hers off the table, never once looking at the cards as she did so;

her eyes remained on him — first to initiate psychological warfare, first in an attempt at getting into the other's head.

"Three," he said as he discarded three of his cards facedown onto the table.

"A pathetic pair, huh?" she said. "Hoping for three of a kind?"

He ignored her and took the three she dealt him, never daring for a second to rearrange his hand once he glanced at them.

She studied his face. She hated it so much but knew it so well.

"I'll *also* take three," she said.

He laughed. "Hypocrite."

She ignored him and took her fresh three after discarding.

He studied her face. He was familiar with her tells and looked desperately for the first sign of one. She too left her cards in the order to which they had been dealt.

There was a moment of pause. Neither spoke; neither wanted to.

What did he have?

What did she have?

The winner was rich, the loser dead.

"All right, let's see 'em," he said.

"Let's see *yours*," she replied.

"What?" he said. "I just told you to lay down your cards."

"And I'm telling you to lay down *yours*."

"What is this?" he said. He frowned. Then he stopped. And then he started to grin — a slow, sinister grin that culminated with the tip of his tongue between his teeth like the deadly snake he suddenly and deliciously felt he was. "You're scared," he said. "Those three didn't help you at all, did they? You've got nothing."

"Don't I?" She grinned back — hers equally sinister, but with a spattering of triumph. "You always *were* an easy one to manipulate — so clumsy and awkward in your attempts at subtlety."

His frown returned. "Taking personal shots isn't going to help you at this point. It's hardly worth it."

"Is it getting under your skin?"

He said nothing; his ever-reddening face was all the reply she needed.

"Then it's worth it," she smirked.

He looked at his cards once more. She at hers.

"Lay them down," he said again, his face now a pulsating beet.

"You first." Her grin was her whole face.

He hated her. *God,* how he hated her.

He looked at the gun.

She caught him and her grin dropped. She knew him so well.

He grabbed for the weapon. She was quicker and seized it first. He latched onto her wrist and shook it violently as the two stood to their feet, knocking the dinner tray over, sending the cards fluttering downward into a scattered mess on the floor.

The struggle was brief; he was far too strong, disarming her with little effort.

There were two shots. One to the chest … and then … a second to the chest—because he hated her so much.

He stood over her dead body, smoking gun in hand.

"Let's see 'em," he said, laughing lightly, then soon, hysterically. "Come, on baby, turn 'em over!"

He was crying with laughter now—eyes wild with delirium, tears streaming down both cheeks. "Let's see that *pathetic pair!*" His stomach was cramping, begging him to stop.

He took a step backward, his free hand wiping the tears from his eyes. "Did that get *under your skin,* my love? You still think I'm *clumsy and awkwa—*"

The heel of his shoe caught the array of slick cards on the wooden floor. Both feet flew out from under him, his head catching the stone base of their fireplace behind him, killing him instantly.

. . .

The gun discharged one last time during his descent—a panicked reflex as he felt himself lose control. The stray bullet pierced the living room window, filling in an ideal detail for the summary of the investigation that followed:

An intruder had silently entered their home while the couple was in the midst of enjoying a pleasant game of cards with one another. The wife was shot twice in the chest, and as the faithful husband came to her rescue, a struggle ensued. The gun discharged once more during the fight, hitting the living room window. Sadly, the intruder managed to overpower the husband, causing him to hit his head on the bottom ledge of the stone fireplace resulting in death by blunt force trauma.

As of this time, the intruder is still at large.

PRINCESS

1

JUNE 2012

John Kearns had a newspaper up to his face but he wasn't reading. Periodically, the paper would drop an inch, John's eyes peering over it, making sure the boy was still there.

And he was, multi-tasking with technology as only teenagers can: text messaging at the speed of a veteran receptionist; head bobbing in slight rhythm to whatever he fiddled with on his iPod; periodically stopping after each text in order to gorge on his tray of burger and fries with all the gusto of fortunate teens who had yet to experience the pitfalls of metabolism.

He was not a perfect match, John thought, but he would do. The food court at the mall was hardly a runway for male models. Besides, he was running out of time. Tonight was the night. He'd been up since dawn, searching. It was now 5:00 P.M., and while the boy was a decent match, there were still no guarantees of a successful delivery—there never were. John only hoped the boy would finish his meal soon, forgo any thoughts of shopping, then get the hell out of Dodge. If John blew it, had to find another one, it would set them back, by several hours at least. And *God help him* if things didn't go as planned.

John shuddered away the thought, looked up and focused on the boy again. The burger and fries were gone. The boy was sucking the last of his soda—John could hear the hollow slurps five tables away. The boy stood, dumped his tray, and headed toward the exit.

John exhaled, actually breathing the words "thank you." He left his paper on the table and hurried after the boy. The mall had two major lots—one above ground and one below. If the boy had parked in the lot below, in the dark, John should have no trouble; he'd be right on schedule, and his wife would be pleased.

2

Samantha Kearns sat in front of her bedroom mirror, weeping. Tammy Kearns stood behind her daughter, brushing Samantha's long blonde hair, every few strokes of the brush followed by a reassuring stroke of the hand.

"I'm sure there's a very good reason, Princess." Tammy stopped brushing and glanced out her daughter's window. She saw no headlights below just yet. Still she said, "He'll be here."

Samantha continued to weep.

Tammy Kearns set the brush down and adjusted the shoulder straps on her daughter's pink prom dress. She took a tissue from its box and dabbed it beneath her daughter's eyes. "You're going to spoil your makeup if you keep this up." She showed the mottled tissue to her daughter. "You want to look like a princess tonight, don't you?"

"Yes."

"Okay then." She dabbed her daughter's eyes a final time. "Stop those tears. I'm sure Daddy will be calling any minute with some good news."

"Mom?"

"Yes?"

"You don't suppose … "

Tammy Kearns moved behind her daughter and began brushing again. "Suppose what?"

"You don't suppose he changed his mind?"

Tammy Kearns slowly set the brush aside. She loomed over her daughter now, spoke with the tone of a loaded gun. "What do you mean?"

"You don't suppose he decided not to show? Decided to go with someone else?"

Tammy Kearns spun the chair with the strength of a man, her meaty hands then clamping down onto the armrests as she thrust her face into her daughter's. "*NO*. No, he did *NOT*." She jostled the chair, once and hard. A lock of Samantha's hair fell over one eye. "You are second to *NO ONE*. Do you understand me?"

"Yes, Mommy."

"DO YOU?"

"Yes, Mommy."

The dark cloud passed and Tammy Kearns became sunshine again. She smiled lovingly at her daughter, reached out with a finger and brushed aside the errant lock of her daughter's hair. "You're my little princess. And a princess *needs* her prince." The lock of hair fell back over Samantha's eye. Tammy brushed it aside again, tried tucking it behind her ear. "And he's going to be here very soon."

Tammy Kearns saw her daughter give a weak smile.

"Oh, come on—you can do better than that," Tammy said, crossing the room, grabbing her favorite of many pictures on Samantha's dresser. "Who's that?" she asked, holding the photo up for her daughter, her syrupy tone suitable for a toddler. *"Who is that?"*

Tammy Kearns saw her daughter start to blush, begin to smile. "Me," Samantha said.

"That's right." Tammy lowered the picture and began looking at it herself. She beamed as she spoke. "My Princess. Only six years old and already everyone knew you were the most beautiful girl in the county." She traced her thick finger over the glass, running it back and forth over the little gold crown atop her daughter's head, the finger leaving the crown, circling the cherub face that was artificially tanned and caked in makeup, leaving the face, caressing the bundle of roses her daughter struggled to hold, leaving the roses, finishing with the trophy that stood next to her daughter, taller than the child by a foot. "My Princess…" she said again. "Your prince will be here soon—you'll see."

3

Thank you, thank you, thank you, John Kearns thought as he followed the boy to the lot below ground. The boy was moving fast and John had to quicken his pace. His forty-four years wasn't exactly over the hill, but his fitness was lacking. His wife constantly ridiculed the paunch that hung over his belt, his breasts that were breasts, his hairline that was in a fast retreat. All signs of sloth, a lack of beauty, a lack of dignity. The paradox—the one he would never dare voice—was that his wife was as heavy as he was, an even guiltier culprit of sloth. Or so it would appear; Tammy Kearns had never perceived it that way. Her world was akin to an editor forced to trim (and often *chop*) a film in order to make inappropriate content suitable for all audiences. Never mind if the chopping came at the expense of plot—when Tammy watched, it always made sense.

It hadn't always been that way. Tammy had once been a catch. Full-figured—perhaps even a bit more so—but worn with a confident beauty capable of enticing any man. And yet *she* had chosen *John.* She was the unmistakable alpha of the two; it was what brought them together. John's shy nature; his inability to take lead of his own life, happily letting someone else steer him towards whatever destination they saw fit; his virginity—all claimed by Tammy with domineering vigor. And he was eternally devoted to her, delighted that someone had finally given him the time of day, given him an alternative to the loneliness he believed to be his inevitable fate.

The gradual change began shortly after the birth of Samantha. Their daughter became everything. Whatever attention Tammy had left for John he accepted with gratitude. He loved his wife and he loved his daughter. And he never dared question the direction his wife was steering Samantha. At times he didn't approve, but a John Kearns simply didn't question a Tammy Kearns. So his mouth remained forever shut. Forced to watch events unfold that had worried him, frightened him, and then ultimately, vanquished him—destroyed whatever manhood he'd had left. Indeed, the precursor for what would eventually become his wife was planted the moment Samantha was born, growing at a terrifying rate where it would reach its incomprehensible pinnacle the moment Samantha was *re*-born.

And tonight was a night where that pinnacle would reach infinite heights. It was Princess's special night after all. A night that came along once in a girl's lifetime, his wife had said. A night that needed to be perfect, his wife had said. *A night he better not screw up,* his wife had said.

John found himself nearly jogging after the boy now. Again, to his delight, John watched the boy proceed deeper into the lot, deeper into the dark. A row of six cars was all that was ahead. One of them had to be the boy's. John took a quick glance around. They were alone.

"Excuse me. Excuse me, son?"

The boy didn't acknowledge; he was still wearing the earbuds to his iPod.

The boy reached his car, a gray Toyota, and began digging for his keys. John waved his arms about, hoping the boy's peripheral vision would catch him now that he stood sideways. It did. The boy removed one earbud and afforded John only a turn of the head.

"What's up?" the boy asked.

John smiled, inched forward and held out a twenty dollar bill. "You dropped this."

The boy looked down at the twenty, then back up at a smiling John. He hadn't dropped it, of course, but John knew he would take it. They always did.

The boy stepped away from his car, went to take the bill. "Thanks," he said. "I didn't realize—"

John released the twenty, letting it flutter to the ground. The boys eyes tracked it, did not see John's other arm pulling the Taser from behind his back. A crackle of blue light, a groan, and the boy dropped. John knew the boy would be stunned, but not out. So he removed the syringe from his coat pocket, crouched beside the boy, and plunged it into his arm. He then fished inside the boy's pockets for his keys, his head periodically popping up from his task, checking his surroundings.

Still alone. *Thank you, thank you, thank you.*

Keys found, trunk open, John braced himself for labor. The boy was only a teenager—seventeen or eighteen he guessed—and was still at that gangly age where a young man had yet to grow into a man's body. He was tall and lanky and limp, like trying to lift a giant Slinky.

But John managed. The boy was tucked into the trunk, and John was now in the driver's seat of the gray Toyota, engine idling. He removed a handkerchief from the inside of his coat pocket and wiped his brow, removed his glasses and sopped up the sweat that had trickled further down and stung his eyes.

It was done. The hard part at least. John then dropped his head into his chest and shook it, closed his eyes, thought of what was ahead. Who the hell was he kidding? This had been the *easy* part.

He took out his cell phone and dialed home to tell his wife and daughter that he'd found him and they were on their way.

4

Tammy Kearns picked up the phone on the first ring. "John," she answered, although the antique phone held no Caller ID. Her lack of pleasantries was irrelevant: telemarketers and the odd wrong number were the only people who contacted the Kearns' farm anymore. What little friends existed before had stopped trying years ago.

"Yeah, it's me," John Kearns said.

"*Well?*" There was anxious anger in her tone, as if her husband dared not blurt his news intentionally.

"I found him."

Tammy threw her head back, slapped a hand to her heart, started to laugh with relief. "So what was it then? Car trouble?"

"That's right—car trouble."

"I knew it. I *knew* it had to be something like that." She put a hand over the receiver, looked at her daughter, mouthed the words: "*He found him. Car trouble.*"

"Why didn't he call?" Samantha asked.

Tammy Kearns frowned. Her daughter had a good point. "John?" she said. "Why didn't you call?"

A brief silence.

"John?"

"He says he tried. He couldn't get a signal."

Tammy Kearns smiled, closed her eyes and nodded. Cell phone reception was often erratic on the farm. She put her palm over the receiver again. "He tried, Princess. He couldn't get a signal."

Tammy watched what was left of her daughter's apprehension melt away.

"Didn't I tell you?" Tammy said to her daughter. "*Didn't I tell you?*"

Samantha smiled and nodded.

"John?" Tammy said. "John? You still there?"

"Still here."

"You did good. Sam is *so* relieved. She wants to talk to you."

"Well, we should be there any minute. Can't you just wait until—"

"*John.*" If she could, she would have slapped her husband through the phone.

An obedient sigh, and then: "Okay—put her on."

Tammy Kearns did not hand the phone to the girl in front of the mirror. Instead, she simply switched the receiver from her right ear to her left. Her face and voice then changed. Became bubblier. "Hi, Daddy," she said to her husband.

Another sigh before: "Hi, Princess."

"Mommy said he had car trouble? That he tried to call but couldn't get a signal?"

"That's right."

Tammy Kearns smiled. "I'm so glad. I was starting to freak out."

"Well you can relax now, Princess. We're going to be there very soon. You should probably start getting ready."

Tammy Kearns now grinned. She sat on the corner of the bed and started to bounce. "Okay, Daddy, I will."

"Okay, Princess. See you soon."

Tammy Kearns hung up and immediately removed the blonde wig from the mannequin sitting in front of the mirror. She began unzipping the back of her daughter's prom dress, began undressing the mannequin completely. Began getting ready for the prom.

5

"Get out."

"*Please.*"

"Get out." John Kearns shoved the gun in the boy's face.

The boy, tied by the wrists and ankles, wormed his way out of the trunk and fell to the ground.

"Put this on."

The boy looked up at the tuxedo as if he'd never seen one before. "What?" he said.

John Kearns shoved the material in his face. Then the gun again. "*Put it on.*"

The boy nodded frantically, pulled at his binds, then looked back up at John, his helpless face and futile struggle saying it all.

John Kearns nodded, felt a little silly for the glaring oversight, and began untying the boy with one hand, gun on him the whole time. Finished, he said, "Now put it on."

The boy was still on the ground, head going in all directions, eyes wide from both fear and to accommodate dusk. Except dusk was no obstacle in gathering one's precise whereabouts out here; the task for virgin eyes was an impossible one, even in daylight. It was a farm. And it went on forever. The end. All dusk added was a celluloid quality to a frightening panorama of isolation that needed none. And, John thought, given what had become of his life these past few years, such a locale of unnerving isolation was a good thing. No. *Good* was a poor choice of words. *Convenient.* That was better. Nothing good about any of this.

"Son," John Kearns said, "are you going to put it on, or am I going to have to dress you myself?"

"I don't get it," the boy said.

"And you don't need to. Now put the damn thing on." John Kearns pressed the tip of the gun to the boy's forehead.

The boy began doing what he was told. He fumbled and struggled in his panicked state, even toppled over after getting caught in a pant leg. But he was completely dressed in five minutes, right down to the shiny black shoes.

"Looks fine," John Kearns said. "Need to get you a corsage now."

"Please," the boy said. "I don't understand what you—"

John Kearns spun the boy, shoved the gun into his back, and began marching him towards the house. "Need to get you a corsage."

.   .   .

"Daddy?" A voice from upstairs the moment John Kearns brought the boy through the front door. "Daddy, is that you?"

"Yes, Princess," John called up. "But we're not ready for you yet. I'll let you know when."

"Is he there with you?"

"Yes, Princess—he's here."

"Hi, Josh," the voice upstairs said. "I was so worried about you."

The boy turned and looked at John.

"Answer her," John said. "Tell her you had car trouble."

The boy's face was wrought with confusion. He did not say what John told him to, only whispered, "My name isn't Josh."

John showed the boy the gun. "Yes it is. Tonight it is. Now say what I told you to say."

The boy turned back towards the staircase, cleared his throat and said: "I had car trouble."

John whispered, "Now tell her everything's going to be okay from here on out."

"Everything's okay … from here on out."

John nodded once. "You go back to your room now, Princess," he called upstairs. "I'll call you soon."

"Okay, Daddy."

John Kearns grabbed the boy's shoulder and stuck the gun back into his spine. "Corsage is in the fridge. Let's go to the kitchen."

6

The mannequin was now wearing Tammy Kearns' clothes, plus a brown wig. All makeup had been removed.

Tammy Kearns was now wearing her daughter's prom dress and her daughter's blonde hair. She wore too much makeup. Too much perfume. Too much jewelry. The pink prom dress was several sizes too small.

The mannequin in Tammy Kearns' clothes was in a seated position on the bed.

Tammy in her daughter's prom dress was far too nervous to sit. She paced the room, biting her lower lip, smiling, giggling. Occasionally, she would look over at her mother seated on the bed. She would see her mother smiling back, bursting with pride, admiring the exquisite beauty that was her daughter.

"Breathtaking," her mother said. "Absolutely breathtaking, Princess. Didn't I say you were second to none?"

"Yes, Mommy."

"The most beautiful girl in the county. Always have been."

"Because of you," Samantha Kearns said.

"Oh, now *stop*," her mother said.

"But it's true, Mommy. I owe everything to you."

"Princess, you're going to make me *cry*."

Samantha joined the mannequin on the bed. She saw her mother welling up, raised a thumb and wiped away tears that weren't there. "Don't cry, Mommy. I'd be nothing without you. Where do you suppose I get my looks?"

"Certainly not from your father."

They shared a naughty giggle.

Samantha then watched her mother's face change. It was nothing dramatic, just a ruminating furrow of the brow, as if trying to decide how to broach a tricky subject.

"What is it, Mommy?"

Samantha watched her mother's expression change again. She looked at her daughter with soulful eyes that carried both love and concern. "You know that tonight is a very big night. A special night."

"I know, Mommy."

"Do you know what I mean by special?"

Samantha blushed. "*Mommy.*"

"Well, Princess, it's important we talk about this. Joshua is a good boy; I'm sure he'll be prepared. But if he isn't … "

Samantha followed her mother's eyes downward. A solitary condom had been placed on the mannequin's lap.

Samantha blushed some more. "Won't it be unladylike if *I'm* the one who has the protection?"

Samantha watched her mother shake her head. "Just shows that you're careful. Responsible. The future for someone like you is limitless, Princess. We don't need to spoil that by being a teenage mommy."

Samantha nodded and took the condom.

"That's my good little Princess." A pause and then: "Now I have one more surprise for you."

Samantha smiled. "What is it?"

"I can't tell you now. Only that it's out in the barn. In fact, I better get out there now—make sure everything is as it should be. You know how I am with detail."

Samantha nodded knowingly. "It's why you're the best. Why we always won."

"Samantha Kearns, you're going to give me the biggest head."

They laughed. And then Samantha suddenly stopped. "Wait," she said. "You're leaving *now*? What about walking down the stairs? Josh seeing me for the first time in my dress? You're going to miss that?"

"Well, I can't be in two places at once now, can I, Princess?"

Samantha hung her head and nodded.

"Oh, don't you start moping on me, missy. Losers mope. And you're not a loser, are you?"

"No, Mommy."

"No, you're not. I'll be waiting for you and Josh after the prom. I'll be there for your big surprise."

Samantha bit her lower lip, fought a grin. "What is it?" she asked again, not expecting, nor wanting an answer, just playing the game.

"You'll just have to wait and see."

Samantha hugged the mannequin. "I love you, Mommy. With all my heart."

"I love you too, Princess."

A male voice, loud and clear calling from downstairs. "Princess? We're ready!"

"Well go on," her mother said. "Best not to keep your prince waiting."

Tammy Kearns, in her daughter's prom dress, smiled lovingly at the mannequin. She then left the bedroom and headed for the stairs to greet her prince.

7

The boy stood at the base of the stairs, corsage ready for his date. John Kearns stood behind the boy, leaned into his ear and said, "She's coming. The gun is in my pocket. If you try anything I will shoot you dead. No hesitation. Understand?"

The boy nodded.

"I will coach you as best I can. Be polite; be respectful; and do what you're told. It will all be over soon."

"You'll let me go after?" the boy said.

"Keep your eyes on the stairs."

"Will you let me go after?"

"Shut up and keep your eyes on the stairs."

The boy turned and faced John, his face frightened yet adamant. Ordinarily, fear provided John with cooperative, yet appalling thespians. And understandably so. It was absurd to think they could perform up to standard (whatever that standard even *was*) in such a frightening carnival, even with—or likely because of—the threat of death shadowing them. They would go on stage, take direction, but the performance would be dreadful. John's saving grace was that his wife never seemed to notice. It was about her, after all. Had always been about her. This particular night, even when it was the real deal five years ago, had always been about Tammy.

Except now something new had fallen into John's weathered lap. The boy was obviously afraid, and that was of course good, but he was also being defiant, a wrong word shy of refusing to go on stage. A poor performance was acceptable, but refusal to go on? Unacceptable.

John's next words were hisses through gritted teeth. "Yes … if you do as you're told, you will walk out of here when it's all over." John stuck the gun into the boy's stomach. "*Now turn around and watch the fucking stairs.*"

"You promise?"

"On my daughter's life."

The boy nodded, then turned and faced the stairs. When Tammy Kearns finally appeared on the landing, the boy looked up and smiled. And it was genuine.

But no theater behind that smile, John thought—fearfully obedient, defiantly assured, or otherwise. He's smiling because he now thinks it's all a joke. Of this John was relatively confident; the boy's smile, which soon became a hearty grin, seemed telling of this assumption. A bit odd that a young man tased, drugged, cuffed, and then forced at gunpoint to put on a tux would not, instead, be furious at this dawning realization and the extremities to which it needed playing out, but what the hell did he know about kids today? He was a tired, beaten man who lived on a farm that was another planet.

When Tammy Kearns began descending each step with the delusional grace of a swan—the reality a lumbering bull—the boy's grin took on a juvenile quality, a '*Ya got me, ya bastards*' quality.

Because he thinks it's an *elaborate* joke. Maybe one of those reality TV shows starring that kid married to Demi Moore. Yes, that would explain his willingness to embrace such extremities for the sake of a good laugh.

When Tammy Kearns hit the final step, and when John watched the boy's eyes go over the worn material of the pink dress, the frayed edges, the stains (food and sweat and soil), the fact that it was several sizes too small, he saw the boy's grin slowly dissolve, saw his eyes go from pleasant, smiling slits, to confused, frowning slits ... because this part of the joke—the dress—doesn't make any sense, does it, son?

The obvious blonde wig, the older woman who outweighed him handily, the bath she apparently took in some god-awful perfume, her face painted in makeup a clown would deem excessive—it could all be accepted as comedy one way or the other, accountability for taste debatable.

But the dress. The thing you can't stop looking at. Something off about it, right, son? Despite all this madness?

"Hi, Josh," Tammy Kearns said behind a blush that competed with her excessive rouge. "You look handsome."

The boy turned and gaped at John. John returned an expression that was a shrug without the shoulders.

Not a joke, son. I wish it was.

"The corsage, Josh," John said. "Maybe you should give my daughter her corsage now."

The boy turned back to Tammy Kearns, his frightened eyes filling up. Tammy's followed seconds later, and she quickly fanned a hand over her face, trying to stem the tears. "Oh, Josh, stop; you've got *me* going now. Daddy?"

John Kearns knew his 'daughter' wanted a tissue, but he dared not move. Dared not even speak. It was all he could do to remain still, to keep from breaking out into hysterics over the twisted irony unfolding in front of him.

.   .   .

Tammy Kearns extended her thick wrist towards the boy. She held it there for several seconds as the boy gawked at it.

John Kearns nudged the boy from behind. "The corsage, son."

"*Daddy.* It's his first time. Be nice."

Again—although by now, he had to know the gesture held no salvation—the boy turned and looked at John, eyes pleading.

"*I* don't want the thing, son," John Kearns quipped. "You're supposed to give it to *her.*"

John and Tammy laughed. John really laughed, released that bottled hysteria he struggled to cork moments ago when the boy and Tammy were both crying for the wrong reasons. Was he enjoying this? Had he tapped into some dark place from within after years of deviant conditioning? Was he becoming like Tammy? Dear God, was he becoming like Tammy?

No. *No.* He knew what was right. What was wrong. What was the *truth.* He stopped laughing instantly. That nudge now became a nurturing pat on the boy's arm.

"Put it on her wrist, son. On her wrist."

The boy began attaching the corsage. Finished, he couldn't pull his hands away fast enough.

Tammy Kearns swooned. "Oh, Josh—it's beautiful."

"Very," John Kearns agreed.

Tammy Kearns grinned, her full cheeks bunching up, swallowing eyes that had been floating in pools of shocking blue eye shadow.

And then the boy asked a question. Two questions in fact. And his questions gave John a moment of pause. In the past, not one of them had ever asked such things. Most of them barely even spoke unless John forced them to.

"Where *is* this prom? How are we getting there?" the boy asked.

And John Kearns had no immediate response. He knew where the prom was being held, of course, and of course he knew how they were getting there, but the boy's simple *asking* had momentarily pinched his tongue. Normally, John would just follow Tammy and a boy down the basement stairs and into the room decorated for the occasion—the room that *was* the prom. Lights, banners, music—it was all there. On the farm. Even the little bedroom adjacent to the dance floor. The bedroom where he would force the boy to have sex with his wife—their daughter's first time.

Except no one had ever asked before. So John Kearns hesitated. He hesitated because he'd never been asked before, and he hesitated because he wondered if the boy thought they might be traveling somewhere, thought there might be an opportunity for escape. He couldn't allow that. The boy was growing nerve, or at least appeared to be; John's suspicions could just be particularly acute for this one. So he needed to thwart it all right now. On the surface, a fearful boy and a cunning boy may seem no different, John thought. Both would go through the motions, but only one would be scheming, looking for opportunities of escape. A fearful boy was a puppet: as long as you promised him freedom when it was over, you had full control of the strings. John needed the puppet, couldn't risk dealing with the other. He was too tired and out of shape to give chase if something happened. Mostly, he was just too tired.

So when John Kearns opened his mouth to give a reply that even he was unsure as to what the contents might be, his wife interrupted him.

And her response was perfect. Had she been in her right mind, he would have thought the fucking thing had been deliberate.

"Daddy's taking us," Tammy said with a chuckle. "He's a chaperone. You knew *that*."

John Kearns inched close to the boy, whispered into his ear. "*Daddy's taking you.*" He then removed the gun from his pocket and stuck it hard into the boy's back, ensuring Tammy was obscured from it all. "*I'm your chaperone.*" John dug the point of the gun into the boy's back as though he meant to stab him with it; he needed the puppet. "*Now—I told you I'd let you go when this was done. But I'm getting the feeling you might give me problems. If you give me problems, you only need to remember where you are. And that's nowhere. And I mean that in both location AND mind, son. Believe me; I know… you're fucking* nowhere."

John lowered the gun, subtly pocketed it as if he'd just stolen it when the clerk's back was turned.

"What are you two whispering about?" Tammy asked.

The boy swallowed hard. His voice shook when he said, "Your father was just telling me how special you were."

Tammy Kearns put a hand over her heart, looked at John and glowed. "*Daddy…*"

John Kearns smiled back, but only because he knew the boy was his puppet again.

8

John Kearns clapped his hands together once. "We all set?"

Tammy Kearns smiled and nodded eagerly. She hooked her arm within the boy's and squeezed it. The boy did not look at John for help this time. He seemed to be accepting it all, his face holding no affect—a drugged patient blindly following his doctor's lead. Puppet indeed, John thought.

"Well then let's get a move on," John said. Except he did not turn towards the front door behind him. He banked right, out of the foyer and into the den.

The couple followed, Tammy Kearns a radiant ball of anticipation, the boy a zombie in a tuxedo.

Through the den, past the dining room, and then stopping in front of the basement door. Above the door was a giant banner. Tammy Kearns—when she was Tammy Kearns—had done it herself, confident the school would allow her to hang it, assuming John didn't muck things up when he presented it to them. John had taken the banner, driven to a nearby corner store where he thumbed through a few magazines, and then returned a short while later to tell his wife the school had happily accepted it. The most prestigious high schools in the state should be so lucky, they'd said.

WELCOME SENIORS CLASS OF 2006! the sign read in every color Crayola knew about.

The boy gazed up at the banner, his mouth falling open a crack as he read. There were muffled sounds of music from below.

"We're here," John Kearns said, opening the door, the music below becoming more audible. John extended his hand with panache like a maître d', gesturing for them to follow.

The bottom of the stairs was boxed off. It contained a table of items carefully laid out, a chair fixed behind the table, and a thick pink curtain strung high along the ceiling and all the way to the floor, the music and flashes of light sneaking past establishing the curtain's role as … the curtain. *Behold!*

John Kearns hurried around the couple and took his seat behind the table. "Forever Young" by Alphaville was playing. Tammy told the boy that the song was one of her favorites. The boy said nothing.

"Well, hello there," John Kearns. "Your names, please?"

"*Daddy.*"

John Kearns wagged a finger. "Tut-tut … I may be your father, but I'm also a chaperone tonight, young lady. Your names, please?"

Tammy Kearns giggled and said, "Samantha Kearns and Joshua Griggs."

John searched the name tags on the table—random names he'd gotten from a phone book, all of them. Except for two. "Ah," he said, scooping them up and handing them over. "Samantha and Joshua."

Tammy Kearns instantly snatched hers. The boy accepted his as if it was ticking.

John Kearns made his way out from behind the table, inched over to the edge of the curtain, gripped a handful of the material, paused and smiled at the couple. "Are we ready?"

Tammy Kearns grinned and nodded like she was having a seizure.

John Kearns whipped back the curtain and officially welcomed the happy couple to their senior prom.

9

The lighting, the music, the food, the décor—it was all there. John took note of the boy's expression. The zombie was gone. In its place was a little boy seeing fireworks for the first time. But John knew the boy's wonder would be fleeting, soon replaced by the frightened bewilderment they all had once things started rolling.

John Kearns hurried towards the DJ booth, grabbed the mic and said: "Hello, seniors … I'd like to welcome everyone here tonight … "

Of course, Tammy Kearns and the boy were the only ones in attendance, and would be, save for the wizard behind the curtain who wielded a gun instead of hopes for a heart, brain, courage, and a way home—the last of which, John mused, drawing freakish parallels to the boy's situation, right down to the fabricated world he was forced to inhabit.

The boy would surely take note at the lack of other 'prom-goers,' had likely expected it, but as far as Tammy Kearns was concerned, there *were* others in attendance on this night, and then again, there *weren't*. It was her and Josh. *Only* her and Josh. Lost within one another. And it was times like this that John Kearns found himself ironically grateful for the workings of the sick and delusional mind, how it could see what it wanted, hear what it wanted. Had John been required to provide some 'extras' at the prom in order to sell the whole farce, he'd likely turn the gun in his pocket on himself.

" … I know this is a very special night for all you guys and gals … "

The boy looked around, looked at John. John smiled back, winked, made a handgun and fired it at the boy as he kept talking.

" … so what I'd like to do now is slow things down, find your one and only, and show this dance floor a little bit o' *ro*-mance … "

Tammy Kearns blushed under the strobe light, held her hand out for the boy. "Crazy for You" by Madonna came on. The boy glanced back over his shoulder at John. John fired the handgun again, no wink or smile this time. The boy turned back, took Tammy Kearns' hand, and started dancing.

10

"Crazy for You" ended and "Keep On Lovin' You" by REO Speedwagon came on next. Tammy Kearns had her head on the boy's shoulder, eyes closed in blissful content, her thick arms tight around the boy's skinny waist as they (she) swayed to the music. John caught the boy's eyes filling up for a second time, but a quick, casual swipe from the sleeve brushed the tears away and alerted Tammy Kearns to nothing. Besides, if she had seen them, she would have likely interpreted them exactly as she'd done before. So John didn't fret. He did, however, approach the couple when "Keep On Lovin' You" was finished and "Let's Get it Started" by The Black Eyed Peas was next. "Let's Get it Started" was a lively dance song that required far more than just hugging and shuffling. John Kearns had no desire to see his wife attempt such a thing.

"Why don't you two grab some punch? Relax a little?"

Tammy Kearns looked up at the boy. "Do you want some punch?"

The boy looked at John Kearns who nodded, and so the boy looked at Tammy and nodded.

Tammy Kearns took the boy by the hand and dragged him towards a table that held two punch bowls—pink punch and blue punch.

John Kearns appeared by their side. "Allow me." He took the ladle from the pink punch, filled a large plastic cup, and handed it to his daughter.

"Thank you, Daddy."

John Kearns took a second cup, filled it from the bowl of blue punch, and handed it to the boy.

The boy took the cup, looked at it, looked at the two bowls, looked at Tammy's cup, and then back at his cup again.

"Something wrong?" John asked.

The boy didn't respond—his gaze shifting from bowl to bowl and cup to cup responded for him. Tammy Kearns chose to register this hesitance. And she chose to address it. Not at its core though—not at the truth behind the reason for the two bowls, the two colors, the two different offerings. The woman, no matter which persona her warped psyche donned, no longer *had* a grasp of the real truth. So she addressed it as plainly and as innocently as a child might if asked why a girl was given pink punch and a boy was given blue.

"You didn't want *pink* punch, did you?" she said. "Pink is for girls and blue is for *boys.*" She took a sip of her pink punch then smiled.

The boy nodded back, seemed to accept her response. And why not? After all the shit he'd seen, that might have been the most logical response he'd gotten all night. And John felt the sudden urge to explain everything to the boy. He didn't know why. To unburden himself maybe? Even if he wanted to, he wasn't sure he'd know how. He could go back to how it all started easily enough, explain that without trouble. But this? What had become the now? Even *he* didn't truly understand it. His wife may have been the Charlie Bucket who found the golden ticket of suppression, thus inheriting the cuckoo factory, but he was left running the damn place, wasn't he? He was the fucking Oompa Loompas. The Oompa Loompas who didn't have the luxury of blissfully deranged ignorance. The Oompa Loompas who did whatever their eccentric master demanded, knew everything that went on behind the scenes, had to live and deal with that knowledge day in and day out, lest the factory implode.

And yet he did it anyway. Did things for his wife that would make most men run and call the police; run and call the asylum; just run. His devotion to his wife's madness had become his world, because the alternative was the real world—a world beyond the farm. He'd heard of prison men becoming institutionalized after long stays, not wanting to be released, afraid to face the world after years of horrific norms. Was that what was going on here? Had he become institutionalized? The farm his prison? He didn't know.

Perhaps it was the lingering fear that had occupied his youth and young adulthood—the fear of being alone. Bad company had now become preferable to no company, the price of placating his wife's madness with such extremities reasonable when seen through eyes so tainted with a fear of loneliness. He didn't know.

"Don't you like it?" Tammy Kearns asked the boy.

The boy hadn't tried the punch yet; he seemed content to merely hold it until Tammy Kearns had finished hers.

"It's fine," the boy said.

John put a hand on the boy's shoulder, squeezed it, showed Tammy a smile, then casually slid his hand to the boy's neck and squeezed. "He loves it," John said. "Go on, son—plenty more where that came from." John squeezed harder.

The boy drank the cup of punch in one go. John said, "I'll get you some more."

11

They were dancing again. "Forever Young" by Alphaville was back on because Tammy had asked for it. The boy was a stalk of despair in Tammy's embrace.

Defeated, John thought as he watched his wife lead the boy's lanky frame on the dance floor. The boy is defeated. That's good. *Puppet* had been essential for the goings-on thus far. *Defeated* was crucial for what lay ahead.

John waited until the song died, did not put on another, then approached the couple. Tammy was still dancing, eyes closed, head on the boy's shoulder, smiling the dreamy smile, the music likely still playing in her head. The boy was limp in her arms, staring off into nothing, allowing it all like a tolerant pet being groped by a child.

"Princess?" John said.

Tammy Kearns lifted her head off the boy's shoulder and looked at John.

"It's getting late. How 'bout you show Josh your photo album?"

Tammy smiled and looked at the boy. "Do you want to see my photo album?"

The boy didn't even bother to look at John this time; he nodded on his own accord.

Defeated puppet. Good.

"Come on, kids," John said. "I'll show you the way."

He walked the couple all of six feet towards the only door in the basement, opened it, and extended his arm like the maître d' again. The couple entered with John close behind.

The room belonged in a dollhouse. Pink and more pink. Antique furniture for looking and never touching. Porcelain dolls on display in every direction. A king-sized bed with more lacy throw pillows at the head than one could count at first glance.

No window.

Tammy offered the boy a seat on the bed. He took it without bother. Tammy happily joined him a second later, her girth squeaking the bed and bouncing the boy.

"Do you have it, Daddy?"

John Kearns handed over a thick album dressed in white material, its ornate texture like a doily. The word "Princess," sewn in pink lettering and an extravagant font, took up most of the cover. Tammy Kearns opened the album.

The first page:

A little girl, dressed like a woman; looking like neither.

A heavy woman standing next to the little girl.

The little girl smiling a fake smile. The heavy woman next to her, a triumphant smile.

The little girl clearly not Tammy Kearns—because the heavy woman next to the girl, brandishing the first place trophy as if it were her own, clearly was.

And John Kearns watched the boy closely as he did with every boy after the first picture had been revealed. He watched the boy's glazed expression fall on the picture with no interest, then with a little interest, then with curiosity, and then, like most, with a dawning fear that the nightmare he found himself in was far deeper than he could have ever imagined.

12

The second page:

Dated one year later. Similar to the first. The same little girl, her outfit, her makeup, still woefully inappropriate for a child. Tammy Kearns next to her, the triumphant smile her whole face. The child, a gold crown resting on her teased bleached-blonde hair, smiling a practiced smile. Tammy Kearns holding another first place trophy, cradling it.

The third page; the fourth page; the fifth page:

More of the same, each subsequent page dated one year after its predecessor.

The sixth page:

Second place. The little girl is heavier. Tammy Kearns is smiling while she holds the second place trophy, but now she is the one who smiles with effort.

The seventh page:

Third place. The little girl is heavier still—her body starting to resemble Tammy Kearns'. The third place trophy stands alone on the floor, nearly out of frame. Tammy Kearns' smile is a thin lipless smile. Her eyes have a leashed intensity behind them.

The eighth and final page:

Fifth place. It is now very obvious the little girl and Tammy Kearns are related. No trophy. No smiles. Tammy Kearns appears the embodiment of rage.

.   .   .

Tammy Kearns closed the photo album and stared at it while she spoke. "Mommy stopped putting pictures in after that last one. She said the contests were all rigged and that everyone was just jealous of me. She said the other girls were all cheating and using special diet pills. She was even going to throw the last couple of pictures away, but then she reconsidered. She said that the pictures should stay, so that everyone could *see* how wrong the stupid judges were. How they favored the girls who cheated. How I was still the best, the *real* winner."

John Kearns looked on. He'd heard the explanations before, often varying in detail, but never in theme. He was never truly sure if what he was hearing from his wife was the product of her essence: a stubborn justification that could never be abated, even at the deepest possible level of suppression. Or perhaps it was some form of subconscious guilt, which harvested that justification in order to cope.

But did it really matter? The motives could be different, yet the end result was always the same. And the truth was that his wife *had* forced their daughter to dietary extremes (a single light meal every other day at one point). She *had* forced their daughter to take prescription pills.

None of it worked. His daughter had his wife's impenetrable genes—exacerbated and unrelenting once puberty arrived. His daughter was one of the unfortunates that was eternally fixed in the chassis she'd been given. Detail work could be done, but nothing would ever change the frame that displayed it.

John dropped his head and wrung his hands, willing the truth away.

"Mommy said I was too pretty to be in stupid contests anymore anyway," Tammy Kearns continued. "She said I was going to be a model. She even went to my high school and yelled at the gym teacher for making me play dodge ball with the other girls. '*What if I got hit in the face?*' she said. The other girls laughed and made fun of me, but Mommy told me they were just jealous I was so pretty and that I had a mother who loved me so much."

Tammy Kearns lifted her head and looked at the boy, eyes glassy. "I doubted things sometimes. People can be so cruel." She wiped away a tear. "But when you asked me to the prom, I knew Mommy had been right all along. I *was* the prettiest girl in the whole school. This *would* be the most special night of my life."

Tammy Kearns leaned in for a kiss. The boy instantly pulled away.

"What's wrong?" she asked.

The boy said nothing, his torso still leaning away from her.

"Are you shy?"

The boy looked at John. John stood.

"Princess?" John said. "Would you excuse Josh and me for a minute?"

"Why?"

"Man-to-man stuff," John said with a strained smile.

Tammy Kearns blushed and nodded.

John Kearns took the boy by the arm and led him out of the room. He made sure the door was closed before he fronted the boy and spoke in a firm whisper.

"This isn't an option, son. Go in and get it over with."

"Get *what* over with?"

John chewed his thumbnail, spoke while it was still between his teeth. "I think you know."

"You want me to *hook up* with that lady?"

Without pause, John said, "Yes."

"That's crazy. This is all crazy. Who *is* that lady? Who was that little girl in the pictures? Why are you doing this? Why—"

John grabbed the boy's face, bunching his cheeks. "I told you from the beginning—you don't need to understand any of it; just do as you're told."

"You're insane."

John said, "If only. Now go on. This is a no-brainer for most men. Get laid or get shot." John pulled the gun from the back of his waistline.

The boy's eyes skittered all over the basement.

"You're not going anywhere, son." He then threw a thumb over his shoulder towards the door where Tammy Kearns was waiting. "And I'm sure you noticed that room had no windows—you're not going anywhere once the two of you are alone either."

The boy made a go at defiance. "How do you know I won't hurt her once we're alone?"

"Because there's only one way out..." John pointed the gun in the boy's face. "That's through me."

The boy's defiance visibly drained.

"Get laid or get shot, son," John said.

The boy stuttered. "I won't be able...I won't be able to...you know...*perform*."

"Already taken care of," John said.

The boy frowned, confused.

"Pink is for girls and blue is for boys," John said.

The boy's frown changed to a look of terrible revelation.

"Go in and get it over with."

"*Please*."

John cocked the hammer back on the pistol.

The boy started to cry again.

John felt a twinge of sympathy for the boy, then a powerful wave of self-loathing. He pressed the barrel to the boy's forehead. "*Go*."

The boy dropped his head, turned, and started towards the room. When he opened the door and entered, John caught a glimpse of his wife: she was already naked, waiting.

13

The door opened a half hour later. Tammy Kearns walked out, closed the door behind her. She was back in her prom dress, her blonde wig slightly mussed.

"Hi, Princess," John Kearns said.

Tammy Kearns blushed, lowered her head and said, "Hi, Daddy."

"I just spoke to your mother. Your surprise in the barn is ready."

Tammy Kearns' head shot up, excited. "It is?"

"Yup. Why don't you go up to your bedroom and talk to Mommy. She's up there waiting for you. She'll bring you out to the barn when it's time."

"What about Josh?"

"Josh will be with me, Princess. All part of the surprise."

Tammy Kearns said nothing else, just giggled and thundered her way up the basement stairs.

John Kearns took a deep breath, let it out slow, cheeks puffing, chest hurting. He withdrew the pistol from his waistline and entered the room.

The boy lay naked on the bed, face-up, indifferent to his nudity. His eyes were glazed and lost.

"You okay?" John asked the boy.

The boy nodded but did not look at John.

"Everything go all right?"

Now the boy turned his head and stared at John. His eyes were still glazed, still distant, but close enough to convey the contempt for John's words.

John nodded an unspoken apology. "Well, it's over," he said. "You can get dressed."

The boy's eyes were still on John, contempt suddenly becoming hope. "You're taking me home?"

John shook his head. "I meant this . . . " He waved a hand around the room as if fanning away a smell, and in a way he was; the room smelled of sex. "*This* is over. We've still got more to do."

The hope in the boy's eyes left as quickly as it had arrived.

He's still defeated, John thought. More so. Still, he could not lower his guard. He needed to watch the puppet with scrutiny now more than ever—desperation could be dangerously unpredictable.

The boy rolled his head back and began staring at the ceiling again. "What more do I have to do?"

"Not much. We're almost done. Put the tux back on."

Eyes still on the ceiling, the boy asked: "You still going to let me go?"

"Yes."

The boy's head rolled towards John again. "I miss my mom. I want to see my mom."

The boy's words, regressing to the womb, his naked body and soulful eyes giving John Kearns the wrenching image of innocence lost—at his hand. It was a pile-driving punch to the gut, and John instantly thought he would vomit.

He turned his back to the boy, saw the trash can, picked it up, and spotted the used condom inside. The nausea immediately left. What remained was a familiar empty—the puppet master who took no joy in his craft, performed for a solitary audience member that was indeed *his* puppet master.

John Kearns set the trash can down. Sighed. Turned back to the boy and did not look at him when he said, "Just get dressed. We're almost done."

14

John Kearns led the boy out of the house and towards the barn. Outside, the barn was a barn. Inside, it was an extension of the basement—a replica of a senior prom. And while the décor was as fitting as it had been in the basement, one item in particular dominated the scene, a towering item, the purpose of relocating from the basement to the barn.

Ten feet high and six feet wide, an enormous arch adorned in pink and white flowers stood atop a small stage, the top of the arch hosting a gorgeous banner, its message making as much sense as the evening thus far:

CONGRATULATIONS HOMECOMING KING AND QUEEN 2006

John Kearns marched the boy towards the arch, holding the gun but not pressing it into the boy's back as he'd been doing all night. He wondered if he even needed such strong-arm tactics anymore. And that was fine by him. They didn't come natural—not from the very first time; not this time.

They climbed the small wooden stairs of the stage and stood beneath the flowering arch, the giant banner looming overhead. John handed the boy a crown—big and extravagant and gold. The boy surprised John by putting the crown on his head without question. He's still defeated, John thought, but he's also hopeful. He thinks the night is coming to an end. He's doing as told without bother in hopes to get it over with. He thinks he's going home.

"Looks fine," John said.

The boy actually gave a smile in return. It was quick and small and thin, but it was there.

John looked away. "Looks fine," he said again, dusting the boy's tux down with pats and swipes of his hands.

"Where is … ?" the boy asked.

"They should be here any moment now."

The boy frowned. "*They?*"

John said, "You'll understand when you see."

"You assume a lot, sir."

John genuinely laughed. "Touché, son."

A heavy thud and a clank by the barn door. John stopped laughing.

"Here," John said, positioning the boy beneath the arch. "Stand here and don't move."

He then jumped off the stage and waited for the barn door to open. When it finally did, and when Tammy *and* Samantha Kearns both entered, John heard the boy mutter: "*What the fuck … ?*"

15

Tammy Kearns entered dressed as Tammy Kearns, her hair its natural brown. The prom dress she'd been wearing was now on a mannequin, its hair a familiar blonde wig. Tammy Kearns carried the mannequin as though it walked on its own, any grunt or inconvenience hidden behind a blazing smile from another world.

"Hi, Princess," John Kearns said to the mannequin before motioning to the arch, and of course, the banner's message. "What do you think?"

Tammy Kearns, holding the mannequin tight to her side, said, "Oh, Daddy!"

John Kearns hit a switch on the wall as casually as he could. A round of cheers and applause boomed from unseen speakers overhead. There were even whooping shouts of Samantha's name on the recording—John's voice, recorded while projecting inside an empty fruit jar and with a cloth over the mic to make them sound distant and foreign.

John clicked off the switch and the applause died. He then told perhaps one of the biggest lies he'd told all night. "Don't thank me, Princess. Mommy did all the work."

Tammy Kearns acted as if the mannequin had suddenly pulled her into an embrace. Tammy laughed as they hugged. "Oh, Mommy! It's so wonderful!"

John hit the switch on the wall again; the crowd erupted again.

"Second to none, Princess," Tammy Kearns said over the noise, still hugging the mannequin tight. "The people have voted." Tammy then took the mannequin by the shoulders, held it at arms' length, looked into its lifeless eyes. "*Second to none.* Always and forever."

John stole a glance at the boy. His expression now was the same one John had seen in all the others. It wasn't fear, and it wasn't confusion. It was an expression John had never seemed to be able to define. Until tonight. And ironically, it was the boy's mutterings moments ago that defined it perfectly.

What the fuck?

The boy's expression (*all* of the past expressions upon first witnessing both Tammy and Samantha in the same room together) now had a name. And John could think of no other name that was as blunt and as apt and … hell, as shamefully amusing, as *What the fuck?*

John killed the switch again. "Don't keep your prince waiting, Princess." He then popped a look of playful discovery. "Or should I say: Don't keep your prom king waiting, prom *queen*."

"Oh John," Tammy Kearns said. "You've made her blush." Tammy Kearns stroked the mannequin's face.

John said, "Camera's getting cold."

Tammy Kearns assisted the mannequin on stage, stood it beneath the arch, next to the boy. She then extended her hand. "Hello, Josh. I'm Tammy Kearns; Samantha's mother."

The boy held out a limp hand on reflex, *What the fuck?* now stamped on every inch of his body. Tammy took hold of the boy's hand and shook it vigorously.

"I believe," John Kearns began, hopping on stage, "that a queen needs her crown." He pulled a gold crown from behind his back, smaller and daintier than the boy's, but no less magnificent. "Tammy, would you like to do the honors?"

Tammy Kearns took the crown and placed it gently on the manne-quin's blonde wig. She then put a hand to her mouth, tears in her eyes. "Oh, Princess, you look so—"

"*Queen,* Tammy," John said to his wife. "Queen."

Tammy Kearns wiped away tears. "Right you are, John. Tonight our princess is a queen."

"Well then," John Kearns said, brandishing his camera. "Shall we make it official?"

16

They were gone. John and the boy remained.

"It's over now," John said.

The boy nodded but showed no relief. He looked at John as if he wanted to ask something.

"What is it?" John said.

"Seriously? Do I really need to ask?"

John smiled, dropped his head and shook it. "No—I suppose you don't." He then raised his head, pulled the gun, and stuck it in the boy's face.

The boy immediately raised both hands. "What are you doing?"

John pursed his lips. "Come on, son—you had to know."

"You said—"

"Of *course* I did. What else was I going to say?"

The boy backed up, removed his crown and pulled it to his chest as though it might protect him from a bullet. "You *promised.*"

"It's either you or her," John said. "I think you know what *her* is like."

The boy started to cry again. "Please … you don't have to do this … I won't tell … "

"I'm sorry." He steadied the gun.

The boy shifted from pleading to desperate logic. "People will come," he said. "People will look for me."

"I'm sorry, son—but they won't." John flicked his chin towards the arch. "Five boys have stood beneath that thing before you. Five boys wearing the same exact tux you're wearing now…"

The boy looked down at his attire, dumbfounded.

"I was certain someone would come looking for that first boy. I didn't even bother burying him; just hid him. Figured the police *had* to eventually show up." He splayed his hand and gun. "No one ever came knocking. Not once… not for any of 'em."

"You've done this before." The boy's words were a statement of disbelief, not a question.

"Unfortunately," John said.

"Why?"

John chuckled to himself. And there it was. The elusive question he still didn't have an answer to. He could tell the boy *how*. He could tell him *what*. And he could tell him *when*. But still no definitive answer to *why*. So John just shook his head. "It doesn't matter."

"Yeah—so you keep saying," the boy said. "Well it matters to *me*."

John's chin retracted, startled by the boy's sudden assertion in the face of death.

"You're gonna kill me anyway, right?" the boy said. "So fucking tell me."

John could not fight a little smile. Goddammit if he didn't admire the kid. Still he pointed the gun, cocked it. "I'm sorry."

The boy whipped his crown into John's face. John flinched away, the gun discharging, flying out of his hands. The boy dove at John's waist, launching them off the stage, the pair thudding hard onto the dirt floor, John going *oomph!* beneath the boy, his wind knocked from his lungs. The boy scrambled to his feet, eyes frantic, searching for the gun. John struggled to his feet, grabbed the boy from behind in a bear hug. The boy kicked and flailed. John had weight on the boy, but the boy had youth. He needed to end it quickly; John could not afford a battle of attrition.

Summoning what might have been the last of his strength, John lifted the boy off his feet and slammed him to the ground. The boy let out a groan and a hiss, his breath leaving him. John immediately scurried towards the gun on all fours. He could see the boy trying to find his legs in his periphery. He snatched the gun, wheeled around, pointed and fired a shot at the boy's feet. The boy froze. They *both* froze. Remained like that for almost a minute: the boy standing, hands raised, panting; John on his knees, gun pointed, panting harder.

John eventually waved the boy away from the exit with the gun. The boy obeyed. John did not get back to his feet. Instead he slumped backwards onto his butt and started to cry.

17

"2006," John said. "That's when it happened. It was all a joke. We thought it was real, but it was all a joke. I should have known ... " He wiped his eyes. "My daughter wasn't a popular girl."

Still breathing hard, the boy took a cautious step forward. "A joke?" he said.

John nodded. "That guy—*Josh*—never showed up." He took a deep breath. "Tammy insisted the boy was lost or had broken down or run out of gas or some other slice of denial that fed her daily life." John picked a stone up off the ground and flung it away. "So Sam called the boy, and he answered, and he started laughing. Started *laughing*. Sam said you could hear his friends laughing in the background too." John clenched his teeth. "The kid then tells Sam that he's going to the prom with someone else. Starts ripping into my daughter, and God help me for saying this, but there was plenty of ammunition for the son of a bitch. My daughter was ... well she was ... let's just say she was a product of my wife. Need I explain what that means?"

The boy shook his head.

"Now—you'd think that after such cruelty, after such ... such fucking *cruelty*, my daughter would be entitled to some sympathy, yes? To put it mildly?"

The boy nodded.

John Kearns flashed a look of disgust, looked like he wanted to spit. "Wrong. My wife knew no gray—her world was black and white; winning and losing; beautiful and ugly." Now he did spit. "She *destroyed* my daughter that night. Told her she was stood up because she wasn't pretty enough; wasn't thin enough; was second-best to some other girl. Was a *loser*."

John felt his throat tightening, cleared it so his voice wouldn't crack. "Sam ran out of the house. I went to go after her but Tammy stopped me. She told me her words to our daughter were harsh but necessary. That Sam needed some time alone to process them." John gave a pathetic chuckle. "And I obeyed. I obeyed like I always do. Like the pathetic..." His upper lip curled in disgust as he searched for any word but 'man.' "Like the pathetic *waste* that I am."

"Where is she?" the boy asked. "Where's Sam?"

"Dead," John said matter-of-factly. "She ran in here." He gestured to their surroundings, then pointed to a wooden beam near the entrance. "Hung herself there."

The boy swallowed hard, his Adam's apple bobbing in his skinny neck.

John wiped away more tears. "Tammy found her... and from that day on..." He let out a short bray of laughter that made the boy flinch. "If I thought things were bad before, yeah? *Yeah?*"

The boy nodded quickly, showed a quick smile that wasn't a smile.

John hung his head. "I saw the way you looked at the dress when she first came down the stairs." He cleared his throat again, head still down. "She never washes it. Seeing as how meticulous my wife is you'd think she would, but she doesn't. She never washes out the food and drink stains because each time is the first time. She never irons out the wrinkles because each time is the first time." John lifted his head and stared at the boy. "And she never washes out the soil stains because I never had to cut my daughter down from that beam over there and watch her fall to the earth in a lifeless heap."

The boy gnawed at a fingernail, his gaze never leaving John.

John shrugged helplessly. "Her eyes see what they see, and her mind accepts what it accepts." He then hung his head again. "I miss my little girl so much."

The boy said, "I'm so sorry for your loss, sir. I can assure you, if you let me go, I won't say a word... out of respect for your daughter."

John lifted his head and locked eyes with the boy: the boy's blue looked desperate and hopeful; John's brown were assuredly dead.

"I give you my word," the boy added.

John Kearns chuckled softly through his nose. He looked at the gun in his hand.

18

John Kearns walked into his daughter's room. Tammy Kearns was sitting in a chair reading a fashion magazine. The mannequin was in bed.

Tammy held a finger to her lips, mimed a hush gesture to her husband, then used the same finger to point to the mannequin under the covers. "She's asleep," she whispered. Tammy Kearns then set the magazine aside and placed both hands across her chest as though her heart might burst. "She had such a magical time, John."

John Kearns didn't respond. He strolled past his wife and towards his daughter's dresser.

"Did you take Josh home?" Tammy asked.

His back to his wife, John said, "He's gone."

"Lovely boy," Tammy said. "For Sam to even *think* he wasn't going to show..."

John said nothing. He picked up a picture of his daughter from the dresser. He remembered it well. Their first trip to Florida. Samantha was four. She stood by the pool in a pink bathing suit, grinning, deliriously happy. No practiced smile. No flash, no glamour. His little girl being a little girl—and loving it.

John started to cry. He faced his wife. Held up the picture. "I miss her so much."

Tammy Kearns returned a curious look. "Miss who?"

John dropped his head, turned back to the dresser and set the picture down. When he faced his wife again, he shot her three times. He then stuck the gun into his own mouth and pulled the trigger.

JEREMY'S LOSS

1

Jeremy met Bret Fallon for the first time in a bar right after his mother's funeral. Despite condolences, Jeremy made no attempt at pleasantries with the stranger. He questioned if he could ever be pleasant to anyone again. His bedrock, his one source of unconditional love and support had been taken from him in a tragic car accident, and right now Jeremy had but two goals—to hate the world and to drink himself into oblivion. Until Bret Fallon told him his mother was murdered.

.   .   .

"What do you know about my mother?"

The man moved a barstool closer to Jeremy. He leaned in and spoke in a whisper. His breath was foul.

"She treated me at the hospital," he said. "A good nurse. A good woman."

So you're a veteran, are you? Jeremy thought. He studied the man's face. His hair was dark and ragged, eyes deep and sullen. Yet these features were unavoidably diminutive, lost in the surroundings of the man's most dominant feature—his complexion. It was horrid. The man had what appeared to be abnormally deep acne scars scattered throughout his face, some old, some raw and weeping. Jeremy had seen this in some unfortunates before and usually found the scars limited to areas around the cheeks and forehead. A second, sneakier glance showed Jeremy that this man's entire face and neck were drilled with these flesh-pits. Even his ears.

There was something else too—a familiarity about the man like he had seen him before.

The day after his mother's death Jeremy had desperately tried to occupy his mind with his school work. He would stare blindly at the pages of his medical books, highlighting random text indiscriminately as though the simple act of pushing the yellow marker was therapeutic.

When school work failed as a distraction, he resorted to pacing throughout his mother's home. He walked aimless routes, head down, palms mashed over both ears to stop the walls from crying out. Seconds later he saw the man.

Just as Jeremy felt the breath of madness whisper its threat into the nape of his neck, he lifted his head and spotted someone from his bedroom window. The man was standing and staring from the street, his image a dim silhouette traced by a nearby lamppost. Still, despite this lack of clarity, one thing was certain: the man was watching the house. He was watching Jeremy.

The next morning the memory of the man at his window—no less ingrained, no less unsettling—was forcefully demoted to nothing but paranoia; Jeremy's bastard grief taunting him. Yet when he stopped at the newsstand that morning to buy a paper, the paranoia's return was like a winter blast shaking his body to the core. There were eyes on his back, he was sure of it.

Jeremy spun and he was there, across the street, watching. Was it the man from last night? Jeremy couldn't be sure. He *appeared* to be. Jeremy turned and tossed the paper back onto its pile, whipped back around. The man was gone. Vanished completely, almost impossibly, like something out of a ghost story.

And now? Was the man who Jeremy believed to be following him this same man approaching him in a bar? No. Not with this man's complexion. Despite the feeling of familiarity he was *sure* he would have remembered the complexion. But then … on both occasions he *had* spotted him from a distance, one of those two occasions the middle of the night.

Jeremy sipped his bourbon and winced from its bite. His status as a drinker was amateur at best. "So what do you want? You just giving condolences?"

The man leaned in closer. "Your mother's death? That was no accident..." He made the sign of the cross on his chest and sighed. "It was murder."

Jeremy was not a fighter. But those words, the audacity of them, from a stranger. Jeremy was seconds from hitting someone for the first time in his life.

The man seemed to sense this and leaned away. "This is no joke, Jeremy."

"How do you know my name?"

"Your mother—she confided in me. Told me to find you if anything happened."

Jeremy squinted. "*Who* are you again?"

The man held out a hand. Jeremy didn't take it. The man didn't appear offended when he retracted it and said, "Fallon. Bret Oliver Fallon. And you're Jeremy Marsh. Your mother, Anne Marsh, was buried today after a car accident. I'm here to tell you it wasn't an accident."

Jeremy tightened his fist. "If this is your idea of some sick—"

"I already told you it wasn't." The man's eyes were stone, no longer wary.

Jeremy jabbed at Fallon's claim. "Well then if what you're telling me is true, then I assume you went to the police already?"

Fallon smiled a row of rotted teeth. "No way, kid. There are higher powers involved here. Powers that supersede any authority the police might have."

Jeremy scoffed. "*Higher powers?*"

Fallon stayed firm. "I'm telling you this in order to save your life."

"*My* life? You're telling me *my* life is in danger?"

Fallon nodded once.

"Why?"

"Your mother was killed for what she knew. For what she found out. You're her only son, her only family. No husband, no relatives, just you. You might have been her only confidant. That makes you a liability."

"You just said she confided in *you*," Jeremy said.

Fallon snorted. "Yeah, that's true—and it's also why I'm *here*, away from that place and running for my *own* life."

Jeremy was still numb from the funeral and the whiskey was proving an efficient catalyst in expediting that feeling, but what this man was saying, the intensity in his eyes. Was he a shell-shocked veteran talking gibberish? Or was he someone who really *did* know something crucial about the death of his mother? The accurate details he had divulged thus far were certainly solidifying his claims as a resident in the VA hospital where his mother worked, however anything beyond that was fantastic—a story whose authenticity needed more than mere words for acceptance.

"Well she never mentioned anything to me," Jeremy said.

"*Nothing at all?*"

"Well, I'm a med student and she's … " He swallowed hard. "She *was* a nurse, so yeah; of course she talked about her job. But it was just clinical chat about medicine and psychiatry and such. Never anything … " He held up both hands and made quotation marks. "*Top secret.*"

"You don't have to believe me, kid. Hell, after what you've just been through, I'd be shocked if you were anything but skeptical. However, with or without me, you're gonna find out on your own."

"Find out what?"

Fallon didn't lean in and whisper this time. His posture was straight, his expression ice. "That people are looking for you."

Jeremy shook his head slowly, an incredulous smile on the side of his mouth. He finished the remainder of his drink, *refused* to wince, then waved the bartender over with a writing gesture. "Well then I'll have to find out on my own," he said.

The bartender brought over the tab. Jeremy slapped two twenties on the bar, pushed back his stool and stood up.

"You're making a big mistake, kid. I can help you."

"Yeah, well, maybe I am. I don't doubt my mother treated you at the hospital, but this other stuff you're selling is just a little too *X-Files* for me. Have a nice night."

Jeremy walked past Fallon towards the exit. He half expected Fallon to make a desperate grab as he passed him, or perhaps call out one final plea as Jeremy reached the door, but he did not. Fallon let him go peacefully.

2

Jeremy stopped cold just as he was about to put his key into the car door—all four plastic thumbs in his Toyota were tall and unlocked. He frowned. Had he forgotten to lock his car? Maybe. After all, he certainly had a solid excuse for carelessness after leaving his mother's funeral. But all four locks on all four doors? And in a neighborhood like this, outside a bar that catered to men who were more adept at swinging their fists than their dicks? Jeremy was admittedly a fish out of water in such a place, but that was precisely why he sought it out. He wanted anonymity, not condolences from people he hardly knew in some yuppie bar. There was even a part of him that silently wished he'd get into a fight here; have someone break his goddamn nose just so he could taste a *different* kind of pain, no matter how fleeting.

"Something wrong?"

Jeremy spun. It was Fallon—a cautious five feet from Jeremy and the car. The lot was fairly dark save for a giant lamppost that flickered and buzzed from above like a nest of metallic bees.

Fallon stepped out of the dark and into the iridescent glow, highlighting his pock-marked skin; Jeremy questioned if it was actually getting worse by the minute.

"My car's unlocked," Jeremy said.

Fallon said nothing.

"I didn't unlock it yet."

"I'm not surprised," Fallon said.

"What?"

"They were here."

"Who?"

"The ones who took your mother from you. The ones who are after *you* now."

Jeremy turned his torso away from Fallon and looked over both shoulders. There was no activity in the lot. "There's no one here," he said. "I probably left the doors unlocked by mistake. My mind was on my mother."

Fallon nodded. "Fair enough—if you want to believe that."

"So what are you saying? Someone went through my car?"

"Yes."

Jeremy turned back towards the driver's side window, cupped a hand over his brow and peered inside. His CD case lay on the passenger seat. His phone charger was still plugged into the lighter. "Looks okay in there to me. Nothing missing."

"You don't know what they were looking for."

"Do *you?*"

Fallon said nothing.

Jeremy shook his head and opened the driver's side door. "Good night, Bart, or Bret, or whoever the hell you are."

A car pulled into the lot some fifty yards away. It moved slowly and deliberately towards the two of them, its high beams on.

Jeremy squinted and muttered, "*Assholes.*"

Fallon did not squint through the glare. Instead, he pivoted like a slammed door, his back to the approaching lights, his face projecting fear.

Jeremy thought he looked like a boy caught stealing. "Ohhh…" he hummed with a smirk. "Is that *them?*"

Fallon didn't reply, just kept his back to the high beams.

The car eventually stopped, yet remained idling twenty yards back, its high beams still on, obscuring the details of its model.

Jeremy's mocking wit faded. He shielded his eyes to the high beams and frowned. "What the hell is their problem?"

"We need to go," Fallon said.

"*We?* You can do whatever the hell you want. I'm going home."

Fallon still kept his back to the headlights but spoke loud and with a purpose. "Goddammit, kid, I can *help* you!" He moved to the unlocked passenger door and opened it.

"Whoa!" Jeremy said. "No way. Get out."

Fallon seemed not to hear, his attention was now fixed curiously on his own feet.

"What?" Jeremy said.

Fallon bent down. When he stood upright he showed Jeremy a cell phone. "What's this?" he asked.

Jeremy pecked his neck forward. "That's my cell phone. *How did you get that?*"

"It was on the ground."

Jeremy shot Fallon a look. "Well, can I have it back, please?"

Fallon held the phone like it was a hollow wafer, slowly turning it over in his hands for fear it may break apart. "I'm not sure that's such a good idea," he said.

"What? Why? Give me my phone, man."

Fallon ignored him; all of his attention was on the phone.

Jeremy looked up at the strange car in the distance again. It was still there, its idle purr loud and clear behind its blinding eyes.

"What do those assholes *want?*" Jeremy asked, himself more than Fallon.

The phone rang. Fallon jumped then fumbled with it.

"Give it to me," Jeremy said once Fallon had steadied his grip on the cell.

Fallon read the small rectangular window on the front of the device. "It's an unavailable number."

"*Give it to me.*"

The phone continued to ring.

"If you answer this phone, we're dead," Fallon said.

"*Give. Me. My. Phone.*"

Fallon extended his arm over the roof of the car and handed Jeremy the phone. He then took a few cautious steps back, his expression of someone about to watch a balloon pop, his stance of a man ready to sprint.

Jeremy flipped the phone open. Fallon flinched.

"Hello?"

"Jeremy?" A man's voice.

"Yeah?"

"Jeremy Marsh?"

"Yeah—who's this?"

The line went dead.

"Who is it?" Fallon asked, still in a ready stance. "*Who is it?*"

In the movies Jeremy had always thought it ridiculous when someone continued trying to speak to the other end of a dead phone, sometimes even *after* the dial tone had sounded. Now it seemed to make sense. It wasn't ignorance that kept you talking and trying in the face of sure futility; it was a desperate fear, an innate response that was out of his *own* mouth before he could draw ironic similarities between he and the celluloid dummies he used to mock on the big screen. "Hello? *Hello?*"

The engine revved on the idling car making its headlights jump.

Fallon hollered over the engine. "*What did they say?!*"

The car roared a final time then slammed into reverse, semi-circling backwards, its tires screeching, its rear shimmying like a thick metallic tail.

The white and red lights on the rear of the car faced them now. There was a brief pause where neither man breathed. A second screech—both men jumped—and the car shot from its spot as though on a race track.

Jeremy watched the car speed away. Checking the license plate occurred far too late to him and he cursed himself for it. He lowered the phone from his ear, and looked at Fallon over the hood of his car. "Was that ... ?"

Fallon nodded, a strange mix of gratification and fear on his ugly face. "You believe me now, kid?"

Jeremy looked down at his phone, brought it to his ear one last time, and then finally snapped it shut. "I don't ... I don't understand ... "

"Well that's a start I guess. Come on, we need to go." Fallon moved the CD case, lowered himself into the passenger seat, and closed the door.

Jeremy paused, standing by the driver's side. On any other night in his life he would have already been on the road with this stranger left far behind. Yet something tugged at his psyche—stoked the growing fire that was his paranoia. This man, this Bret Oliver Fallon, did not seem the con man or unstable veteran Jeremy had originally pegged him to be. Perhaps there was validity to his wild allegations. The mystery car and anonymous phone call certainly added weight to those claims.

Fallon leaned to his left and rapped his knuckles on the driver's window, shaking Jeremy from his daze. "Let's go!"

Jeremy's instincts told him to obey; to go forward so he could hear the man's entire story concerning the death of his mother. And if Jeremy believed that story to be credible? If all the facts were presented, seemed legit, and pointed to murder? Well, then he would ask for two things from Fallon:

First, he would take Fallon up on his earlier offer for help so that Jeremy would not become the next 'accident.'

And second, he would ask the former soldier for his *professional* advice—to help him avenge the murder of his beloved mother.

As it would turn out, Fallon's earlier offer involved accomplishing both those things.

3

Jeremy and Fallon sat in his mother's living room—Fallon on the sofa, Jeremy across from him on the edge of the coffee table, his hands wringing one another dry.

"You sure it was a good idea to come *here?*" Jeremy asked. "Wouldn't this be the first place they'd look?"

Fallon shook his head and leaned back into the sofa. He looked painfully exhausted, his skin worse than before—of this Jeremy was now certain. It reminded him of barnacles on the underside of an old boat. He even spotted it on his hands. His fingernails looked recently gone; the tips seeped and glistened puss.

"No," Fallon said. "They're not stupid. Taking you out here would be blatant and foolish. They want it to look like an accident. Like your mother."

Jeremy rubbed his hands back and forth over his knees. Sitting still was impossible. "Okay," he said, "I'm listening."

Fallon licked his lips. "I could really use a drink."

Jeremy was annoyed with the request. He was eager to hear what Fallon had to say, but if a drink would hurry things up, then so be it. "I think there's whiskey and wine."

"Whiskey."

Jeremy went to his mother's liquor cabinet, and returned with a tall Collins glass filled to the rim with whiskey; he did not want to have to get up in the middle of things to fetch him a refill.

Fallon thanked him, and gulped a third of it as if it were iced tea. "I was shot through the lung in Iraq," he said. "I suppose I was lucky. One inch over and it would have split my spine in two."

"So you were ultimately sent to my mom's hospital."

Fallon nodded, took another gulp. "We hit it off fairly quick. She was different than most nurses. She truly seemed to care, you know?"

Jeremy hung his head. He no longer felt capable of crying, but the pain still vibrated throughout his head and shook his vision.

"You all right?" Fallon asked.

Jeremy brought his head up quickly and breathed in. "Keep going."

"We talked a lot. She told me all about you—that you wanted to be a doctor. Told me that your father left when you were young, and that it's been just you and her ever since." He paused for a moment, seemingly sure that Jeremy may need another minute to collect himself. When Jeremy didn't flinch he continued.

"I had trouble breathing and was in constant pain. So one day your mom says that me and a few other veterans are going to be transferred to a different wing to undergo some new kind of treatment that would speed up our recovery and help with the pain.

"I had no problem with that. Hell, I'd have taken heroin if they offered it, I was hurting so bad." He took another gulp of whiskey. "So they start giving us these shots. Once a week we got them—and they were absolutely wonderful. Stopped the pain instantly and made you feel like you could hop out of bed and dance … for a little while. But you know, the stuff may as well have *been* heroin because once that blissful feeling wore off you were worse than before—like coming down from the ultimate high. And it wasn't just a feeling of withdrawal, it was like a *true illness*, you know? Guys were puking blood and shaking something awful. One guy had a seizure.

"I used to ask your mom if she could give us more than the usual once a week, but she said it was out of her hands; she was following specific orders from Dr. Tate. He was the main man in charge of this whole thing—the move to the new wing, the new drug.

"During the third week I knew something was wrong. We were getting *sicker*. The highs were short-lived, and when we came down, we came down *hard*. Your mom suspected something was wrong too. She asked around—wanted to know just what it was they were giving us, and most importantly, why we were getting *worse*."

Fallon looked off and went into a daze. Jeremy knew he was back at the hospital, reliving it. Fallon blinked, shook his head, and took another swallow from his glass.

"Your mom got the runaround—a bunch of shrugs and 'I don't knows.' So she did some digging of her own." Fallon reached into his coat and pulled out a bunch of papers rolled tight into a tube. "She found this." He handed it to Jeremy.

Jeremy thumbed through the papers. One particular bit of text stood out. He lifted his eyes off the paper and looked at Fallon. "*Chemical warfare?*"

"We were guinea pigs," Fallon said. "We were literally melting from the inside out."

Jeremy pointed to Fallon's face. "Is that … is that why … " He didn't know the right way to ask such a thing. Suppose it wasn't?

But it was. And as Fallon ran his hand over his rotted skin he confirmed it. "I'm deteriorating by the day. After the fourth treatment everyone in that wing died—dissolved like an overhead sprinkler of acid had been set off. I'll never forget the smell."

"But not you," Jeremy said.

Fallon sipped his whiskey. The big glass was nearly empty now. "I never *got* the fourth treatment. Once your mom found out what was going on, she got me the hell out of there. Snuck me out during her nightshift, and then checked me into a motel. She wanted to save the others but they were too far gone. She wept hard for them."

Jeremy looked down at the pages again. "You've been following me, haven't you?" He looked up. "Ever since my mom died."

Fallon nodded and continued as though the question was irrelevant, and by now Jeremy supposed it was.

"Your mom said she was going to get me help," Fallon said. "All things considered, I suppose I'm actually worse off than everyone back at the hospital—they melted after that fourth treatment like wax in a microwave. After only three treatments I'm melting, but it's more like a candle that drips slowly. Sometimes I wonder if I'd be better off in the microwave just to put an end to it." He looked away again before continuing. "Anyway, your mom told me she'd meet up with me back at the motel the next day. She never showed up … I don't need to tell you why."

Jeremy held up the papers. "We need to show someone this. Expose these bastards."

Fallon smiled a pitiful smile. "Like I said, kid—there are higher powers at work here. It would be the very definition of useless."

"Then we at least need to try and get you some help. Get you to a hospital or—"

Fallon shook his head, cutting Jeremy off. "I'm already dead, kid. If it wasn't for you, I'd do myself right now and end it all."

"*Wasn't for me?*"

"I wanna help you, like your mom tried to help me. This Dr. Tate is the epitome of evil—I saw it in his eyes even *before* they started treating us. I'd put him right up there with Mengele, twisted experiments and all." Fallon finished his whiskey in one giant gulp. "He'll come looking for you. I'm absolutely certain of it."

"Because he thinks my mother told me everything."

"Yep."

"So what do I do? I mean how could you possibly help me?"

"I'm gonna help you kill Tate," he said as matter-of-factly as someone offering help with a simple chore.

"You what?"

"You need to get rid of Tate before he gets rid of *you*."

Jeremy's eyes grew wide with fear, but only for a tick. They soon narrowed when previous thoughts of vengeance surfaced. He stared hard at Fallon with an indignation that was foreign to him. "He's the one who's responsible for my mother's murder?"

Fallon stared back, his steel expression providing a better response than words.

"Then I'll do it," Jeremy said.

Fallon nodded once.

"And afterwards?" Jeremy asked.

"What do you mean?"

"After I get rid of Tate. There's going to be others, aren't there? *The higher powers?*"

"Getting rid of Tate is a good start—he carries a lot of weight. It will definitely slow them down and buy us time."

"But you don't *have* much time."

"I know. But I promise you, I *will not* leave this earth until I know a madman like Dr. Tate is dead … and I figured you just might be the one who wanted to do it … to save your ass for the time being … " He sneered and looked like he wanted to spit " … and to kill the son of a bitch who murdered your mother."

Jeremy matched his sneer. "You figured right."

.   .   .

Fallon pulled a second something from his coat pocket that night. It was a Bluetooth mobile phone.

"What's that for?"

"Your cell phone is already compromised. This is a new number—something inconspicuous you can wear on your ear when I talk you through everything."

"Talk me through what?"

"You ever killed anyone before, Jeremy?"

Jeremy dropped his head and shook it.

"If we're gonna track down Tate and get rid of him, then you're gonna need someone like me to talk you through it."

Fallon handed the Bluetooth to Jeremy. He held it in his palm and studied it.

"You still think you can do it?" Fallon asked. "If not, then I—"

"I can do it," Jeremy said. The words came easier than he thought—he only needed to think about his mother for a split second before they shot from his mouth.

"You'll have to get physical, Jeremy; I don't have a gun. But you're young and fit, and Tate is old. You shouldn't have any trouble. The tricky part will be entering his home and catching him by surprise before he has a chance to call for help. Again, I can talk you through that."

"How do you know where he lives?"

"Did some digging of my own."

"So no gun," Jeremy said. "What will I use? A knife?"

"No—not in the hands of a novice. It would get messy and take forever. We should go blunt trauma all the way. A few good whacks and it's done."

"My mother bought me a cricket bat when we visited England two years ago."

"A gift from your mom?" Fallon smirked. "How appropriate."

4

3 A.M.

Jeremy was parked a block from Dr. Tate's home, the Bluetooth snug against his ear, the cricket bat in the back seat. Fallon was still at Jeremy's mother's house, his health fading.

"You there?" Jeremy asked.

"I'm here. You all right?"

"Scared."

"I know. Use the memory of your mother to give you strength. I'll be with you the entire time."

"Okay." Jeremy reached up and clicked off the interior light so it would not shine when he opened the door. He moved swiftly, exiting the driver's side then snatching the cricket bat from the back seat in seconds. He headed down the sidewalk towards Tate's home, the cricket bat tight to the length of his body to hide its protrusion.

He could feel his pulse in his head and chest—pounding thumps blocking out all else. The faster he walked, the harder the thumps. He questioned his ability to hear.

"You still there?" he asked Fallon.

The voice came back shockingly loud and clear and Jeremy flinched. *"I'm here, kid, I'm here. Where are you?"*

Jeremy was close to jogging now. His adrenaline was surging—blood flooding his skin and burning it, his stomach a swirled mess. "I'm nearly there. His house is just ahead."

"Okay—now remember, he's sure to have an alarm system. You know how to get past that."

"You're sure about this?"

"The last thing he would expect is for you to ring his doorbell."

Jeremy was one house away. He felt his bladder and bowels threaten to empty. "He'll recognize me through the window. Won't he recognize me through the window?"

"We've been through this, Jeremy. His curiosity will open the door, I promise you. When he does you can't hesitate. Move inside quickly and shut the door behind you. His confusion will buy you time. Don't waste it. Hit his head—nothing else. Keep hitting until he doesn't have a pulse. You can do this. Think about your mother, Jeremy. This man murdered your mother…"

"I'm—"

" … And unless you do this, you're going to be next."

He was outside the front door. His voice was a cracked whisper. "I'm here."

"Do it."

Jeremy rang the doorbell. He could hear it echo from inside—a melodic symphony of chimes. There was an agonizing pause. Jeremy gripped the bat's handle so hard his hands cramped. He felt feverish. He wanted to puke.

An outdoor light clicked on. Jeremy winced.

"He's coming."

"*Do it, Jeremy.*"

An older man wearing rimless glasses appeared at the thin rectangular window parallel to the front door. He looked confused and annoyed. He did not open the door; he spoke through the glass.

"Can I help you?" he called.

Jeremy's voice was a frantic whisper now. "He's not opening the door, he's not opening the door ... "

"*Kick it down! Kick it down!*"

Jeremy did not hesitate. He took a step back and rammed his foot into the wood. The door exploded open knocking Dr. Tate backward, tumbling to the ground. An alarm sounded. Tate scooted backwards across his foyer, his mouth opening and closing, presumably pleading for help; Jeremy couldn't hear. He could only hear Fallon—his roars of approval fueling Jeremy's limbs and replacing all trepidations with bloodlust.

Jeremy brought the cricket bat high into the air and whipped it down with an almighty force onto the crown of Tate's head—the alarm and Fallon's shouts robbing Jeremy of the sickening crack that filled the room. The old man's legs shook violently as he convulsed.

Jeremy was hardly finished.

He smashed down onto Tate's skull repeatedly, deforming its shape, releasing spatters of red in all directions. He thought of his mother, and although he was now sure Tate *had* to be dead, he raised the bat again to deliver a final, righteous blow for her memory. But instead his world went black.

5

The only reason Detective Cooper was standing in the middle of Anne Marsh's living room was because of the assailant's mention of an accomplice during questioning. Otherwise it would be an open and shut case:

Jeremy Marsh had broken into an elderly man's home and beaten him to death with a cricket bat.

What didn't sit well with Cooper was the story Marsh told. It was bizarre—of that there could be no doubt—but it wasn't a lie. Cooper was as wily as they came; a veteran of over thirty years. He had a keen gift of seeing things from different perspectives that brought closure to even the most baffling of cold cases. And something told him that Jeremy Marsh was telling the truth. Or at least Marsh *believed* he was telling the truth.

That was the hunch Cooper was going on right now. And after some rudimentary checking into Marsh's story, he had a few useful bits of information to support the theory that was slowly coming together in his head. He just needed a few more pieces in order to make it solid.

So as he walked slowly throughout the living room and took everything in—the full glass of whiskey on the coffee table, the rolled-up sheets of an old term paper next to the glass, and most importantly, the open medical books riddled with yellow on specific parts of text—his theory began to gel. But it was only when Cooper took out his notebook and began scribbling onto the pad while looking at those medical books that everything solidified at once.

Cooper stared at what he had just written, eventually lowered the pen and notebook, sighed and said: "Son of a bitch."

.   .   .

Jeremy waited alone in the interrogation room. Cooper and a second detective watched him from the two-way mirror.

"Has his story changed any?" Cooper asked.

"Nope. He must have told it ten times now. Not *one word* has changed."

"I'm not surprised." Cooper pinched the bridge of his nose, his usual chocolate skin now ashen.

"You okay, Coop?"

Cooper nodded, his eyes closed, his fingers still pinching his nose. "Just not looking forward to what I'm about to do."

.   .   .

Cooper entered the interrogation room carrying a large cardboard box under his arm. He set the box on the floor, and sat across from Jeremy.

"How are you feeling?" Cooper asked.

The boy looked exhausted. His face was a milky-white; dark purple rimmed his eyes.

"Tired," the boy said.

"How's your head?"

The first officer on the scene had rendered Jeremy unconscious with his night stick when he saw the bloodied cricket bat ascend for the umpteenth blow.

"Sore."

"Jeremy, I've got your confession. I've heard it several times now. So have the other detectives. The reason I'm—"

"Officer, I know what I did was wrong. I committed premeditated murder. I won't ever deny that. But it was either *me* or *him*. If I didn't get Tate, he would have eventually gotten me … just like he got my mother."

Cooper dipped to one side and pulled a photograph from the box on the floor. He slid it across the table to Jeremy.

"You know who that is, Jeremy?"

Jeremy looked at it. "It's the man I killed tonight. His name is Dr. Tate. He works at the VA hospital where my mother worked."

Cooper breathed in deep and slow. "His name was Arnold Becker. He was a retired school teacher."

"*What?*"

"His name was Arnold—"

"Are you telling me I killed the wrong man? Or did … *holy shit* … " He looked away, went into a brief daze, blinked and looked back. "Did Fallon set me up?"

Cooper said nothing. He dipped to one side again. This time he pulled the rolled-up papers and Jeremy's school books from the box. He smoothed out the papers then opened to the pages in the medical books marked with highlighter.

Cooper slid the papers to Jeremy first. "What is this, Jeremy?"

Jeremy took the papers but didn't look at them. "Those are the documents Fallon gave me."

"And you read them?"

"Yeah."

"And you claim they revealed information about chemical warfare, using veterans as test subjects?"

"That's right."

"It's an old term paper you wrote in medical school, Jeremy. There's nothing in there about chemical warfare and experimental testing."

"Huh?" Jeremy whipped his head down onto the paper. His eyes raced feverishly over the text. "Are you *blind?*" He thrust the papers back at Cooper and pointed at them. "It's all *right there.*"

Cooper took the papers, did not look at them, and slid the open medical books towards Jeremy. The books were open to various chapters on the human brain. "Look at what you have highlighted here, Jeremy. The sections deal specifically with the cause and effects of schizophrenia. You highlighted the words '*frontal lobe*' repeatedly."

"So? *So?*"

"People who suffer from schizophrenia see a gradual deterioration of the frontal lobe in the brain," Cooper said.

"I know that. *I know all about that.*"

"I know you do. And it took me awhile to get it. And I don't think you were consciously aware that Bret Fallon—Bret O Fallon—is an *anagram* for frontal lobe." Cooper showed Jeremy what he had scribbled in his notebook the night he was in Anne Marsh's living room. The word 'frontal lobe' had been written then rearranged numerous times until it spelled out 'Bret O Fallon.'

Jeremy's mouth fell open a crack.

"Even your story about the chemical warfare makes sense, Jeremy—Fallon, like the frontal lobe in patients with schizophrenia, was deteriorating. Your subconscious concocted a story to accommodate your visual and auditory hallucinations."

Jeremy finally spoke. "You are out of your—"

"There *is* no Bret Oliver Fallon, Jeremy. He exists only in your mind."

"*Bullshit, bullshit, bullshit.*"

"Jeremy, the symptoms of schizophrenia usually don't become prevalent until well into the late teens—sometimes the early twenties. It's not uncommon for a traumatic event to trigger those symptoms. In your case the loss of your mother was too much to bear. You unknowingly developed the entire conspiracy idea and created Bret Fallon from your existing knowledge of psychology and the brain."

Jeremy barked out a laugh. "So Fallon isn't real, huh? Well then do me a favor and go down to Frank's Tavern on Chestnut and check with the bartender there. I'm sure he wouldn't forget a face like that. Oh, and check the phone record of the Bluetooth! I'm sure—"

"We *did* go to Frank's Tavern, Jeremy. The bartender remembers. He remembers *you*…talking to yourself for fifteen minutes. He said you were alone."

Jeremy opened his mouth but Cooper kept going.

"As for the Bluetooth…?" Cooper said. "It didn't even have a *battery* in it when we took it from you, Jeremy."

"You're lying."

"I'm not lying."

"My cell phone," Jeremy said, "not the Bluetooth, but *my cell phone*. It rang that night. There was a car with high beams and the phone rang and some guy wanted to know who I was and then he hung up and then—"

"We checked your phone records. You had no incoming calls that night."

"But what about the car?"

"A guy outside a place like Frank's Tavern with his high beams pointed at you? You're lucky that's *all* he pointed at you. Not the safest of neighborhoods."

Jeremy lowered his head. When he brought it back up he looked like a child. "So what does all this mean?"

Cooper stared at Jeremy; there was a twinge of sorrow in the detective's eyes. "It means you murdered an innocent man, son. You're very sick…you're very sick and you need help."

Jeremy looked at the two-way mirror, then at Cooper, back at the mirror, then finally Cooper again. His last words before he clammed up for the night were: "I don't believe you. I don't believe any of this. In fact, I wouldn't be surprised if you were one of the higher powers Fallon was talking about."

6

Cooper made it a point to visit Jeremy in the forensic unit at the state hospital two weeks later. They sat across from one another in the lounge area not far from Jeremy's room. Each man had a cup of coffee.

"How are you feeling?" Cooper asked.

"Not too good."

"I understand they're treating you with Haldol."

"That's right. I used to read about it in books—never thought I'd end up taking it."

"Any recurring doubts?" Cooper asked.

Jeremy sipped his coffee then stared at the cup as he answered. "No. I know Fallon wasn't real. I know I murdered an innocent man."

"You weren't well at the time, Jeremy. I'm not justifying what you did, but you have to understand that you were very sick when it happened."

He kept his head down. "I know."

Cooper reached into his coat pocket and pulled out the Bluetooth. He set it on the table between the two of them and gauged Jeremy's reaction. "It's over now. With proper treatment you can get better."

Jeremy picked up the Bluetooth and clicked it open. There was no battery inside. "I heard a man's voice in this."

"I know."

Jeremy clicked the battery compartment shut. "Can I keep this?"

"It's evidence."

"Then why did you bring it?"

Cooper succumbed to a smirk. "A little test, I suppose. Guess I'm always on the clock."

Jeremy smiled. Then his face went flat. "I'm a murderer."

"But when you thought it was your mother's killer?"

Jeremy shrugged. "It felt right then. But now? I don't know if I can live with this."

"Give it time." Cooper sipped the remainder of his coffee, stood up, and pointed to the Bluetooth in Jeremy's hand. "Tell you what—keep it. I'll just say I lost it." He tossed his coffee cup in the trash. "How 'bout I drop by for another coffee sometime?"

Jeremy nodded. Cooper extended his hand. "Take care, Jeremy."

"Goodbye, Detective Cooper."

7

For the past four days Jeremy had been cheeking his medication and then flushing it at the first opportunity. When he felt ready, he returned to his room and took the Bluetooth out from under his mattress. He didn't know why Cooper let him have it that day, but now he did. Cooper liked Jeremy; he was trying to protect him.

Jeremy fixed the device snug to his ear and took a deep breath. "Are you there?"

Fallon's voice came through brilliantly. "*I'm here, kid, I'm here.*"

Jeremy smiled. "I'm not safe in here, am I?"

"*No—Tate's boys will find a way to get to you.*"

Jeremy gave one hard emphatic nod. "Then I think I'm gonna need your help again."

JOB INTERVIEW

1

Monica Kemp stood and faced the table of prospective employers. Behind that table sat a man and a woman—middle-aged, meticulously groomed, straight-faced. They whispered to one another about Monica's performance.

"Miss Kemp," the woman began once the whispering was done, "your performance was exemplary. All areas—exemplary."

Monica nodded. "Thank you."

"Your training?"

"My father."

The woman nodded approval. "You would be our youngest female asset."

"That would be something," Monica said.

"Assuming we take you on, of course."

"Of course."

"If we did, you'd be in the two percentile of applicants we greenlighted for immediate assignment," the man said.

Monica gave a polite smile. "I like to think there's always more I can learn."

"And there will be—more to learn."

"Of course," Monica said again.

"So," the woman said, "that would leave us with the final hurdle."

"The final hurdle?"

"What weeds out those ninety-eight percent," the man said. "*Despite* stellar prerequisites like the ones you've exhibited today."

"I'm confident," Monica said.

"Most are."

"Perception and moral flexibility," the woman said.

"I'm sorry?"

"All of our applicants know what's expected of them when they walk through these doors. More often than not, it is their moral compass that fails them when perception gets foggy."

The man added: "Any decent asset can eliminate a target when they are certain it *is* the target. Most—ninety-eight percent—cannot when they are uncertain." He splayed his hands. "Perception—" He brought his hands together with a soft clap "—and moral flexibility."

"How's your moral compass, Miss Kemp?" the woman asked.

"Your perception?" the man added.

"I guess we'll see," Monica said.

The man smirked. It was a smirk he'd no doubt given to dozens of confident applicants before him. There was a solitary landline on the table. The man picked up the receiver and said, "Send them in."

2

Monica stayed put when the door opened. A line of five people—all of them gagged, cuffed from behind—were marched inside by a large man in a black suit. All five people stood next to one another against the furthest wall like a police lineup.

There were three men and two women in the group. All of them white, all of them dressed in identical gray sweats. One of the two women wept into her gag. One man's head was tilted skyward, his eyes closed, appearing to be in prayer. The remaining three stared straight ahead with indifferent eyes.

"There are four innocent people standing over there, Miss Kemp," the man at the table said. "One of them is not. The specifics to his or her guilt are irrelevant; it is not an asset's job to question an assignment, only to carry it out with proficiency."

The large man in the black suit stepped forward and handed Monica a pistol.

The woman at the table leaned forward. "Your target is in that lineup, Miss Kemp. So are four innocent people. We need to determine your sense of perception in identifying that guilty target, while reading your moral compass when it comes to the very real possibility of killing an innocent person."

"Do you understand your assignment?" the man asked.

"Yes," Monica said.

The man leaned back in his seat. "Whenever you're ready then."

Monica popped the clip on the Beretta she'd been given, checking to see if it was loaded. It was, and she popped the clip back home. She then considered the five people along the wall.

The one woman still wept into her gag. The man in prayer had since lowered his head and tried appealing to Monica through pleading eyes. The second woman dropped her head and kept her eyes on the floor. The remaining two men stared straight ahead, but avoided eye contact with their potential dispatcher.

Monica raised the gun and waved it down the line of five. All but one flinched: the woman who kept her eyes on the floor.

Monica smirked, and then shot all five until they were dead.

"My perception was that the target was confirmed to be in the lineup," she said to her prospective employers. "I killed all five to ensure my target was dead." Then, after handing the gun back to the big man in the black suit, she said: "And I have no moral compass."

Monica got the job.

GET OFF MY ASS

1

"Get off my ass, fucker."

"*Arthur.*"

"Sorry, Ma. Guy's riding my butt."

Maria Fannelli looked in her side-view mirror. All headlights. Ever the optimist, she said, "Maybe they're lost and trying to get your attention."

"They're not lost, Ma."

Boom. High beams.

"Mother-*fucker.*"

"*Arthur!*"

Arty squinted into the rearview as he spoke. "Sorry, Ma, but come on, this is dangerous. I don't like people pulling this stuff with you in the car."

"Pull over and let them pass."

"Why? I'm going—" Arty glanced down at the speedometer "—five miles *over* the speed limit."

"Maybe they need help."

They're gonna need some fucking help, he thought.

Horns now. Not one or two burps, but a long blare. "Oh, you gotta be fucking kidding me."

Maria gave up chastising her son's mouth and resorted to a sign of the cross on her chest instead. Finished his salvation, she said, "Pull over and let them pass, Arthur."

Arty said and did nothing. *Oh, God how I wish Mom was home and Jim was here. The things we would do to these people.*

"It's probably an emergency, Arthur." Ever the optimist.

The high beams flickered now, horn wailing in five second intervals, nose inches from their bumper. With Jim in the car, Arty would have stomped the brakes, and then he and Jim would have stomped whatever pulse beat behind the wheel. The inevitable collision from such a sudden stop would have mattered little to the two brothers; the reward lying in wait would be more than enough compensation for a busted rear.

But Mom was in the car. This meant eggshells. Arty lifted his foot off the accelerator. There was a chance the high beams would swerve into the opposing lane and speed past, but Arty's gut felt otherwise; the hand on that horn wanted Arty to know he was incompetent. Arty even made a little bet with himself: some wealthy douchebag would be behind the wheel, the car a pricey one (high beams and night had obscured the model), and there would be a woman in the passenger seat. A bitch. As angry and as entitled as the driver.

When Arty eventually slowed to a stop on the shoulder of the road, the car slowed to a stop behind them. When the passengers emerged from the car, Arty smiled inside. He'd won his bet.

"Who the fuck taught you how to drive, man?" The kid looked mid-twenties, not fat, but well-fed. Handsome enough so that whoever had his arm that night didn't have to think exclusively of his bank account in order to get wet. Arty spotted the kid's watch as he pointed and threatened Arty. *I could fetch you and Jim some damn good Eagles season tickets* that watch said. The car was a black Mercedes, only the second or third trip out of the showroom from the looks of it.

Arty held up a calm hand. "Easy there, pal."

The passenger door opened. Out stepped the woman, adorned in money, and with a face that was about to ruin the beauty it held by opening its mouth. "What is *wrong* with you? Do you know people who drive that slow cause more accidents than people who drive *fast*?"

"I didn't know that, no," Arty said.

"Well they *do*."

"I find that hard to believe," Arty said.

The woman's disgust looked as if she meant to spit on Arty; he still hadn't ruled it out as a possibility. "Well *I* find it hard to believe you even *have* a license," she said.

Arty splayed his hands and sighed. "Well I do. And I pulled over for you to pass. So why are you still here?"

The kid stepped forward. "Fuck you, man. We'll leave whenever the fuck we feel like leaving."

"I'd appreciate it if you watched the language. My mother is in the car. She was the reason I was driving so cautiously."

"Man, fuck your mom."

Arty's face changed. He was not aware of the specifics of the change, but knew it had to reflect the rage he felt the instant his mother was cursed. That, and both the kid and his date took two cautious steps back.

Slowly and clearly, Arty said, "I think it would be best if you got in your car and left now."

Still the cautious two steps back, but no less deterred, a lifetime of spoils superseding common sense, the kid said: "Do you know who I am?"

Arty shook his head. "I don't. But I'd love to know."

The woman now, her moment of wariness effortlessly back to bitchiness. "His name is Kyle Bonnar." She pecked her head forward and nodded emphatically with each condescending syllable. "You might wanna look it up."

"Never heard of you," Arty said. "I imagine the name is supposed to mean something to me?"

"What it means," Kyle Bonnar began, "is that I could have you, *and* your mother disappear if I fucking wanted."

Arty dropped his head and nodded. "I see." He lifted his head. "What was the name again?"

"*Bonnar*," the woman blurted. "B-o-n-n-a-r." She smiled with great pleasure after spelling the name.

Arty nodded again. "Got it. Sorry for the inconvenience."

The kid opened the driver's door and puffed out his chest. "Damn right you're sorry."

The woman opened the passenger door. "Asshole."

The black Mercedes sped away. Arty stood very still for a moment. He took several deep, calming breaths to tame the atrocities in his mind that begged letting. Certain he had them leashed—and *only* leashed; not caged, no way—he headed back to the car.

"What happened?" Maria Fannelli asked. "I couldn't hear much. Were they shouting at you?"

"Everything's fine, Ma. It was like you said; they were lost. They were only shouting because we were outside, you know? Cars going past and everything?"

Except no cars *had* gone past. Strange … and sad. Such a missed opportunity. If Jim had been here, dickhead and bitch would be in the trunk of their own Mercedes right now. A missed opportunity, but not a lost one. It could and would be salvaged—somehow. Fuck whatever connections the little prick boasted.

"Ma, do you mind if we skip ice cream tonight? I'm not feeling so hot."

Maria Fannelli immediately placed a hand to her son's forehead. "Do you feel like you're coming down with something?"

"Maybe, I don't know. You mind if we just head home?"

"Of course not."

"Ma, do you know the name Bonnar?"

"Bonnar?"

"B-o-n-n-a-r."

"The name does sound familiar."

"Politicians?"

Maria scrunched her brow in thought. "I don't think so. I *have* heard it before though. I wonder if it's not the people who own that restaurant."

"What restaurant?"

"There's a restaurant on the Mainline called Bonnar's. Very swanky. I hear that big director from around here goes often. The one who did the film about the boy who sees ghosts."

"So these Bonnars … they're just people from the Mainline who own a restaurant? That's it?"

"Assuming it's who I'm thinking of."

"No politicians or judges or … ?"

"Arthur, what on Earth are you getting at?"

"Nothing, Ma. Never mind." So that was it. Mere restaurateurs. The kid he'd encountered a spoiled little prick from the Mainline who fancied himself untouchable. Probably didn't lift a finger in the place unless it was to help himself to his folks' income.

Arty headed home. He hoped Jim was there so they could start right away. He wondered what Jim would say when he told him what the prick had said about Mom. He wondered what Jim would *do*. Even Arty's mind had trouble fathoming.

2

Kyle Bonnar stood naked at the oak bar in his bedroom, pouring himself a scotch. His girlfriend Amber was showering.

The doorbell rang, followed by three hard knocks.

Kyle cursed under his breath as he gathered his scattered clothes off the floor.

The doorbell rang again. More knocks.

"All right!" he yelled downstairs, hopping on one leg as he snaked the other through his jeans. Screw a shirt, let whoever it is see him bare-chested; see what kind of inconvenience they're causing knocking on his door at this time of night. *His* door of all things. Better be a goddamn emergency.

Kyle arrived at the front door and peeked through the adjacent window. He saw a cop.

"Christ," he muttered, opening the door.

The cop was solid. Nearly six feet. His head was shaved.

"Mr. Bonnar?"

"Yeah?"

"We're following up on a traffic complaint; wondered if you could help us out?"

"Traffic complaint? What the hell is that?"

The cop ignored the question and dove in with his own. "Were you involved in an incident earlier this evening with another motorist?"

"What're you talking about?"

"Did you, or did you not tell a motorist to go fuck his mother?"

Kyle retracted his chin in disbelief. "Is this a joke?"

"No, sir, this is no joke. Please answer the question."

Kyle snorted. "Since when is telling some guy to go fuck his mother against the law?"

"Anyone else in the house with you, Mr. Bonnar?"

"Yeah, my girlfriend. What's that got to do with anything?"

The officer dipped his torso to one side and snuck a peek around Kyle, into the house. "And where is she now, sir?"

Kyle dipped too, blocking the officer's view. "Well, not that it's any of your business, but she's in the shower."

"Nice," the officer said.

"*What?*"

The officer pulled his baton and rammed the butt into Kyle's solar plexus. Kyle stumbled back into his house, doubled-over and struggling to breathe.

"So you told my brother to go fuck my mother, huh?" The officer raised the baton. A split second before turning Kyle's world black, he added: "You have *no* idea how fun this is going to be."

3

Amber Calloway was applying an expensive color-care shampoo to her long blonde hair when she heard the bathroom door open.

Eyes shut tight for fear of the shampoo dripping its way in, she asked: "That you, sexy?"

A hungry groan was her reply.

She smiled. "You gonna join me?"

She heard the glass door slide open behind her. Then a pause. Then a waft of cool air entered the steamy glass box, and she turned her front into the stream of hot water. She continued shampooing blind. "Are you just gonna watch, you perv?"

She heard him enter the shower behind her. Heard the glass door slide shut. Felt his hands reach around and begin kneading her breasts. Felt his erection pressing against her.

And it was all wrong.

The hands were too rough, the erection too large.

Amber spun and opened her eyes. She screamed.

.   .   .

Arty heard the scream from the bedroom. He could only assume Kyle Bonnar did too—bound and gagged on the floor, the kid writhed and grunted and fought his binds the moment it sounded.

The screaming soon stopped. Arty stood over Kyle and grinned down at him. "She's quiet now. Maybe she's diggin' it, yeah?"

Kyle hollered something incoherent into his gag.

"What are they doing, you ask? Well..." Arty mimed holding a pad and pen, began running down a list of citations. "We have you on three charges, Mr. Bonnar. Riding one's ass; high beams; and incessant honking of the horn. Now, my brother is handling the 'riding one's ass' punishment—good thing they're in the shower; soap will help such a tight squeeze—but I'm afraid you will be receiving the brunt of the remaining two charges." Arty put away his imaginary notebook, and produced a very real ice pick. "Ready to pay your debt to society?"

4

Jim exited the bathroom as naked as he'd entered.

"All good?" Arty asked.

"For me? Oh yes."

Arty smirked. "What about her?"

"You know that joke, how does a real man know if a woman has an orgasm? A real man doesn't care?"

Arty bit back laughter. "I do."

Jim touched the tip of his nose and grinned.

Arty lost it. He was still laughing as he walked past his brother and into the bathroom. Before their visit tonight, the bathroom had been an extravagant show of décor. It resembled a crime scene now. Arty could only wonder how his brother had managed blood on all four walls. And with his bare hands no less.

"So what's up with hotshot here?" Jim asked, still nude, his birthday suit like a badge of honor commemorating his recent conquest.

"Cited him for high beams and horns," Arty said, reentering the bedroom.

"He's still alive," Jim said, kicking Kyle Bonnar's fetal body and getting a moan in return.

"Yes, I know."

Jim squatted next to Kyle and inspected him. Kyle's eyeballs had been punctured. Blood leaked from both ears. "High beams and horns," Jim said.

Arty twirled the ice pick between his fingers. "I did his eardrums first. I wanted to see the pain in his eyes before I did those."

Jim stood and faced his brother. "But he's still alive."

"We don't have to kill everyone, Jim."

Jim cocked his head. "This wasn't a game though. This was for Mom. They deserve to be dead."

"It's always a game. We simply adjust the rules accordingly." Arty stopped twirling the ice pick and gripped the handle. "And who said I was done with him?

.   .   .

Both brothers stood over Kyle Bonnar's corpse. His entire torso was slick with red. His face was unrecognizable.

"This was pretty big, bro," Arty said.

Jim, still naked, said, "Yeah."

Arty turned and looked at his brother. "We're gonna have to lay low for a while. Leave Philly."

Jim frowned. "This isn't Philly. It's the Mainline."

"Exactly. They're going to turn the world upside down to find out who did this."

Jim's frown faded. He gave a reluctant nod.

Arty said: "Maybe now might be the perfect time to move Mom where she wants."

Jim groaned. "Western PA? We're gonna be out in the fucking sticks, man."

"Don't be so down on it yet, Jim," Arty said, rubbing his brother's shoulder. "We might have some fun."

AUTHOR'S NOTE

Thank you so much for reading *Warped*, my friends. I truly hope you found at least a couple of stories that will stay with you. As for the last two stories, if you want to know more about those mean old Fannelli brothers and Miss Monica Kemp, then check out my *Bad Games* series and get your fill!

Please know that every single reader is important to me. Whenever I'm asked what my writing goals are, my number one answer, without pause, is to entertain. I want you to have fun reading what I write. I want to make your heart race. I want you to get paper cuts (or Kindle thumb?) from turning the pages so fast. Again—I want to entertain you.

If I succeeded in doing that, I would be very grateful if you took a few minutes to write a review on Amazon for *Warped*. Good reviews can be very helpful, and I absolutely love to read the various insights from satisfied readers.

Thank you so very much, my friends.

Until next time…
Jeff Menapace

ABOUT THE AUTHOR

A native of the Philadelphia area, Jeff Menapace has published multiple works in both fiction and non-fiction. In 2011 he was the recipient of the Red Adept Reviews Indie Award for Horror.

Jeff's terrifying debut novel *Bad Games* became a #1 Kindle bestseller that spawned three acclaimed sequels, and now the first three books in the series have been optioned for feature film and translated for foreign audiences.

His other novels, along with his award-winning short works, have also received international acclaim and are eagerly waiting to give you plenty of sleepless nights.

Free time for Jeff is spent watching horror movies, The Three Stooges, and mixed martial arts. He loves steak and more steak, thinks the original 1974 *Texas Chainsaw Massacre* is the greatest movie ever, wants to pet a lion someday, and hates spiders.

He currently lives in Pennsylvania with his wife Kelly and their cats Sammy and Bear.

Jeff loves to hear from his readers. Please feel free to contact him to discuss anything and everything, and be sure to visit his website to sign up for his FREE newsletter (no spam, not ever) where you will receive updates and sneak peeks on all future works along with the occasional free goodie!

Connect with Jeff on Facebook, Twitter,
LinkedIn, Goodreads, and Instagram

http://www.facebook.com/JeffMenapace.writer

http://twitter.com/JeffMenapace

https://www.linkedin.com/in/jeffmenapace

https://www.goodreads.com/jeffmenapace

https://www.instagram.com/jeffmenapace

OTHER WORKS BY JEFF MENAPACE

Please visit Jeff's Amazon Author Page or his website for a complete list of all available works!

http://author.to/Jeffsauthorpage

http://www.jeffmenapace.com

92006446R00165

Made in the USA
Middletown, DE
05 October 2018